To Dare the I

The Daring Daughters

By Emma V. Leech

Published by Emma V. Leech.

Editing Services Magpie Literary Services

Cover Art: Victoria Cooper

ASIN No: B09XJ9PLGT

ISBN No: 978-2-492133-43-5

About Me!

I started this incredible journey way back in 2010 with The Key to Erebus but didn't summon the courage to hit publish until October 2012. For anyone who's done it, you'll know publishing your first title is a terribly scary thing! I still get butterflies on the morning a new title releases, but the terror has subsided at least. Now I just live in dread of the day my daughters are old enough to read them.

The horror! (On both sides I suspect.)

2017 marked the year that I made my first foray into Historical Romance and the world of the Regency Romance, and my word what a year! I was delighted by the response to this series and can't wait to add more titles. Paranormal Romance readers need not despair, however, as there is much more to come there too. Writing has become an addiction and as soon as one book is over, I'm hugely excited to start the next so you can expect plenty more in the future.

As many of my works reflect, I am greatly influenced by the beautiful French countryside in which I live. I've been here in the Southwest since 1998, though I was born and raised in England. My three gorgeous girls are all bilingual and my husband Pat, myself, and our four cats consider ourselves very fortunate to have made such a lovely place our home.

KEEP READING TO DISCOVER MY OTHER BOOKS!

Other Works by Emma V. Leech

Daring Daughters

Daring Daughters Series

Girls Who Dare

Girls Who Dare Series

Rogues & Gentlemen

Rogues & Gentlemen Series

The Regency Romance Mysteries

The Regency Romance Mysteries Series

The French Vampire Legend

The French Vampire Legend Series

The French Fae Legend

The French Fae Legend Series

Stand Alone

The Book Lover (a paranormal novella)

The Girl is Not for Christmas (Regency Romance)

Audio Books

Don't have time to read but still need your romance fix? The wait is over…

By popular demand, get many of your favourite Emma V Leech Regency Romance books on audio as performed by the incomparable Philip Battley and Gerard Marzilli. Several titles available and more added each month!

Find them at your favourite audiobook retailer!

Acknowledgements

Thanks, of course, to my wonderful editor Kezia Cole with Magpie Literary Services

To Victoria Cooper for all your hard work, amazing artwork and above all your unending patience!!! Thank you so much. You are amazing!

To my BFF, PA, personal cheerleader and bringer of chocolate, Varsi Appel, for moral support, confidence boosting and for reading my work more times than I have. I love you loads!

A huge thank you to all of Emma's Book Club members! You guys are the best!

I'm always so happy to hear from you so do email or message me :)

emmavleech@orange.fr

To my husband Pat and my family … For always being proud of me.

Table of Contents

Family Trees

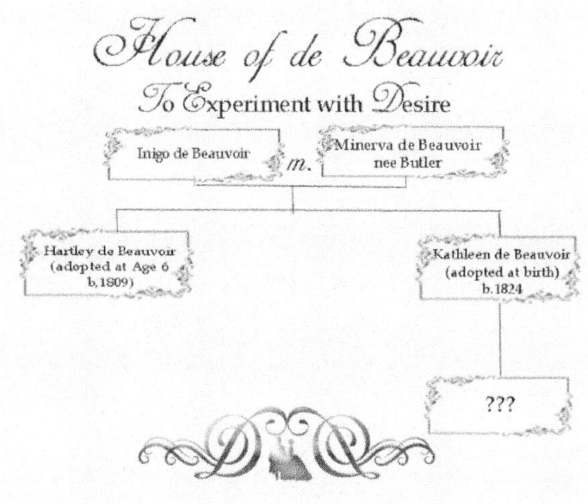

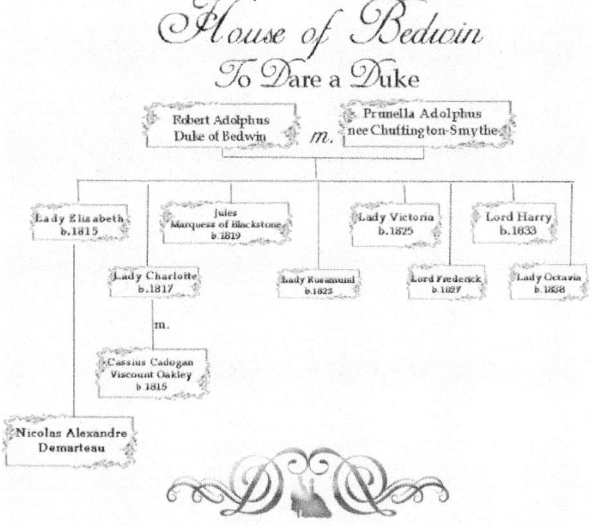

House of Cavendish
To Break the Rules
Silas Anson
Viscount Cavendish
m.
Aashini Anson
aka: Lucia de Feria
Twins
Ashton Anson
b.1816
Vivien Anson
b.1816
m.
August Lane-Fox
House of Hunt
To Steal a Kiss
Nathaniel Hunt
m.
Alice Hunt
nee Dowding
Leo Hunt
b.1815
Arabella "Bella" Hunt
b.1820
m.
Lawrence Grenville
Marquess of Bainbridge

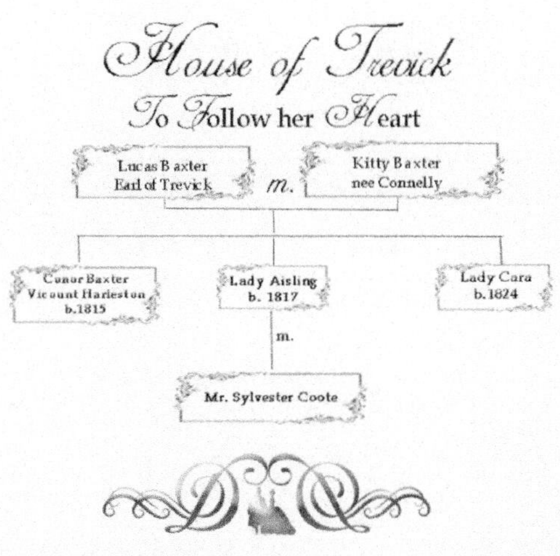
House of Trevick
To Follow her Heart
Lucas Baxter
Earl of Trevick
m.
Kitty Baxter
nee Connelly
Conor Baxter
Vicount Harleston
b.1815
Lady Aisling
b. 1817
Lady Cara
b.1824
m.
Mr. Sylvester Coote

House of St Clair
To Wager with Love
Jasper Cadogan
Earl of St Clair
m.
Harriet Cadogan
nee Stanhope
Cassius Cadogan
Viscount Oakley
b.1815
m.
Lady Charlotte Adolphus
b.1817

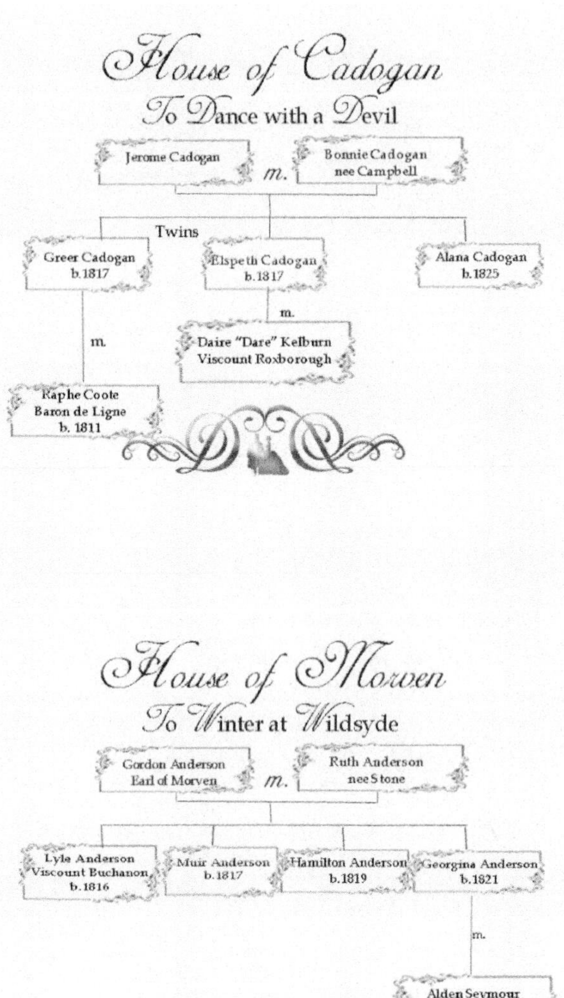
House of Cadogan
To Dance with a Devil
Jerome Cadogan
m.
Bonnie Cadogan
nee Campbell
Twins
Greer Cadogan
b.1817
Elspeth Cadogan
b.1817
Alana Cadogan
b.1825
m.
Daire "Dare" Kelburn
Viscount Roxborough
m.
Raphe Coote
Baron de Ligne
b. 1811
House of Morven
To Winter at Wildsyde
Gordon Anderson
Earl of Morven
m.
Ruth Anderson
nee Stone
Lyle Anderson
Viscount Buchanon
b.1816
Muir Anderson
b.1817
Hamilton Anderson
b.1819
Georgina Anderson
b.1821
m.
Alden Seymour
The Duke of Rochford
b.1814

House of Rothborn
To Bed the Baron
Solo Weston
Baron of Rothborn
m.
Jemima Weston
nee Fernside
Larkin Weston
b.1816
Grace Weston
b.1821
m.
Mr Sterling Oak
b. 1813
House of Knight
To Ride with the Knight
Gabriel Knight
m.
Lady Helena Knight
nee Adolphus
Florence Knight
b.1817
Evie Knight
b.1822
Felix Knight
b.1824
Emmaline Knight
b.1826
m.
Henry Stanhope
b.1799

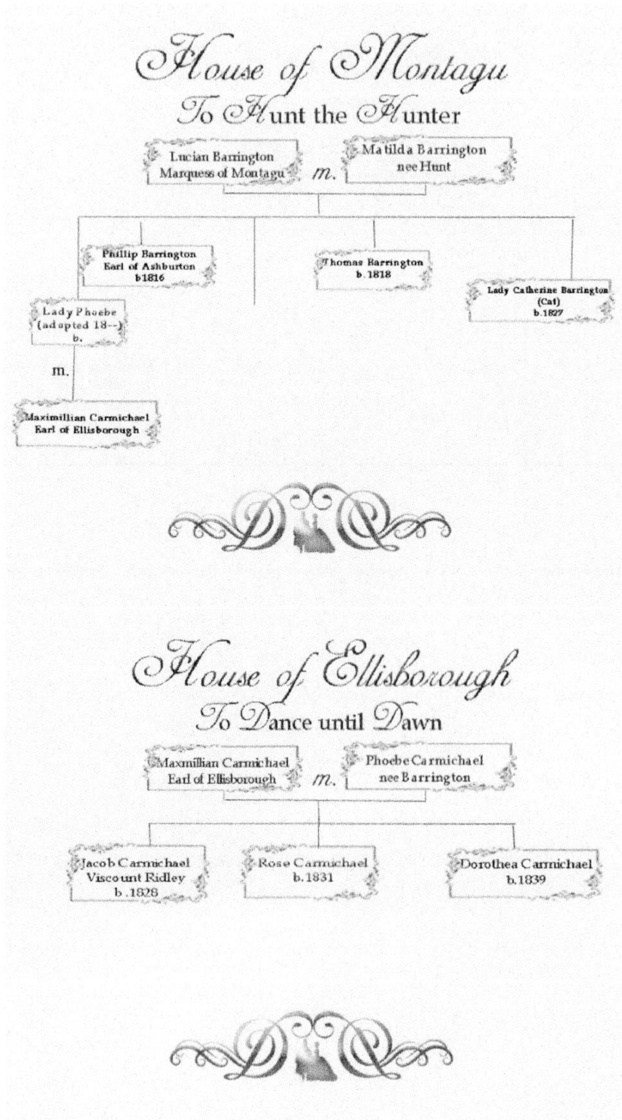

House of Montagu
To Hunt the Hunter
Lucian Barrington
Marquess of Montagu
m.
Matilda Barrington
nee Hunt
Phillip Barrington
Earl of Ashburton
b1816
Thomas Barrington
b.1818
Lady Catherine Barrington
(Cat)
b.1827
Lady Phoebe
(adopted 18--)
b.
m.
Maximillian Carmichael
Earl of Ellisborough
House of Ellisborough
To Dance until Dawn
Maxmillian Carmichael
Earl of Ellisborough
m.
Phoebe Carmichael
nee Barrington
Jacob Carmichael
Viscount Ridley
b.1828
Rose Carmichael
b.1831
Dorothea Carmichael
b.1839

Chapter 1

Nic,

Knight has taken his family and left London. I have just received a note from Evie. She knows not where they go or why or for how long. I fear he has discovered my interest in her and seeks to take her from my reach. They will cut her off from me, Nic, I know it. They'll not see another letter reach me, nor allow us to be within ten miles of each other. I will lose her.

Please, I know I have begged you to keep my feelings to yourself, and this does not change, but I pray you will ask Eliza to discover where they have gone. Surely, she would know where her aunt had disappeared to in such a ramshackle manner?

I do not know how I will endure months without her, brother, when I do not know where she is or if she thinks of me at all.

—Excerpt of a letter from Louis César de Montluc, Comte de Villen, to his brother, Monsieur Nicolas-Alexandre Demarteau.

15th February 1842, Church Street, Isleworth, London.

Kathy took a deep breath and closed her eyes. Light filtered through her eyelids, flickering in gaudy shades of pink and red. The scent in the glasshouse was a pleasing mix of damp earth, vegetation, and the subtle perfumes of vanilla and cinnamon. Humidity lent the air weight enough to touch her skin like a caress, cocooning and cosy on a bright, wet day. Outside, the weather was chilly, rain falling on the glass with a soft patter, but inside it was warm and peaceful, making her languid and a little melancholy. She liked it here, liked the serenity of it, even if the large, uncompromising figure who dominated the space was not the most relaxing person to spend time with.

Hartley de Beauvoir was her brother, though they shared no blood. Inigo and Minerva de Beauvoir had adopted both him and Kathleen, Hart when he was six years old, and Kathy within hours of her birth some years later. An act of charity by two of the most loving parents they could possibly have wished for. They were a happy if unconventional family, and they both knew their lives could have been horribly different. Hart strove to repay them for their unconditional love and support by working all hours to make a success of himself, by making their parents proud. His gratitude and love for them made him push himself to succeed, no matter that Mama and Papa would have loved him no matter what and wanted nothing but his happiness.

It was easier for a man to find a role in life, however. At least, it seemed that way to Kathy. She wished she had Hart's passion for his work, for his purpose… or that she had a purpose at all. Her parents had encouraged her to take an interest in science, but it had never sparked in her mind as it did for Papa and for Hart, though Hart's interest had shifted to the science of plant propagation and gardening. It was an incongruous sight, to watch her big brother, built like a warrior of old, delicately nurturing his orchids with the tender care of a fretful nursemaid.

"Stop sighing. It's like living with a defective windmill," Hart grumbled, not looking up from his work repotting a peculiar tangle of roots. "Orchids don't like draughts."

Kathy rolled her eyes.

"And don't roll your eyes at me. If you're bored, find something to do."

"I didn't roll my eyes," she lied, folding her arms and shifting on the stool.

"Yes, you did."

"You weren't even looking, Hart," she retorted, reaching for a small wooden dibber and turning it in her hands.

Hart looked up, snatched the dibber from her and set it back where it had been on the workbench. "I don't need to look. You sigh, you roll your eyes, throw your hands in the air, tut and toss your pretty curls. Haven't you a dress fitting to go to?"

"This afternoon," Kathy grumbled. "And a fat lot of good it will do me."

"Tell Mother you don't want to go," Hart said, a weary note to his words that suggested he might plant her in the compost headfirst if she didn't change the subject. She had worn it rather thin.

"And disappoint her after everything she's done to prepare me for the season? I'm not so spoilt as that."

Hart snorted, so Kathy kicked him in the shin, muttering a curse as her thin slippers offered no protection to her toes. Hart didn't even blink.

"You're supposed to get married and produce babies too, I might remind you. Two and thirty next birthday," she added in a singsong voice.

Hart glowered at her. "I'm not marrying, which is why you need to find a bloody husband. We can't both disappoint her.

She'll be heartbroken if she doesn't get grandchildren, and you love babies, so you can do it."

Kathy frowned. Hart was an independent man with a home of his own and a successful business propagating and selling exotic plant specimens. The orchid house he'd commissioned built at his new premises was not yet ready for use, which was why he was often back home, tending the overspill which he'd left here with his parents. She couldn't argue with his logic, for she could not imagine him married. He held himself too separate, had never gained the knack of sharing his thoughts and feelings. It would leave any wife out in the cold, unlike the blasted orchids. And she *did* love children and babies, but, surely… there was something more than that?

Mama had found more. Though no scientist herself, she was a brilliant organiser and the motivating force behind many of their father's and other leading scientists' publications, also in securing sponsors and funding for many budding scientists and inventors. Kathy had tried to find an interest in that too, she really had, but though she also had a knack for organising, the subject did not inspire her. Reading was a delight, and she devoured anything that landed in her lap, finding a particular delight in ghoulish medical texts, but nothing stuck. She needed something else.

"If you don't stop fidgeting, I shall throw you out," Hart muttered, his dark eyes glinting with irritation.

Kathy sighed and slid off the stool, admitting defeat. "Don't bother. I shall throw myself out. I'm going to make a nuisance of myself in the kitchen."

"If you're baking something, make some gingerbread," he demanded as she headed for the door.

She snorted, shaking her head. "What, so you can eat the lot? I think not."

"You're mean," he grumbled, turning back to his orchids.

"And you're a big oaf," she returned sweetly, and hurried out through the rain to the kitchen to make gingerbread.

15th February 1842, Lower Square, Isleworth, London.

"Not that I'm complaining, but I assume there is a reason you've brought us to a muddy field on a cold, wet day," Lady Elizabeth said, her lips quirking into a smile.

Maxwell Drake, seventh Earl of Vane, laughed, admiring the picture the young woman made against the rain-swept surroundings. Lady Elizabeth Demarteau might have married a bastard nobody in the eyes of the *ton*, but she was the daughter of a duke and everything about her screamed good breeding and wealth. Her outfit was the height of fashion, her cheeks glowed with health, her green eyes sparkled, and the considering look her husband was giving him reminded Max that he was behaving himself these days.

"There is, my lady," he assured her earnestly. "As the buildings we have visited to date have been less than satisfactory, I thought perhaps a different option might work better for us. I own this land and I would be happy to donate it to the cause and use the funds I have already promised to build a school here. Something that would perfectly meet your requirements. I know you wanted to begin at once and it would take far longer, of course, but I think in the long run, this would be the best option."

Lady Elizabeth's eyes widened, and she gave a little gasp. "Well, I wished to begin at once, yes, but I know that is my impatience at work. Building the perfect school would be better, only finding the land close enough to town and— Oh, Lord Vane, this is simply marvellous! Thank you."

Maxwell grinned. There was certainly something in this do-gooding lark. He had never realised that making other people happy made him feel good too, but then he'd never tried it until after he'd come so close to losing everything. Until recently, he would have lived up to every description of a spoiled, vain, self-centred and loathsome parasite of an aristocrat, but no longer. Some beneficent deity had given him a second chance, a chance to redeem himself, and he'd grabbed hold of that chance with both hands.

"I have taken the liberty of having some preliminary plans drawn up, if you'd like to see them," he offered.

Lady Elizabeth was practically bouncing on her toes, and her enthusiasm for her project, for life itself, made Maxwell want to hug her. Well, obviously that would be unwelcome and inappropriate coming from him. Her husband obviously felt the same impulse however, and put his arm about her shoulders, leaning down to kiss her temple. Despite all his good intentions, Max could not help a little envy creeping into his soul as she gazed up at her husband with adoration. His old self would have seen that as a challenge and immediately set out to charm and seduce the lady into his bed. These days it chagrined him to discover that not only did he not wish to spoil what was obviously a happy marriage, but he rather thought *that* was the bit he envied. He desired the closeness, the obvious affection and accord between her and her husband. It must be nice not to be alone in everything, to have someone to share your days, your triumphs and your disasters.

Maxwell blinked, disconcerted to discover Mr Demarteau had spoken to him and he'd not heard a word.

"I beg your pardon, I was wool-gathering," he said, feeling like a prize twit.

"I said, could we discuss this somewhere warm and out of the rain before my lady catches pneumonia?" the big man replied dryly.

Maxwell nodded at once. "Of course, forgive me. I'm afraid the weather is not being kind to us today."

"It's of no matter. I won't dissolve under this brief shower, and I am so pleased you brought us to see it, my lord. It will be quite perfect, thank you," Lady Elizabeth said with a warm smile, laying her hand on his arm in a friendly gesture. Maxwell darted a glance at her husband, who regarded him, his placid expression daring him to read anything into the touch beyond her gratitude and a naturally welcoming nature. Maxwell damned his own vile reputation, smiled and handed the lady up into the carriage.

"Forgive me, Mr Demarteau. Let's get your wife out of the cold. I have an excellent brandy, which I believe will chase the worst of it away."

Mr Demarteau nodded his agreement. "I'll not refuse such an offer," he said politely.

Maxwell hesitated and then decided to give being honest a go. It was something else he was working on, and it had produced mixed results thus far. He did not discount the possibility of getting his nose broken, but it was clear to him this man was well aware of his reputation and feared he would make inappropriate advances to his wife given the opportunity. "You're a lucky man, Mr Demarteau. Lady Elizabeth is quite remarkable. I've met no one like her before. Beautiful and clever, and so very determined."

"That she is," Demarteau replied, the tone of his voice at once a warning, and giving Maxwell the distinct impression the man could not quite believe his own luck.

"I envy you," Maxwell admitted in a rush. "I think… I think I should like to marry, if I could find something close to what you two have."

Demarteau's expression relaxed, and his smile was somewhat warmer this time. "Then this new Lord Vane is here to stay? I can't say I shall miss the old one."

Maxwell rubbed the back of his neck, his expression wry. "Yes. I'm still finding my way, to be honest, and I am aware I have many bridges to mend, and some that are beyond repair, but I mean to do everything I can to make amends. I know you've no reason to think well of me. The gossip mill never ceases and I cannot pretend most of it isn't true."

Demarteau shrugged. "We all have a past. Make amends where you can, and marry a woman who will love you despite everything *and* hold you to account. Perhaps you'll sleep at night. Worked for me," he added with rather more honesty than Maxwell had been expecting.

"I'd like to try that," Maxwell said, meaning it. "She doesn't have a sister, does she?" he added with a grin.

"She does, as I'm sure you are aware, my lord," Demarteau said, laughing.

"Oh, call me Maxwell. No need to be formal if we're to be working so closely together."

"Right you are, Max, old man. In which case, I'm Nic," he said with a grin that showed his teeth, before climbing into the carriage.

Maxwell snorted, feeling rather encouraged, and followed him inside.

Chapter 2

Louis,

Eliza is as puzzled as you it appears. I have asked her to discover the reason, but I cannot press the matter without revealing my interest. If you would let me confide in her, I might have better luck, though I hesitate to do so.

Eliza will keep a secret if I insist, but it may sit ill with her. She adores her aunt and uncle and is a friend to her cousin Evie. However, as your happiness is at stake, I will do so if you will allow it.

Why not come and stay with us, brother? Living alone does you no good and we should be delighted to have you here. Remember, I know how much you hate being by yourself, Louis. Please come, even if only for a short while. And lay off the brandy. When Evie comes home, you'll not want her to discover you've become a sot in her absence.

—Excerpt of a letter from Monsieur Nicolas-Alexandre Demarteau to his brother Louis César de Montluc, Comte de Villen.

Two and a half years earlier…

7th June 1839, The Crown, Great St Andrew's Street, Covent Garden. Parish of St Giles.

The pub was a god-awful place by Mayfair standards, but many fine young bucks like to drink in it all the same. The company was lively and held an edge of danger irresistible to many young men. Max was not in the mood for lively company however, and the underlying stench of despair, and unwashed bodies was so thick he could taste it. He took another large swallow of gin to wash it away. The relief lasted only briefly, and the foul miasma settled about him again, invading his nostrils, inveigling its way down his throat to his guts, laying upon his tongue like decay. More gin, then. That ought to improve his mood. It was the only way, as most residents of St Giles came to realise eventually.

Not that Max was a resident. Oh, no. He did not belong among the filth and squalor, not he with his shiny boots and his gilt buttons and his bank accounts groaning under the weight of gold and prosperity. His work, all that prosperity. Not that his bloody mother appreciated his hard work. Miserable bitch. What had he been thinking, trying to impress her? He'd never managed it before. Neither she nor his dear departed father had ever been interested in anything he achieved. *His father.* That was a laugh, as it turned out. But he was the best they'd had. No. He was *all* they'd had. Their only option despite years of trying and trying for another. No wonder they didn't care. Fate would let him live or it wouldn't. What his life looked like, if he was happy or successful, well, that was his affair. He bit back a curse as he considered the news he had to tell her. He'd made a mess of things again, not that it would surprise her. It was what she expected of him, after all. At one and twenty he was already dissipated and cynical, and now he'd made someone else's life a misery too. He snorted and filled his glass again, reminding himself he liked it here. No one could look down at him from this low pit of vice. Slumming it, that's what he was doing. Drowning his sorrows in a dingy pub before he forced himself to do the right thing for once in his misbegotten life.

The barmaid winked at him and jiggled her tits suggestively and Max considered taking her upstairs. Sally had been trying to get him upstairs for weeks, her interest obvious enough. But she'd had Humphrey Price last night and the fellow was notoriously jealous about his women. Price was here tonight, and Max didn't need the aggravation. Sally caught his eye again and jerked her head towards the stairs. Temptation nagged at him until a face swam into his mind, full of accusation. He shoved it down again. Badly done, Vane. Regret niggled, suggesting he needed more to drink. He'd killed his conscience—or perhaps pickled it—many years ago, and he wasn't about to let the damn thing bother him again. Besides, he'd resigned himself to the inevitable. He'd get it done within the week, so he'd not waste time feeling guilty about it.

Where the hell was Kilbane, anyway? The devil was supposed to have met him here an hour ago. No doubt he'd found something, or someone, more interesting to do. Max chuckled and lifted the bottle to pour himself another and found it empty. *Bollocks.*

He lifted his hand to order another, and the barmaid sashayed over and set it on the table in front of him. She leaned towards him, arms braced on the table to give him an eyeful of her abundant charms.

"Anything else you want, ducks?" she asked, her voice low. She licked her lips, looking him over.

Max reached out and squeezed one of her tits. She gasped, cheeks flushing.

"Come upstairs, handsome," she said, her voice urgent now.

With a laugh, Max shook his head. "No love, no pox for me tonight. Just the gin. Here, though, for your trouble." He took out a silver crown and slid his hand under the low neckline of her gown, settling the coin against her plump flesh and getting a good feel of her breast at the same time.

She covered his hand, holding it in place. "You sure? I've never tupped an earl, and you're easy on the eye I'll give you that. I'd treat you real nice."

"No thanks, love. Not interested. Now, sod off and leave me be," he said, enjoying the flash of anger in her eyes.

"Suit yourself. Bet you couldn't get it up anyway," she retorted cattily as she stalked away.

Max laughed and got to his feet, leaning against the chair to steady himself as the room lurched. Or was that him? He shook his head and took a breath. Shouldn't have got so bloody drunk in this pit, but he knew better than to pass out here. He'd find himself bare arsed in an alley somewhere he if wasn't careful, robbed of everything… or worse. Snatching up the gin bottle, he made for the door, relieved to be outside. The cloying heat of the pub diminished somewhat, though the air outside was only sweet by comparison. What the devil was he doing in town still? He couldn't remember what kept him here in June, but the stink of the Thames rolled over London like a bolt of damp felt, smothering everything beneath a heavy fug.

He stared up at the night sky, squinting to see if the stars were visible, but that was a laugh. No one in the Dials could see anything bright. Nothing survived the squalor. He took a deep draught from the gin bottle and then cast it aside, hearing it smash against the wall. Max lurched forwards, taking one of the seven streets for which the Dials were named. He walked quickly, knowing better than to linger. Two small, filthy children played in the gutters even at this late hour, whatever the hour was. Their mother sat on the steps of a dilapidated building with a ragged blanket for a door, crooning a melancholy lullaby off-key, clutching an empty bottle of gin to her breast. Max stuck his hands in his pockets, feeling the jingle of coin, and walked on. The children looked up as he passed, staring at him with wide, old eyes.

He could hear two women arguing, voices raising to a pitch that threatened violence, and the sound of breaking glass followed. He turned right and strode on, following his usual path except… no… this wasn't it.

Confused, he turned in a circle, frowning. Wrong road. Must have been the next he wanted, and he struck off at an angle down some narrow alley. Footsteps followed him and the darkness seemed suddenly thicker than the stench. Max hurried on, the hair on the back of his neck prickling as the footsteps got closer. He didn't look back, just walked faster. Damn him for a drunken fool, taking a wrong turn after all these years of carousing in low places. The alley took a sudden dart to the right, but the road Max had hoped to find was not there, just another long stretch of bleak, reeking alleyway.

He took a breath, trying to force his gin-sodden limbs to move, but there was a sudden pressure in his side, a hand covering his mouth, forcing the cry of pain to remain in his throat where it burned and choked him. The hand released him and, overwhelmed by dizziness, Max crumpled to the filthy cobbles.

Distantly, he heard footsteps running away as others got closer. Hands moved over him, checking his pockets, taking the coins, his grandfather's pocket watch, and tearing the buttons from his clothes.

"Help me," he pleaded, "*Please*… help…." He struggled to focus, to hold on to consciousness as pain rose in a razor-sharp wave and bore down on him, cutting and shredding as it pressed into tender flesh and organs. He was so damned cold, shivering. Warm wetness poured over his fingers. Blood. His blood. He was dying, here in the gutter, like some mongrel dog, another corpse to add to the stench of rot and decay.

The two children stared down at him, eyes too large in their heads, incongruous how old those eyes were, staring at him like judgement. He ought to have spared them a coin. Words tumbled about in his head, pleas to a god he'd barely acknowledged in his too short, wicked, decadent life before. Not until now, not until it was too late. All the same, he closed his eyes and prayed.

I'll change, he promised, weeping with fear and sorrow. *I'll be better. I swear I'll be better if you give me another chance. Please, give me another chance.*

He opened his eyes, but there was no beneficent god staring down at him, only the two dead-eyed children, watching him with curiosity.

"Please…" he whispered, raising a trembling hand. Such effort it took, that gesture of supplication, of desperation. The smallest child took a hesitant step closer, reaching for him.

Yes! Yes, please. I'll buy you a house and food and….

The small fingers firmed around his, tugging.

His ring. His signet ring.

He huffed out a laugh and closed his eyes. Dead, then. The last Earl of Vane, dead in a ditch, the end of his glorious line. Fate had won after all, despite his parent's little secret. What a grand joke on them both. Well, so be it.

"Oi! Get away from him, you vile little beggars! Clear off before I clout ye good!"

There was a metallic clatter against the cobbles and then different hands tugged at him, forcing him up. Max shook his head, protesting weakly.

"Dying. Dead in a ditch… mongrel…" he murmured, just wishing they'd leave him be. Dying seemed an awful tedious business, and he'd just as soon get it over with.

"You ain't dead yet, my lad. Come on, now. Christ, but you're heavy. Pike, run and get Jimmy. Quick smart now, lad."

More footsteps running away, fast as lightening, but Max didn't open his eyes. Curiosity was for the living, and he had dying to do.

20th July 1839, The Crown, Great St Andrew's Street, Covent Garden. Parish of St Giles.

Kathy stood on the unfamiliar street, staring about her with wide eyes. This was not Hatchards. To her horror, she realised the carriage had already driven away, and Hart was striding at his usual impossible pace, rounding a corner. With a gasp of panic, she ran after him.

"Hart!"

He turned just as she barrelled into the back of him, nearly breaking her nose on his elbow.

"Kathy! What in the name of God?"

He gave her a hard shake and did not hold back in his observations of her character and general lack of intelligence.

"You stupid, pig-headed, ignorant, spoiled little brat!"

Kathy's cheeks burned as her brother railed at her, though she could hardly blame him. It had been rather reckless. She had to admit that now. It had seemed a great lark until she'd seen where they were.

"This is how you repay our parents, is it? You're so grateful they saved you from the workhouse, you've decided to get yourself murdered in the Dials, is that it?"

His eyes burned with such fury that Kathy swallowed. But then that was Hart. He was only angry because she'd frightened him to death. For all his scowling and moody ways, he loved her and was protective of his family, of his annoying little sister.

Kathy folded her arms, quailing inwardly, but determined to stand her ground.

"I didn't know you were coming here, did I?" she retorted. "I thought you were going to Hatchards like you told Mama, but you lied," she accused him, narrowing her eyes.

"Of course I lied. She worries when I come here, you little sneak."

Kathy folded her arms, scowling. "I only wanted a new book. I've read all of ours twice."

Hart snorted and shook his head. "Yes, even the ones you didn't understand." His expression softened a degree, which still left him looking fiercer than most people. "Promise me you'll not do such a daft thing again."

Kathy considered this as she kicked at a stray pebble.

"You didn't ought to have to think about it!" he exclaimed, incensed.

"Oh, fine. I promise. But why are you here, Hart?"

Hart sighed. "To call in on Burt."

"Burt Clump? *Your* Burt?" Kathy exclaimed eagerly, naming the man who had done his best to keep Hart alive when he'd run away from the workhouse, before their parents had adopted him.

Her brother grinned. "The very same. I couldn't believe it, but I was meeting a friend here a few nights ago and… there he was."

"But why didn't you tell us?"

His expression became troubled, and he rubbed the back of his neck. "I don't know, it felt… disloyal somehow. Is that stupid?"

Kathy shook her head, taking her brother's hand. "No. It sounds like you, trying to protect everyone from being hurt. But they wouldn't mind, Hart. They'd be pleased. They know how much he meant to you."

Hart shrugged. "I suppose."

"Can I meet him too? Please, Hart?"

"It isn't a place for—"

"Don't you dare say it!" Kathy waved a finger in his face. "I'm not a child, nor a proper lady. Not really."

Hart's expression darkened. "That's exactly what you are, no matter how you argue the toss. Oh, stop pouting. I can hardly leave you here, and Burt's expecting me. Come on, now, but for the love of God, stay close and keep your eyes down."

Grinning with triumph, Kathy hurried beside her brother, staying close like he'd asked but finding it impossible not to stare about her. Her eyes widened with growing astonishment and horror as he led her down the narrow, filthy roads. The jingle of a costermonger's cart and the weary tread of a flea-bitten donkey echoed through the high-sided streets, where the buildings leant close to each other as if whispering secrets. It was a sunny morning, but the light barely penetrated the skinny thoroughfares of the Dials. Though the refuse was thick underfoot, Kathy did her best to avoid it, stepping around an especially large and mouldering pile of manure and rotten cabbage leaves and inadvertently stepping on something that squelched unpleasantly under her boot. Grimacing, she hurried on, increasingly overwhelmed by the noise that seemed to boil together into a constant hum of sound, of men shouting, dogs barking, basket women chattering as they hurried to market. Turning a corner, a pie man shouted, inviting people to try the quality of his wares for themselves. The smell of cooked meat melded with the general stench of the streets, and Kathy's stomach gave an uneasy growl of disquiet.

"Mornin,' handsome! Want some company?"

Kathy looked up to discover a barely clad woman leaning out of a first-floor window, grinning at Hart. Her hair was loose, hanging in lank curls, and she held a gaudy shawl about her naked shoulders.

"No, thanks," Hart replied, darting a glance at Kathy. "Eyes down," he hissed.

Sighing, Kathy complied, mostly so she didn't tread in anything else, though it was nigh on impossible when the streets were so thick with waste and… ugh! Swallowing a shriek, she grabbed her brother's arm as an enormous rat ran in front of them and disappeared down an open drain.

"Still glad you came?" Hart asked her dryly.

"Yes," Kathy shot back. "It's fascinating and dreadful. How these poor people live, Hart. My word, how *you* lived."

She stared up at him, only now realising the true horror of what his life had been, why he worked so hard to repay their parents by making a success of himself. Surely, more of these people could do the same with a little help?

Hart shrugged. "I was lucky, I barely remember it," he lied.

"You remembered Burt well enough," she pointed out.

Hart laughed, which was a rare enough sound for her to stare at him in surprise. "I did, but then Burt is hard to forget."

She discovered the truth of that a moment later when Hart knocked on a sturdy oak door. It appeared to be the only sturdy thing about the building, at least from the outside. They waited until the door swung open and a small boy of perhaps seven or eight years old peered owlishly up at them.

"Whatcha want?" he demanded.

"I'm here to see Burt," Hart said. "He's expecting me."

The boy's eyes narrowed and then widened as they looked at Kathy. "Are you a lady?" he demanded, gawking at her.

Kathy blushed, wondering if he was mocking her for a moment until she realised his expression was one of sincere interest.

"Yes," Hart told the boy firmly.

Kathy snorted. "No. Just a Miss. Miss de Beauvoir, pleased to meet you, Master…?"

"I'm Pike," the boy said, standing a bit taller.

"Master Pike," Kathy repeated with a smile.

Another voice called from inside the gloomy building. "Pike? What's all… Well, I'm blowed. You came!"

Burt—as Kathy assumed this was he—hurried to the door, gesticulating madly. "Come in, come in! Don't jus' stand there. Put the wood in the 'ole afore all the world knows our business."

The fellow was whip thin and all angles, and Kathy could not begin to guess his age beyond somewhere between fifty and seventy. His face, wrinkled with glee upon the sight of Hart, had creased like old leather, the deep grooves about his eyes and mouth giving him the look of a malnourished gargoyle. His clothes hung off his narrow frame, worn and with patches over patches about the elbows. He and the building they entered were clean if threadbare, however, at least compared with the alley they'd just left.

Burt clucked, shaking his head and walking a circle about Hart, looking him over.

"I still can't get over it. Whatever did they feed you? Lord, but you're as big as a bleedin' horse, and such a skinny bit of bone you was too. But… never tell me this is your sister. What the devil did you bring such a pretty child to this hellhole for? You 'ad more sense at six, my lad."

Hart snorted and sent Kathy a doleful glare. "I didn't bring her. She smuggled herself along."

"I thought he was going to buy books!" Kathy retorted defensively, and then realised that might seem as though she was disappointed to be here, which she most definitely was not. It was the most fascinating thing that had ever happened to her. "But I'm glad he didn't. It's very nice to meet you, Mr Burt, and I'm so glad you took care of Hart for us. You were very kind to do so."

"Hark at her," the boy called Pike said, staring at Kathy as if she was a circus sideshow.

"Aye, you mind your manners, Pike, my boy. P'raps she'll teach you to talk nice, like a gentleman. Like our Hart here."

Pike's expression grew mutinous, and he folded his arms.

"Well, offer the young lady a chair, then, like a proper gent would," Burt muttered, shooing Pike until he pulled out one of the few pieces of furniture in the place and made a great show of dusting it off with a grubby handkerchief.

"Thank you very much," Kathy said, perching gingerly on the rickety chair. It gave an ominous creak beneath her.

Pike's annoyed expression eased a tad, and he sat on the floor in front of her, cross-legged, staring at her, clearly as fascinated by her as she was by him.

"If you'll excuse us, Miss de Beauvoir, Hart and I have some things to discuss. Pike, you entertain our guest, and mind your tongue."

"Yes, Burt," Pike said with a sigh.

Hart followed Burt out of the room and down the dark corridor, leaving Kathy with Pike.

Kathy cleared her throat, wondering what to do now.

"Do you live in a big house?" Pike asked.

"Well, it's quite big," Kathy admitted. "I'm very lucky, but it's not terribly grand, cosier and more comfortable. Aunt Prue is a duchess, though, and her house is vast. A palace, really. And she and Bedwin have lots of other houses too."

"More than one house?" Pike exclaimed, looking stunned. "What do they want wiv all them houses? Can't live in more than one at a time, can they?"

Kathy laughed, unable to contradict the logic of that. "No, but the houses take a lot of looking after, and they employ lots of people to do it, so that's a good thing, isn't it?"

"Dunno. P'raps," Pike said, though he still looked dubious, and they subsided into an awkward silence.

A low groan broke the uncomfortable peace, and the hair on the back of Kathy's neck stood on end.

"What was that?" she exclaimed, leaping to her feet.

Pike's expression lit up, his eyes sparkling. "You ever see a fellow what's been murdered?" he asked.

Kathy's hand flew to her throat. "No, of course not."

"Want to see?" he asked eagerly.

"To see?" she repeated faintly. "But… no, that's silly. How can a murdered man make a noise like that? He'd be dead."

Pike scowled, plainly irritated by this observation. "Well, all right, he ain't dead yet, but he ought to be. Will be soon, I reckon. Someone stabbed him wiv a knife. Blood everywhere, there was. And he's a toff, like you."

"I'm not a toff," Kathy said automatically, but she was already moving towards the door that separated this room from the next. The sound came again, low and raw, heavy with pain. The poor man. "Who is he?" she asked.

"Dunno," Pike said, pushing the door open. "He tried to say afore the fever got him. Began with a V, but we couldn't understand him. Mrs Wilkes, what comes to help with him, named him Valentine on account of him being so pretty, she says. Come on. He's off his head with laudynum, so he won't know you're here."

Kathy hesitated in the doorway, not wanting to disturb the poor man's misery, but Pike grabbed her hand and yanked her into the room.

Her breath caught. Pretty indeed. The man in the bed was white as death, though two bright spots of colour burned on his high cheekbones. He looked as if he was sculpted from marble or carved in alabaster, his handsome face chiselled by the hand of a master craftsman. His torso was bare, and Kathy stared in fascination, never having seen a naked man before. Even to her innocent eye, this fellow seemed a grand specimen, all long limbs and lean muscle.

"But he's so young," she said in horror, for surely he could not be more than twenty years old, and it seemed a travesty that such a handsome, fit young man should die in such a squalid manner.

A sharp intake of breath from behind them had both she and Pike leaping with guilt.

"What the devil are you doing? You was supposed to be entertaining the girl, not subjecting her to this poor devil's misery," Burt raged, giving Pike a swift clip round the ear.

"For the love of God, Kathy!" Hart said, striding over to grasp her arm, moving her away from the bed as Burt hurried over to cover the man up.

Kathy spoke before she could think better of it. "Wait!"

Her cheeks turned crimson as Burt hesitated with the sheet in his hand and everyone stared at her.

"H-His dressing," she stammered, putting her chin up to mask her embarrassment at being found staring at a naked man and then objecting to him being covered. But the dressing was dark with blood and looked none too clean. "It needs changing."

Burt's expression darkened. "Might be a blessing not to do it. He'll die of fever soon enough. May as well make it swift."

"Oh! Oh, no!" Kathy exclaimed, her heart aching at the idea this beautiful young man might die here, with none of his family any the wiser. "But if you keep the wound clean…."

She regarded the grubby-looking cloths wrapped around his ribs. They might have been white once, she thought uncertainly, but they were far from pristine now, blood notwithstanding.

"I done what I could," the old man said regretfully. "Wish I could do more, but—"

"Honey!" Kathy said desperately, turning to him. "I read that clean linen and honey can heal a wound."

"Honey?" the old man said, wrinkling his nose.

Hart stepped closer and nodded. He'd looked thunderous ever since he'd stepped into the room and found her there, with a dying man, but he would not let the fellow die if they could save him. "She's a prodigious reader, and I believe she's right. The Egyptians and the Greeks both used honey for healing."

"Do you have any?" Kathy asked him, her heart twisting at another low moan of pain from the beautiful man on the bed.

"Oh, aye. I keep it with the butter and cream," Burt said wryly, though his tone was not cruel at least, which was somehow worse. Kathy blanched as she realised how thoughtless she'd been.

"Hart!" she said, pleading in her voice. "We must help him."

Her brother sighed, recognising a battle he couldn't win. "Fine. I'll fetch honey and clean linen, but you're coming with me."

Kathy folded her arms and shook her head. "No. I want to see it's properly done."

"Kathy," Hart said, a warning note to his voice most people would have balked at.

"No." Kathy planted her feet. "I'm not going anywhere, and if you try to force me, I'll tell Mama all about this little trip to the Dials."

Hart's expression darkened. "Why, you little devil! You don't seriously believe she'll blame me? That she'll believe I *brought* you here?"

"Of course not," Kathy said impatiently. "But she'll lose sleep fretting about all the terrible things that might have happened if you'd not seen me, or if I'd got lost following you, or kidnapped, or—"

"Argh! Fine," he snapped, dark eyes glinting with fury. "Machiavelli had nothing on you, you little viper."

"Thank you, Hart," Kathy said sweetly, and watched him stalk away.

She turned back to the bed, where the man twitched fretfully, murmuring incoherent words, and settled in to wait for her brother's return.

Kathy reached out and smoothed back the once golden hair. It was dark with sweat and the young man fretted and muttered as the fever wore him down. He was burning up, blazing away what remained of his life in one last burst of heat. She doubted he could survive it, but she prayed anyway, blinking away tears. In the past hours, she had grown sick of the sound of her own voice as she talked to him, telling him stories, telling him secrets about herself, anything to keep him with her, tied to this life. She felt as if she were weaving threads about him, binding him to her, but they were too fragile to keep him here, no matter how hard she tried.

"Stay with me," she pleaded, certain he could hear her. "Stay with me and I'll be here for you. You're not alone. I am waiting for you."

It was foolish, she knew it. She did not know him, not really, but her heart refused to accept that. Her heart had taken one look at the beautiful young man, dying too young, and had bled as though she were wounded too. Kathy wanted to make him better, to fix him and make him whole again. She could not abide to see anyone in distress, to watch suffering and do nothing. It was beyond her to endure it, so she had nagged and nagged Hart until he had grudgingly brought her back to watch over her golden boy.

He groaned, writhing on the thin pallet in misery.

"I'm here," she soothed him, unable to fight the tears that streamed down her cheeks, as she wiped his face with a cool cloth.

"Hold on now. You must hold on, and then you'll see. I won't leave you."

His eyes flicked open then, too bright, febrile and full of terror. A firm hand gripped her wrist, and she gasped.

"Do you forgive me?" he rasped, his hold on her too tight. "Absolution for the devil?"

"What?" Kathy stared at him, her heart beating fast. She tried to tug her wrist free, but his grip was strong considering how weak he'd seemed. "You're not the devil."

He moaned and closed his eyes. "You don't know. You don't know. I'm going to hell. I'm burning, burning in hell."

"It's just the fever. That's why you're so hot. It's just a fever. Someone has hurt you. You're injured."

He thrashed, kicking the sheet away, shaking his head. "Forgive me," he demanded, his agitation worsening by the second. "Forgive me."

"I don't know what to forgive you for, but I'm sure it's not so terrible," Kathy told him, wanting only to ease his suffering.

He laughed at that, a desperate sound that tore at her.

"Tell me, then," she said, laying her hand over his, where he gripped her wrist so painfully. "Tell me and I shall forgive you."

He relaxed and did as she asked, but his confession was more than Kathy could have bargained for. He told her all the vile things he'd done, his language crude and uncompromising. With ugly words, he drew a picture of a spoiled, selfish creature, of a life of dissipation, of whoring and fighting and gambling, of adultery and the ruination of anything good in him or in others.

The fever broke not long after, as if purging himself of the poisonous words had healed his soul. But the poison seeped into Kathy, into her heart, spoiling her vision of the world, of a place where a man who looked like an angel could be the devil himself.

He had made her feel stupid and weak and so very innocent of reality. She tugged her arm free of his grip and stood, her legs trembling as Hart came to fetch her.

"Kathy?" he asked, his eyes full of concern for her. "Is he…"

"He'll live," she said, her voice hard as she fought to keep her composure. "We can go now."

"Thank God for that, and don't go asking me to bring you back again, Kathy, because—"

"I shan't," Kathy replied, interrupting him. She closed her eyes for a moment, forcing down the guilt of breaking her promise to be there when he woke. That promise had been made to another man, one she had spun from daydreams and her own ignorance of reality. She had not understood, coming from the warmth and protection of her loving home, how cruel the world could be, or how cruel a man like him could be. Coming here to the Dials had opened her eyes. He had opened her eyes. And she would never be so ignorant of the cruelties of life again.

Chapter 3

Monsieur Le Comte,

By the time this reaches you, it may be too late to do you any good, but I have noticed someone asking a few too many questions. He's discreet, a professional for sure, but he seems a deal too interested in your past. Thought I ought to let you know.

Rouge et Noir is still the black diamond of Parisian Society. When you finally tire of all that English Roast Beef, she'll be here waiting for you, like the best and most wicked of mistresses.

—Excerpt of a letter to Louis César de Montluc, Comte de Villen, from Jacques Toussaint, Manager of Rogue et Noir, Paris.

Present Day …

12th May 1842, Lower Square, Isleworth, London.

Kathy stared out at what had been an empty field a few weeks ago, but was now a hive of activity. Busy workmen thronged the place, and carts trundled back and forth, bringing endless supplies of materials. The first signs of a large building's foundations had already appeared amid the chaos. The weather was mild today, the sky blue and dotted with fluffy white clouds that scudded overhead, trailing shadows upon the open ground as they went. A breeze fluttered Kathy's skirts and tugged at her bonnet, and she lifted her hand to keep it in place.

This was to be the new school. Eliza's school for boys, though Eliza refused to take credit for it, giving that honour to some mysterious benefactor she refused to unmask. Kathy chewed at her lip, considering the possibilities. Behind her, the sound of carriage wheels and the smart clip of hooves rang out, but Kathy didn't turn, too intent on her thoughts until the carriage stopped behind her. She turned then and, too late, saw the crest upon the door.

"Blast," she muttered under her breath, turning to leave.

She'd barely taken two steps before the carriage door swung open and the occupant leapt down. "Wait, Miss de Beauvoir!"

Kathy froze, wincing. *Damn. Damn. Damn.* One benefit of having an older brother was gaining a terrific ability to curse when the occasion warranted it. And this occasion definitely needed a damn, blast, and quite possibly a *bloody hell.*

"It is Miss de Beauvoir, I think?"

Kathy turned, glowering, already knowing what she was going to face. Maxwell Drake, the Earl of Vane. He was tall and infuriatingly handsome, his blonde hair shining gold in the spring sunshine. Eyes of cornflower blue stared at her, his gaze intent.

"It is," she replied, her voice cold, well aware that she was being horribly rude and not caring a jot.

He swallowed, his blond brows tugging together. "I apologise for accosting you like this. I know it's highly irregular."

"Highly," she agreed, crossing her arms.

"Yes," he said, obviously discomfited by her animosity. "Only, I've tried several times to make your acquaintance, and each time you slip through my fingers. It's like trying to catch an eel. Every time I get close, you dart in the other direction."

"An eel?" she demanded, narrowing her eyes at him. "What a delightful description. So that's how you think of me, is it?"

She was quite aware he'd meant nothing of the sort, but the quicker she could offend him into leaving her be, the better.

He gave a startled laugh. "No! Not in the least. Far from it. I think you perfectly lovely," he added, giving her what he probably believed was a charming smile, boyish and a little crooked.

Kathy's scowl deepened. She was not lovely. Not in the conventional sense, at least. She had no illusions or false modesty. Yes, she was attractive, but her nose was too long for beauty and her slanting eyebrows, set over dark grey eyes, gave her a rather fierce countenance.

"Well, you've made my acquaintance at long last, my lord," she said, giving a cursory dip in lieu of a curtsey and turning to leave.

"Wait!"

Heaving an audible sigh of irritation, Kathy turned back to him.

"I know we've never been formally introduced but… I *do* know you, though, don't I?"

There was something so close to fear in his eyes. Kathy hesitated.

"You don't remember if you know me or not?" she asked, curious despite herself.

Pike had told her he remembered nothing of her, of the fever that had almost killed him, but she'd assumed the memories would return to him, eventually. Apparently not. Which was for the best.

He shook his head. "I had an accident a few years ago. Since then, my memory is patchy in places but, whenever I see you, there's something about you that… resonates."

Kathy just about stifled a bark of laughter, but it was a close-run thing. She did not doubt her expression was contemptuous, though, and his expression faltered.

"Christ," he muttered. He took off his hat and ran a hand through his hair, staring at his feet, his expression so bleak Kathy had to admit herself surprised. She waited, too interested to know what came next to move. "Miss de Beauvoir, if…."

He broke off and swallowed, looking rather like he might be ill.

"If?" she echoed, wondering what was making him look as if he'd cast up his accounts at any moment.

"If I have wronged you, in *any* way, you have my most sincere apologies, and… and as pitiful a recompense as it may be, if there is anything I can do to make amends, I would do so in a heartbeat."

Kathy stared at him, too entertained to be insulted. The idiot thought he'd taken liberties with her.

"Are you implying that you doubt my innocence, my lord?" she demanded, keeping her voice icy with contempt, though in truth she was enjoying his discomfort enormously. It wouldn't hurt the arrogant sod from being taken down a peg or two.

"What? *No*!" he exclaimed, his expression increasingly horrified. "I…. Damnation, this is harder than I thought. I—"

He broke off, turned and strode away muttering curses and then walked back to stand in front of her.

"Ready to try again?" she asked sweetly.

He nodded. "Miss de Beauvoir. I am aware that my past is nothing to be proud of. I have spent most of my life taking what I wanted with a complete disregard for how it affected anyone else. I was cruel and selfish, profligate—"

The earl broke off again, the self-loathing in his voice taking her by surprise. He took a deep breath, rubbing a hand over his face, and she realised how much he had aged since that time, though it was not quite three years ago. Yet there were fine lines of strain about his blue eyes and there was a bleak air about him that spoke of experience, and that she suspected had not been there before.

"Carry on," she said, interested now. What was he doing here in Isleworth? Was this the mysterious benefactor Eliza had spoken about? "You were cruel, selfish, and profligate."

"Yes," he said, a frown creasing his brow. "All of that and more, and the worst of it is I cannot remember much of the harm I did, the people I hurt. Not only because of my unreliable memory, but because I spent a good deal of my life—"

"Half seas over?" she suggested tartly.

He nodded, his expression increasingly grim. "Yes, which makes atoning for my sins somewhat difficult."

"So you're doing good works, building a school?" Kathy gestured to the building works. He did not reply, so she carried on. "Eliza is family. She mentioned an anonymous rich patron funding the build."

"I would appreciate it if you would not speak of my involvement," he said.

Kathy regarded him with interest. He stood stiffly, every line of his body radiating tension and unease. He wanted no credit for the school, she realised. Was he truly punishing himself? The man she had known so briefly had turned her young heart upside down and inside out. Not that it had been his fault, exactly. She had known him for such a short time, barely three days, and for all of it, he'd either been unconscious or out of his mind with delirium. But she had woven romantic stories about the sleeping prince, only to discover he was the devil himself. He had shattered her innocent illusions about love, and though it was foolish, she realised now that she had still not forgiven him for it. She stared at him now, seeing not a devil, but only a deeply flawed man, trying to do his best.

"Well then, I wish you success with your endeavours, my lord."

Kathy discovered she meant it. If he was truly repentant, then he deserved credit for it. It had not been his fault she had assumed him to be something he wasn't.

"Wait, you still haven't told me if—"

"No. You did not debauch me in a dark corner," she cut in, her voice harder than she'd intended, admitting herself shocked to see the flush that rose high on his cheeks.

He let out a shaky breath. "I am relieved if I have never offered you any insult or done you any harm, Miss de Beauvoir, but I cannot shake the feeling that… I *know* you."

There was something, some depth of feeling behind the words that troubled her and made her snap out a response.

"You do not."

Perhaps it was the intensity of his gaze, or the emphasis he put on that one word, which gave it too many intimate connotations. Not that they had ever been intimate, not physically, though she had sat with him and sponged his fevered body, changed his dressings and tried to calm him when he was afraid and in pain. She had sung to him and held his hand, told him stories, told him her secrets as though he'd been as sweetly innocent of wrongdoing as she. And then he'd burst out of his sleeping fever to spill his poison in her ears. To confess his darkest secrets to her, ranting and furious with pain and confusion, and she'd been frightened and appalled and so horribly disillusioned. His confessions might have been good for his soul, but they had tainted some part of her she'd not been ready to let go of and she was still angry about the loss she'd felt.

"No," he said, letting out a breath. Was that disappointment in his eyes? "No, of course not. Forgive me for bothering you."

He gave her a polite bow and had turned to walk away when the idea struck her out of nowhere. Here was her opportunity. Here was something she could do, something that interested her, that could make the most of her skills.

"My lord?"

He turned at once, a hopeful glint in his eyes that made her remember that sleeping prince and the foolish stories she'd told herself. Worse, that she'd told *him.*

Annoyed to discover herself fighting a blush, Kathy put up her chin. "If you think you can keep your interest in this project a secret and monitor progress on it too, you're mad. It won't take any time at all for people to notice your frequent visits."

"I know that, but I have yet to employ someone to do the job for me. The truth is, Miss de Beauvoir, I'm not quite used to being a responsible human being. I am trying to get my life in order, to undo years of bad behaviour and idiocy, and getting good staff is—"

"I'll do it," she said, aware she was interrupting him again and not giving a damn.

He blinked at her, and she glared at him, daring him to tell she was hardly qualified.

"I have worked for both my father and brother, my lord. My father, as I am sure even you must be aware, is a brilliant scientist. However, his filing skills are non-existent. He has no concept of time, and loathes dealing with correspondence. If I say so myself, my organisational skills are exemplary, I am hard working and I enjoy getting things done and done properly."

"Yes, but why—"

Kathy didn't allow him to finish, too determined to get her point across. "I have been looking for just such an opportunity. I have long wanted to improve the lot of those less fortunate, but I have neither the power nor the finances to do so. For example I have tried to raise awareness of the vile conditions in the workhouse here in Isleworth. You noticed, perhaps, how much money has been spent on the elegant building you passed. What a pretty confection it is, so as not to offend its rich neighbours, and yet conditions inside are appalling. The poor creatures who inhabit that pretty edifice are starving and ill-treated, living in filth, and despite endless visits and writing dozens of letters, I am ignored by the dull old men in charge. With your name, and your money, I could make them listen. I could do some good. We can begin with this school project. I will liaise with Eliza and give you regular reports. I will make the very best use of your money and perhaps, if I can prove my worth, you will allow me to pursue other avenues on your behalf."

He frowned, looking more than a little stunned. She supposed she could hardly blame him; that *had* been something of a tirade. Kathy did not fool herself into thinking she'd won him over. Once the shock of her outburst had subsided, she assumed he would pat her on the head, laugh at the very idea, and walk away.

She was wrong.

"And you would report to me. *Personally.*"

Kathy hesitated. Having to spend more time in this man's company was not a comfortable idea, and yet, she wanted this opportunity to do some good. She had wanted to do *something* since that ill-fated day she'd followed her brother into the Dials and had her eyes opened to what her life might have been if fate had not been so kind. The day she'd met *him.* If she could use this opportunity to make a name for herself, she might really do some good for the people who lived in such terrible conditions, and perhaps then she could stand beside her brilliant parents and brother without feeling so horribly ordinary in comparison.

With her heart beating in her throat, she gave a taut nod. "Yes, my lord. I would."

Maxwell stared at the girl, temptation an itch under his skin. She was too delicious, a heady combination of wilful temper and innocence. She disliked him, no matter her claims that they did not know each other. Perhaps she just knew him by reputation, but he doubted it. She was lying. He was certain of it. Max had lied often enough himself not to recognise it in others. He had hurt her, or insulted her, or someone she cared about. The truth of that weighed him down, reminding him he must do better.

In the past he would not have hesitated to do all in his power to charm her, to beguile her and seduce her, and to get beneath her skirts as quickly as possible. The idea made guilt squirm in his chest, but did not quench the heat flickering in his veins. It was a bad idea to let her within a mile of him, but then that was part of it, was it not? Part of becoming a better man was not to just avoid temptation, but to resist it because it was the right thing to do. It was not supposed to be easy. But if he failed, it would not be him who suffered, as ever.

It would be safer for her to keep her distance.

"I have no doubt you would be an excellent choice, Miss de Beauvoir, but I don't think it's a very good idea."

"Liar," she threw back at him, and he suspected she'd shocked herself with her outburst as much as she'd shocked him by the widening of her stormy grey eyes. He'd seen the clouds gathering there before him as he spoke. It was quite fascinating to watch. "You know it's a good idea. You just don't want me around, but… but you owe me this."

Maxwell recoiled as though she'd slapped him. Well, there it was then. He'd been right all along.

"Why?" he asked, his voice rough. "What did I do?"

She shook her head, waving this away. "It's of no matter now. But this is."

"It matters to me," he said furiously, and then calmed himself. Losing his temper was hardly a way of making amends, even if frustration was snapping at his heels. If she wanted to torment him, he could hardly blame her for it. He deserved to suffer, for so many things. "I beg your pardon, Miss de Beauvoir."

"There's no need. I prefer plain speaking, my lord, and I want this job. I'll do it well. You have my word."

"And if I agree. Will you forgive me for whatever harm I did to you?"

Her gaze slid away from him, and her eyebrows drew together. A moment later she looked up, her reply firm.

"I do forgive you."

Well, he could hardly ask for more than that, but…. "And will you tell me what it was I did to hurt you?"

She shook her head. "It was a long time ago. You did not dishonour me, and any hurt you inflicted was not intentional."

"And yet it has coloured your life," he said, the burden of that knowledge settling upon him with such weight it was hard to breathe.

She held his gaze, and when she spoke her voice was softer, her forgiveness implied in the words. "You opened my eyes, my lord, that is all. I suspect you did me a great favour, perhaps even saved me from my own foolishness. It simply did not feel that way at the time, but I can see it now, and so I forgive you. And that is the last time we shall speak of it. Do we have an agreement?"

Maxwell looked down at the slender hand she held out to seal the deal. Encased in soft grey kid gloves, her hand looked small and fragile, and he took it carefully, barely squeezing her fingers for fear of doing greater harm.

"We do."

She let out a breath, which he suspected she'd been holding for some time, and smiled and the force of it nearly knocked him down. Good God, but he'd been kidding himself. She was not merely lovely, she—

His startled brain thrashed about for a word to describe the sensation in his heart, the one that told him he *knew* her. He knew her heart, her soul, like he knew his own. Except that didn't make the least bit of sense. Lust, he told himself. That was all it was. He was a disgusting excuse of a man and he wanted her in his bed and that was all there was to it. Well, not this time. This time he would behave like the gentleman his title proclaimed him to be, and that was the end of it.

Chapter 4

Dear Eliza,

You'll never guess what. I've just had the most interesting conversation with The Earl of Vane about the school you are building –

—Excerpt of a letter from Miss Kathleen de Beauvoir (daughter of Mrs Minerva and Mr Inigo de Beauvoir) to Lady Elizabeth Demarteau (daughter of Their Graces, Prudence and Robert Adolphus, The Duke and Duchess of Bedwin).

12th May 1842, Heart's Folly, Sussex.

"Thank you for coming, Mr Godwin," Elton said, taking Barnaby's hat and gloves from him.

"Well, of course. I came as soon as I read your note. I've been worried sick these past weeks, wondering where the devil he'd got to."

Barnaby hurried after Louis' valet. He'd known something was amiss when Louis had vanished without a word. He'd thought they were friends. Though he knew well enough that most people only tolerated his company, thinking him a fool, he'd thought Louis was different. Yet he'd not heard a word from him for weeks, and being so thoroughly abandoned had hurt until he'd realised that this was not about him. A fine friend he'd been, licking his own wounds when he ought to have known Louis needed him. Except, by then, he'd not known where to look. He'd been here to Heart's Folly two weeks ago, only to find the place empty.

"Monsieur has been blue devilled for some time and so had been staying with his brother at Mr Demarteau's insistence," Elton said, speaking over his shoulder as they hurried up the stairs. "Except something happened two nights ago. He'd been waiting for something, I think. Information. Whatever it was, I don't think it was what he wanted to hear. We left Mr Demarteau's home, though he tried to stop us. I cannot say what happened, but it sent him into a pit of despair so deep, I don't know how to get him out again. He'll drink himself to death if he keeps this up and... well, sir, I am at my wits' end, and that's a fact. I'm only his valet, but you're his friend. His only friend, as far as I know."

Barnaby stared at Elton, a little shaken by that. His *only* friend? That could not be correct, surely? The Comte de Villen was welcomed everywhere, desired by damn near everyone, and yet... and yet now he thought about it, Barnaby could not name a single person Louis truly counted as a friend.

Elton knocked on Louis' bedroom door, but all was silent. Barnaby watched as the man steeled himself and turned the handle. Though it was late in the afternoon, the curtains were closed, and the room was dark. A figure lay before the empty fireplace and, for a moment, Barnaby's heart stopped.

"Louis?" He ran forward, kneeling down and only feeling his heart give a kick of relief in his chest when he discovered the still form warm and breathing, and reeking of brandy. Barnaby looked up. "Coffee, please, Elton. Lots of it, and have a bath prepared."

"At once, sir," Elton said, with obvious relief, and hurried away.

Barnaby turned back to Louis and patted his cheek. "Louis, wake up, old man. It's Barnaby. Can't go about sleeping on the floor where anyone can trip over you. Besides, it's dashed uncomfortable. Come along, wake up now."

Louis stirred and pushed Barnaby's hand away. *"Non."*

Sighing, Barnaby got up and opened the curtains and went to the washstand, picking up the jug of cold water and a towel, and returning to stand over Louis. "I'm sorry, Louis, but it's for your own good."

He upended the jug over Louis' head. What had appeared at first glance to be an inanimate corpse exploded into life and Louis gasped, sitting bolt upright and glaring at Barnaby, his eyes an unholy shade of blue against his pallid countenance.

"*Fils de pute*!" he said, clearly furious.

"I don't reckon that's terribly polite," Barnaby said ruefully. "Not that I blame you. Rotten of me, I know, but I think you need to sober up and explain what's going on. Where've you been? I've worried myself silly fretting over you disappearing like that."

Louis pushed his sodden hair from his eyes with a shaking hand, and regarded Barnaby with a stark expression that did not ease Barnaby's concern. "If I had wanted to be sober, I would not have worked so hard on getting blind drunk," he growled.

Barnaby handed him the towel and sat down, cross-legged, on the floor beside him. "It's Evie, isn't it?" he asked quietly. "I knew she'd gone away, of course, but you've heard something, I reckon."

Louis rubbed the cloth over his face and hair and made a bitter sound. Leaning his elbows on his knees, he pressed the heels of his hands against his eyes. "Yes. She is gone. Gone far from me, and there's damn all I can do about it."

"Well, they can't keep her away forever," Barnaby said, not liking the defeated posture of the man before him.

"No," Louis said, his voice dull. "Just until she's fallen in love with someone else."

"Eh? What do you mean? Where is she?"

"Scotland. Staying with her mother's friend, the Countess of Morven. Both families hope she will make a match with one of their three sons."

"Oh." Barnaby frowned, wishing he knew what to say. "Well, they can't force her to fall in love with one of them."

"*Non*," Louis said, but his expression was one of utter misery. "No more than I can, but they are being given permission and opportunity. From what I hear, they are handsome, eligible young men. Evie will know it is what her parents want, that it will make them happy. More than that, they've made it so she cannot correspond with me. They must have done, for I've had no word and… and even if she has fallen head over ears in love with some damned Scot, she would not forget me, not leave me without a word… *would* she?"

There was a world of pain and doubt behind the question that made Barnaby's chest hurt.

"Of course not!" he said at once. "She's written to you regularly this many years, has she not? She wouldn't stop if she didn't have to."

Louis nodded, though doubt lingered in his eyes. "If that's true, then I am certain her father has discovered our correspondence, or perhaps he found one of the gifts I gave her. I am uncertain whether her maid approved of me. She might have said something to him, might have tattled on Evie behind her back. Someone in Paris has been asking questions, trying to dig up my past. I don't doubt Knight would do such a thing if he knew of my interest in her."

"But why not confront you, then?" Barnaby asked, frowning. "If he thought you were up to no good with his daughter, I would think a man like Knight would call you out? Confront you, at least."

Louis shook his head. "He's not a fool, by any means. Perhaps he might do such a thing if he believed I had compromised her, but if he only suspected we were closer than he would like, he'd never act so rashly. To do so would risk Evie throwing herself into my arms expressly because she'd been forbidden to do so."

"Oh. Yes, I see. Forbidden fruit and all that."

"Taking her out of my reach was his best option, and he knew it. Her father is banking on the fact she's young enough not to be constant in her affections. He's giving her time to forget about me, to find another, more suitable man to take up her time."

Barnaby watched his friend with regret, wishing there was something he could do.

"Morven's son's, you said? Isn't he in the north, up around Wick?"

Louis shrugged, such a defeated gesture Barnaby determined he must do something. "He may as well be on the moon. I've no friends there, no one on whom I could presume, and I fear causing Evie trouble, for I would not do so for the world. I could beg Knight for an audience, for a chance to court her, but even if I assured him my intentions were honourable, I do not believe he will grant me the opportunity. Worse than that, if I declare myself, Evie herself might turn her back on me. On the few occasions I have tried to make my feelings known, I have felt her uncertainty, her desire not to hear what I want to tell her. I think it might frighten her away and straight into the arms of one of those handsome Scotsmen."

"She's very young," Barnaby observed.

"Oui, as are her suitors in the north," he said, stripping off his sodden shirt and casting it aside. "They have no skeletons rattling the bones of their past. Knight knows too much of me to view me with any favour. I can hardly blame him. I'm not good enough for

her and I don't deserve her. I know that better than anyone, but I'm a selfish devil and I *need* her, Barnaby. I cannot bear to consider the future, if…."

Louis' voice cracked, and he choked out a laugh, staring at Barnaby. "Well, are you not glad you made my acquaintance, *mon ami? Merde,* but I am a pitiful wretch. Perhaps Evie has had a lucky escape."

"Now, now. None of that," Barnaby said briskly. "I am glad to be your friend. Proud too, so stop wallowing. First things first. We need to get you sober and tidy you up. When was the last time you shaved? Or bathed, come to that? You smell like the bottom of a brandy barrel."

"That good?" Louis replied with a snort, allowing Barnaby to haul him to his feet. "You astonish me."

"I know. You can't even be disgusting when you're drunk. It's really not fair on the rest of us, Louis.

Barnaby steadied him, slinging an arm about his waist and guiding him to the nearest chair. As he sat, he saw Louis' back and gaped.

"Good Lord!" he said, staring in astonishment. Even more surprising was the embarrassment in Louis' expression. He reached for the discarded towel and went to sling it over his shoulders, but Barnaby stopped him, snatching it from his hands as he gazed at Louis' broad shoulders in consternation. His build alone was a sight surprising enough to make Barnaby stare. Like looking at a Greek god come to life. The fine tailoring he wore highlighted an elegant physique, but the power and muscle beneath that civilised exterior were a shock when revealed in the flesh. This, though, was so scandalous it overcame his innate desire to be polite. "No, show me. Is that… *it is!* It's an eagle. Bless me! But how…?"

"*Un tatouage*—a tattoo. I was very young when it was done," Louis said stiffly.

"It's jolly good," Barnaby said, startled to discover such a thing on his friend but fascinated all the same. The eagle was finely drawn, his wings stretching across Louis' wide shoulders, talons reaching, beak open in a silent cry. The only men he knew of who had tattoos were sailors and criminal types, so to discover such a thing on the refined Comte de Villen was outrageous. He had a hundred questions and very much doubted Louis would answer any of them. "Did it hurt?" was the safest he could come up with.

"At the time, yes."

"But… why?" Barnaby ventured, not expecting an explanation.

"Perhaps another time, *mon ami,"* Louis said with an apologetic smile. "It is a long story."

Barnaby nodded reluctantly, not wanting to let the matter drop, but Elton reappeared. "Ah, and here is the coffee. Good man, Elton," he said with approval as the valet carried in a tray and set it down in front of them.

"The bath will be ready presently, sir," Elton said, casting an anxious glance at Louis.

Barnaby poured out a cup of coffee and put it into Louis' hands. "Drink it," he said firmly.

Louis sighed, but obediently raised the cup to his mouth and took a cautious sip.

"Elton, bring me writing materials, please. I need to send a letter," Barnaby said, aware of Louis' curious gaze upon him.

"At once, Mr Godwin," Elton said, hurrying out again.

Louis opened his mouth to speak, but Barnaby beat him to it, too consumed with curiosity to let the matter drop. "You know, I'm surprised no one has ever mentioned that tattoo before. I assume Elton has seen it, but you've had a good many mistresses, and you know what women are for tattling."

Louis gave him a long-suffering look. "Elton would rather die than let the world know his canvas has the slightest imperfection. As for my romantic interludes, I can trust some women to be discreet and, if not, I keep my shirt on, or employ the use of blindfolds, or the dark, or pleasure the lady from behind. Do you have any other questions?" he asked politely, though the words had an edge.

Barnaby felt colour climb the back of his neck. "Er… no. Not a one," he said, clearing his throat awkwardly.

Louis sighed and then gave a huff of laughter. He shook his head and ran a hand through his damp hair.

"A letter?" he asked, watching Barnaby, who still stood before him, hoping to God he was doing the right thing. "To whom are you writing?"

"Ah. Yes. Now I don't want to get your hopes up, for I've not the slightest idea if she'll agree to it," he warned, wondering if he would live to regret this but Louis stilled, staring up at him, so he carried on.

"I've an aunt, a grand old battleaxe. She's terrified me since I was a boy, but… well, she lives in the Highlands, not a million miles from Wildsyde Castle. I warn you now, Castle Bradwell is a dreadful draughty old pile in the middle of nowhere, with nothing to do but walk and hunt, and catch pneumonia, if I recall. Also, I've not seen her in a decade, and I doubt she's mellowed any, but she's there, and she's family and, if I ask, I reckon we could stay for a few days. It's a long shot, but… well, you'd be in the vicinity, at least. Maybe—"

Louis set down his cup with a clatter and got to his feet, pulling Barnaby into a hug and kissing his cheek. "*Merci*, Barnaby. Thank you, my friend."

Barnaby patted Louis' back awkwardly, very aware of the scandalous tattoo under his hand and not quite certain how to deal with such a show of affection. "Oh, well. That's… think nothing of it, old man. You might not thank me when you get there, though. It's the back end of beyond. You'll be bored stiff, and that's before you even meet Great-Aunt Hester. A frightful old bat."

"I would face a thousand frightful old bats for the slightest chance to speak with Evie again," Louis said, the light of hope shining in his eyes, and making Barnaby glad that he could help, but utterly terrified that it might all be for naught.

One thing seemed certain: Louis was vulnerable where Evie was concerned, and Barnaby feared what losing her for good might do to him.

16th May 1842, Lower Square, Isleworth, London.

"I wanted to speak to you about the gardens next," Kathy said, turning the page of her notebook.

Eliza nodded. "Oh, yes, the gardens have been of vital importance at the girls' school. Many of the children hadn't the slightest notion of how food was grown or where it came from. I'm certain too that being in nature has helped many of them, giving them a sense of peace, a place to calm themselves when things are difficult. And, in a purely practical light, it makes sense for the property to be as self-sufficient as possible. It also provides valuable skills for those who tend the garden, and here there is so much land on offer it would be a crime not to make the most of it. I think even some animals might be possible. Chickens and pigs, at least. Though finding someone willing to design and take charge of it all, when it is only a charitable school and there is little financial reward on offer, is another matter."

Kathy looked around at the overgrown field that Eliza gestured to and smiled.

"I hope you don't think me cheeky for suggesting such a thing, but I believe I have the perfect man for the job."

Eliza raised her dark eyebrows, and Kathy batted down a tiny sliver of envy. Lady Elizabeth was beautiful, stylish, and seemed to know exactly who and what she was. The daughter of a duke, she had defied convention by marrying a nobody, the illegitimate half-brother of the Comte de Villen. The *ton* had been shocked, had giggled and tittered about her marrying beneath herself, and Eliza didn't give a snap of her fingers. She was living life on her terms, as she wanted to, and she appeared blissfully happy.

"You don't mean to say Hart would be interested? I thought he was far too busy with his greenhouses and supplying exotic plants to the world?"

"Yes, but he has always wanted to design a garden, Eliza. We both know it's not his sphere of expertise, but he is so very talented, and he would work day and night to create something splendid for you. And because you would be doing him a favour, giving him a chance to make a name for himself, I rather think he'll be extraordinarily cheap. That is to say, free."

Eliza laughed, looking delighted by the idea. "Well, then, by all means. I'll have copies of the building plans and maps sent over to him, and you arrange a meeting once he's had time to make some preliminary studies."

"Oh, that's wonderful! Thank you, Eliza."

"No, no, thank you. It's a marvellous idea." Eliza took her arm and the two women strolled around the outskirts of the building site, watching the workmen as the bones of the handsome building took shape. "Speaking of marvellous ideas, how on earth did you get Vane to allow you to work on his behalf?"

A glint of curiosity shone in Eliza's eyes, and Kathy avoided her gaze. She shrugged. "Serendipity, that's all. I was here, interested in the project, and he turned up. I guessed at once he must be your mysterious benefactor and told him so. It was obvious that if he wanted his interest to be kept out of the public eye, he needed someone else to oversee it."

Eliza nodded, watching Kathy with interest. "Yes, I admit I was wary of getting involved with him. His reputation precedes him and casts quite a shadow, but I am not as gullible as some people think, and I believe his regret is genuine. He wants to make amends and start over. Easier said than done, naturally. He's discovering now the price for his previous attitudes. The staff who had stayed on whilst he was missing were few, and more than half of them had been lining their own pockets behind his back. Finding good people is never a straightforward task and with his reputation as a neglectful employer, it hardly helps. You must have appeared as manna from heaven."

Kathy snorted at the idea. "Hardly, but I shall prove my worth to him, and once I do, I intend to prey upon his desire to assuage his guilt by spending more of his money on good causes."

"My, you sound positively devious," Eliza said, though her tone was approving. "You won't bankrupt the poor man, though, will you?"

"No, I'll leave him enough for a crust of bread for supper," Kathy said, with a mischievous grin.

"That's a little harsh, love," Eliza chuckled, amused. "I know his reputation was black and, if half the rumours are true, that he was a selfish devil, but we are in the business of charity, are we not? If someone accepts they've done wrong and is sincere in wanting to make amends, ought we not support them and encourage them?"

"Yes. I do agree, truly. What he's doing is admirable and he should be encouraged wholeheartedly, and I ought to find it easier to forgive."

Eliza's gaze sharpened, and Kathy cursed herself.

"To forgive? Do you mean to say *you* have something to forgive him for?"

"Oh, no," she said in a rush. "Not me personally. I was just speaking generally. You are far sweeter in nature than I, that's all," she added, laughing.

Eliza nodded, apparently accepting this, and Kathy heaved a sigh of relief.

Chapter 5

Barnaby,

I've not the slightest idea what you are playing at, but if you must come, you must. I'll expect you by the end of the month.

—Excerpt of a letter to Mr Barnaby Godwin from his Great Aunt Hester Henley, Lady Balderston.

25th May 1842, Vane Hall, Chiswick, London.

"Well, this is most comprehensive, Miss de Beauvoir." Lord Vane's expression was carefully neutral as he perused her report, and Kathy suspected he was working on hiding his surprise.

At least he was trying to be polite. Even so, the knowledge rankled. He looked very much at home here, in the environs of a cosy study. It was all heavy dark wood and velvet curtains, the thick carpets muffling the heaviest of footfalls and the air perfumed with cigar smoke and fine brandy. A masculine room for masculine endeavours, such as speaking of money and business. Things that, in his world, she would be told she need not worry her pretty little head about.

"You employed me, expecting me to make a pig's ear of it, my lord?" she asked with every outward appearance of innocence, whilst sending him a dazzling smile instead of kicking his desk.

His lordship's sensuous mouth twitched, but he held his serious expression with admirable aplomb. "I employed you because you made me feel horribly guilty. A state which I do not doubt I deserve," he hurried to add. "However, you have exceeded my expectations, and I am most pleased. Thank you. Now, as to the matter of schoolbooks. You said you wanted to make some changes?"

Kathy regarded her notes. "Well, the original order you placed comprises six and thirty primers, four and twenty prayer-books, four and twenty testaments, and twelve bibles."

"Miss de Beauvoir, judging by the fierce expression you are sending my way, am I to believe this order does not meet with your approval?"

"Well, really," Kathy said, not bothering to hide her exasperation. "You are seeking to educate boys who've lived on the streets and had to fight for their very survival, and you think to keep them in school by feeding them a diet of prayer and improving stories? Truly? Would that have worked on you, or would you have been out the door the moment your tutor turned his back?"

"Miss de Beauvoir, I *was* out the door, and very well. I take your point. What do you suggest?"

Kathy rifled through her bag and tugged out several leaflets she had collected from various print shops. "Here, there is a set of illustrated encyclopaedias being offered at a very reasonable rate. Just the thing to make boys curious about the world at large. I have negotiated an excellent deal, if you were to buy two copies of the set. There are also some basic texts on science and maths which my father will donate to the cause, and here is a list from the Countess St Clair on books she recommends as simple and educational. I thought perhaps a selection of books on gardening, as there is no point in having such a splendid garden and not teaching the boys how to tend it. Here's a list my brother compiled for me. By the by, he'd be willing to consider employing any able recruits in the future, if they show competence and enthusiasm for the subject. Oh, and also books on animal husbandry. I wrote to a friend whose husband is a farmer and expect to have a list of suggestions by next week. I'm certain there will be plenty of other subjects that ought to be covered, but that at least is a start."

Kathy studied him, waiting.

"It certainly is a start," Lord Vane said, staring at her. "You are something of a force of nature, Miss de Beauvoir."

Kathy blushed, altogether too pleased by his praise until she realised that most men would not have meant it as a compliment. Ladies were supposed to be quiet and demure after all, two things she did not excel at. She shifted uncomfortably in her chair.

"It *was* a compliment," he said gently, only making her more uncomfortable as she realised how easily he'd read her reaction. She supposed that was what had made him such a successful libertine. Knowing what women wanted to hear and gauging their reactions to his words must have gone a long way towards persuading many gullible young ladies into his bed. She supposed she would do well to remember that.

"Then I thank you," she said with a quick smile, gathering up her notes and papers and putting them back in her bag. "Well, that is all for now. I shall begin gathering quotes for the supply of boots and clothing, and I have some ideas for fund-raising efforts, so we do not entirely bankrupt you on this first project. I shall report back to you when there is progress made on the garden design. Good day, my lord."

"Good day, Miss de Beauvoir."

Maxwell watched as the young lady hurried from the room, knowing she was relieved to be out of his company. The knowledge made him uncomfortable, regret an uneasy sensation in his gut. He wished he knew what it was he'd done to hurt her.

Perhaps it was a blessing he didn't remember, because the things that he was aware of were going to take the rest of his damned life to atone for. There was something about her, though, a sense of familiarity that tugged at him. When she entered a room, it seemed as if he could breathe again, as if he'd been waiting for her to return so he could be at ease. He huffed out a laugh and rubbed a hand over his face. He'd not had a drink in weeks. Such sentimental nonsense was likely a result of clean living and behaving himself.

His new regime had him rising early and filling his days with a strict timetable of physical activity and work. Every moment of his day was accounted for so that when evening fell he was too bloody tired to contemplate going out drinking or socialising and risking falling into old habits. He attended the occasional ball or *ton* event when refusing might have caused offence, but mostly, he kept busy and as far from trouble as he could get.

A knock at the door interrupted his musings, which he thought was probably for the best.

"Come."

Jarvis, the butler here at Vane Hall and one of the few members of staff who'd remained, stood in the doorway, looking as regal as always. Vane often thought Jarvis would have made a far better earl than he did. He didn't doubt Jarvis would agree with him.

"The Marquess of Kilbane for you, my lord."

Maxwell hesitated, contemplating not being at home, but that was cowardly. "Send him in."

A moment later, Kilbane strode in, as wickedly stylish as always. "Vane. At last. Where have you been hiding yourself?" he asked, taking the chair before the desk, and arranging his long limbs in an elegant sprawl.

"I've been working," Max replied, gesturing to the paperwork littering his desk. Thankfully, he had put away all that pertained to the school, for he did not need Kilbane poking his nose in there. "You should try it sometime."

Kilbane chuckled, his strange violet eyes glittering in the dim light of the room. "I work," he protested. "The devil knows I work."

"Causing mischief and disrupting other people's lives does not count."

"Oh, but I put so much effort into it, Maxwell. Give me a little credit, surely?" Kilbane said, giving him a charming smile, but the devil *was* charming when he wanted to be.

That was what made him so bloody dangerous.

"What do you want?" Max asked impatiently. Kilbane was an uneasy reminder of the man he'd been, the harm he'd caused, and he did not want him around stirring things up. Ciarán knew too many of his secrets to be a comfortable companion.

"Well, is that any way to greet an old friend? I'm bored, that's all, so I came to see what you were up to these days."

"We were never friends," Max retorted, before he could think better of it. "You don't have friends, Ciarán."

"I've known you since we were boys," Kilbane protested, studying Max with too much interest. "That counts for something, doesn't it?"

Max snorted. "It means we've known each other since we were boys. You're no friend of mine. Friends don't blackmail each other to get what they want."

For a moment, something flickered in the man's violet eyes. Had that been emotion? No. Max rejected the idea as Kilbane gave a little dismissive tut of annoyance.

"And would you have allowed me to attend the Trevick ball if I had not?"

"Would you have destroyed an innocent life if I'd refused?" Max shot back.

Kilbane's expression darkened. "So dramatic, Maxwell. It would never have come to that. I just needed insurance."

"What was so damned important, then?"

Kilbane shrugged and waved an elegant hand. "Personal business. It's all done now."

"And so must I wait until the next time you want something to have the threat dangled beneath my nose again? Is that why you're here?"

Kilbane let out a harsh sound of irritation and got to his feet. "No. I told you. Your pretty little secret is safe with me. I've no interest in her. I'll not use that against you again, Max. My word on it. There, satisfied?"

Max stared at him. "You know as well as I do what your word is worth."

Those violet eyes flashed again and, if he hadn't known better, Max might have believed he'd hurt the fellow's feelings, but Ciarán St Just didn't have feelings like other people.

"What is it you're doing precisely?" Kilbane demanded, gesturing at the paperwork and ledgers piled up around Max's desk.

"Putting my life in order like a normal human being, that's what. I have estates to manage, so do you, if you remember."

Max got to his feet and stalked to the window. He had better things to do than waste his time on a man he wanted left in his past. Kilbane would not entice him back into the dark place he'd been. No one would.

"It sounds dull," Kilbane muttered. "And my estate can go up in flames for all I care. Do you care for a drink? There are entertainments at the Orchid House I believe I shall indulge in this evening."

Max shook his head. There was an itch beneath his skin that reminded him it had been a very long time since he'd had any female companionship, but a visit to an exclusive whorehouse was a bad idea. He knew all too well the vices catered for at the Orchid House, and how easy it was to get drawn in. Besides, he didn't want the company of some clever, practised courtesan. Miss de Beauvoir's lovely grey eyes flickered in his mind, and he slammed the door shut on the idea before it could take hold.

"No, thank you. I have plans for this evening." A small smile flickered at the corner of Max's mouth as he considered those plans, and what Ciarán would make of them if he knew he was turning down the delights of the Orchid House in favour of distinctly different company.

Kilbane's sensuous mouth made a small moue of displeasure.

"Well, then, there's a card game at Grant's tomorrow night. High stakes. Join me then and take your mind off all *this.*" He waved a contemptuous hand at Maxwell's desk. "Whatever it is."

"I have plans for tomorrow night too, Ciarán," he said, his voice flat.

"Fine. Suit yourself." Kilbane got to his feet, his frustration evident. As he made his way to the door, he gave Max a curious, narrow-eyed look. "Come and find me when you grow bored with polishing your halo."

"Goodbye, Ciarán," Max replied, and watched as the door closed behind him.

"Evening, Valentine. Come in, come in."

"Burt, you're looking well," Max said, scrutinising the man to whom he owed his life. He was Valentine here, not Lord Vane, not even Max, but another man entirely. A man he liked far more than the one he'd been before.

"Fit as a flea," Burt said, eyeing the heavy boxes Max's servants were carrying in. "What's all this, then? I told you afore, I don't hold with charity. I do right fine, thank you very much."

"I know you do, Burt, but not everyone else in the Dials can say the same, can they? You do with it what you think is best, but I should be pleased if you'd take what you need. For the boy's sake at least, eh?"

"Ah, now, that's blackmail, is what that is," Burt replied, but his little currant eyes twinkled with satisfaction.

Max let out a sigh of relief, knowing Burt could take what he needed without denting his blasted pride.

"What's for supper, then?" Maxwell asked, though the potent scent of frying answered the question easily enough.

"Got a nice bit o' bacon and some eggs, and I'll fry some bread in the bacon grease." Burt smacked his lips and Maxwell laughed.

"A feast. Hurry up, then, old man. I'm famished."

"Val!" Pike exclaimed, grinning at him from his position guarding the frying pan. "See, I tol' you he'd come, same as always."

"You did," Burt replied, setting out three chipped but clean tin plates on the table. "But sooner or later, he'll realise he can't keep coming back 'ere. Got a life of his own to lead, same as us, but in a different world."

"It's the same world, Burt, and the only reason I've a life at all is down to you. I'm not about to forget that," Max said, taking his usual place at the table.

"Pfft!" was the only response from Burt, who waved the little matter of saving Max's skin away as if it was nothing at all.

"How is your reading coming along, Pike?"

"Much better," Pike told him proudly. "I'll read to you after supper to prove it."

Max nodded and set a small, wrapped parcel on the table. "You can start this, then," he said, pushing it towards the boy.

Pike's eyes lit up, and he abandoned the bacon in favour of snatching up the parcel and tugging at the string. He turned the book in his hands, stroking the leather binding with reverent fingers and touching the tooled gold letters with an expression of awe.

"Robinson Crusoe," he read, his gaze flicking from the book to Max.

"It's a good story. It's got adventure and shipwrecks. Pirates, too," Max added, knowing this would appeal to the lad.

"Pirates?" Pike's eyes grew round. "It's for me? To keep?"

"Yours to keep," Max agreed.

Pike let out a breath. "Thank you."

"It's my pleasure." Max smiled, meaning it. He'd have given the boy a dozen books if he'd had his way, but that wasn't allowed. He came here and shared their supper with them, and if he brought a book or a bottle of wine, that was acceptable. The boxes of food and clothing he'd brought were accepted only because it would go to those less fortunate than Burt and Pike, though anyone Max knew would find it hard to conceive of anyone less fortunate than these two. But that was the point. They had a roof over their heads, and though food was not always plentiful, they did not starve, and they had each other. They looked out for one another and for those around them, and Burt's philosophy of life had taught Max that this was a great deal.

A few moments later and Max had a plate not overburdened but complete with two eggs, two rashers of bacon, and two thick slices of fried bread. A steaming cup of tea sat at his elbow too, and it took no time at all to devour the lot, chasing the golden yolk about the plate with the bread. When he'd finished, Max sat back, licking grease from his fingers with satisfaction.

"Why is it this meal is always the one that tastes the best?" he asked, staring down at his empty plate with bemusement.

Burt shrugged. "Perhaps because you did something to deserve it, aye?"

Max snorted, shaking his head. "I'm not sure about that, but I'm trying."

"It's what counts. Right, lad?" Burt sent the question to Pike, who scratched his nose, looking thoughtful.

"Reckon."

Max sipped his tea, pleased to note it was good and strong, which meant Burt had kept hold of at least some of the tea he'd brought on his last visit.

"When I was here before, after the attack, I mean," Max said, uncertain of what exactly it was he wanted to ask. "When I was—"

"Off your head?" Pike suggested, grinning.

Max laughed, nodding. "Yes, when I was off my head. Did… Did anyone else take care of me?"

"Course not," Burt said at once. "Who else ever comes here, eh? Nah. Just us, eh, Pike?"

Pike stared at his empty plate and nodded.

"No, I suppose not," Max replied, though Burt's answer had been a little too sharp and quickly given. "There wasn't… there wasn't a girl?"

Pike glanced at Burt, a darting, furtive look that Max might have missed if he'd not been paying attention, but then it was gone, and he wondered if he was imagining it.

"We don't hold with girls. This is a bachelors' residence. You get girls in a place, and they start arranging things, eh, Pikey, my lad?"

"Yeah. We don't like girls," Pike muttered, staring fixedly at the book Max had given him.

"Why d'you ask, anyway?" Burt demanded.

Max shook his head, uncertain of the answer to that himself. It had been ridiculous to think a woman of Miss de Beauvoir's class would ever be in a place like this. And she'd have been so young, too. No, he was being foolish and whimsical. "No reason. I just… No. Nothing."

"Can I read to you now?" Pike asked, his eagerness to show off his improving skills enough to make Max forget everything else.

"You can indeed. I'm all ears, Master Pike."

Chapter 6

Dear Aggie,

I hope you are well and enjoying school? How are things with you? Have you been getting lots of good marks? Do write and tell me how you go on.

I am currently in Scotland, spending time with my mother's friends, the Earl and Countess of Morven, and her family. It is beautiful here, though, wild and untamed, rather like the people.

I was so sorry not to visit you as I promised, but our departure was unforeseen – by me, at least – and I had not the time to write and warn you. I hope you will forgive my absence. I promise I will come to see you as soon as I return, though I do not know when that will be. My father wishes me to spend time with the earl's sons. He thinks one of them will make me a good husband. They are all very kind and have made me feel very welcome. Mr Muir Anderson is especially attentive and so very funny. He makes me laugh at his antics, for he is an outdoorsy sort of fellow and seems to have boundless energy.

Have you seen much of your guardian of late? I hope he is in good health. If you do see him, please ~~tell him I miss him~~ give him my fond regards.

—Excerpt of a letter from Miss Evie Knight (daughter of Lady Helena and Mr Gabriel Knight) to Miss Agatha Smith.

26th May 1842, St James', London.

Max sauntered down the steps from White's, following an interesting meeting with the Marquess of Bainbridge about sheep, of all things. Bainbridge—despite somewhat of a reputation in years past for being a loose screw, if not an outright lunatic—had made a grand success of his father's estates since the duke had handed things over. It was a model Maxwell was interested in emulating where possible, and he'd been surprised at how ready the fellow was to share his knowledge. Bainbridge had given him some useful information, and names of people who could help him drag his own estate into the nineteenth century. Max had gotten his financial affairs in order a few years back, and he did not see why he could not tackle this challenge too, with help from the right people. He'd been pondering all he'd learned when a cheerful voice hailed him from across the street.

"Evening, Maxwell, how do?"

"Barnaby. I'm well, thank you, and yourself?"

In fact, Barnaby Godwin was looking quite the elegant man about town these days, no doubt his stylish friend's influence at work.

"Never better, off to Grants for a bite to eat. Meeting Louis there. Fancy joining us?"

Max hesitated. He did not relish the idea of bumping into Kilbane, as he'd already turned down his invitation to play cards, but he liked Barnaby and the enigmatic comte. It would be good to spend a convivial evening with men around whom one could relax, without wondering if they'd an ulterior motive. Besides, it was too early in the evening for Kilbane to show his face for some hours yet.

"I would. Thank you," he said, and fell into step as they walked around the corner to Grants.

They found Louis César had already taken the best table in the establishment and ordered wine, into which he had already made a considerable dent. He greeted Max politely and with apparent pleasure, though Max thought he looked tired. There were shadows beneath his eyes that had not been there before, and his exquisite bone structure seemed sharper than before, suggesting he had lost weight.

The waiter arrived with menus, and Max and Barnaby perused them while the comte watched the comings and goings in the club.

Max made his order and handed back his menu as Barnaby dithered.

"Oh, the game pie, I think," he said at last, frowning as the comte shook his head, indicating he would not be ordering. "And the same for Monsieur," he said firmly, giving his friend a stern look.

"Barnaby, I am not hungry," Louis protested irritably.

"No, but you need something to soak up the wine or you'll have the devil of a head in the morning, and I must share a carriage with you. Besides, you've lost too much weight already."

The comte tsked but said nothing, nursing his glass of wine.

"You're back to Sussex?" Maxwell asked, wondering if they were returning to the Comte's new property there.

"No, Scotland actually." Barnaby replied. "Visiting my aunt. Duty visit. You know how it is, got to keep the ancient ones happy. Not that my company ever makes her happy, but there you are.

She'll enjoy telling me how useless I am and how much better things—especially men — were in her day."

Maxwell laughed, nodding. "Yes, I know exactly what you mean."

"Anyone with extended family would," Barnaby replied with a grin.

"What about you, Louis?" Max asked. "Do you have an endless catalogue of ancient relatives to placate?"

The comte toyed with his meal, not looking up. "Not a one. My kin did not fare well during the revolution, and my father was remiss in providing heirs. Myself and my brother are all that remain. I am the last of my line."

"I'm sorry," Max said, not having realised quite how alone he was. Though Max's extended family were mostly a source of irritation, and certainly a drain on the coffers, he did not like to consider what it might feel like not to have those links, those roots going back generations.

Louis snorted, shaking his head. "Don't be. If my father was anything to go by, I doubt the world has lost anything of value."

They ate, with Barnaby a convivial companion and Louis César picking at his food and saying little. He was never a man who chattered about nothing, but neither was he this withdrawn and remote. Barnaby sent him anxious glances from time to time, encouraged him to eat a few bites of dinner like some anxious mama, and frowned when Louis ordered another bottle. Max wondered what the trouble was and regretted that he knew neither of them well enough to ask if he could help.

Once their plates had been taken, with Louis' practically untouched, Max thought it about time he made his excuses and left. Before he could, a familiar voice greeted them.

"Gentlemen, what a surprise. Vane, did you not have other plans for this evening? Or was it just other company you were seeking?"

Max suppressed a sigh as he looked up. Kilbane's expression was bland, but Max could sense the man's annoyance at finding him here.

"A last-minute change of plans, that's all. We only came to eat. I'm still not playing cards," he added, just in case Kilbane thought to manipulate him into playing.

"Cards? There's a game?" Louis demanded.

Max looked up in surprise, for the comte was known for never playing cards.

"Really, Louis? You *want* to play?" Barnaby said, echoing Max's disbelief. "When I cannot even get a game of whist out of you?"

"Oh, yes, *monsieur*. Do come and play with me," Kilbane said with a wink, smiling with an expression that made all the hairs on the back of Max's neck stand on end.

"No. Don't," Max said, alarmed now. Kilbane was a terrifyingly good card player, and that was before he cheated. Max often suspected he didn't need to cheat to win, he just enjoyed behaving as people expected him to… i.e., badly.

Louis glanced at him, interest flickering in his eyes. "Why not?"

Max hesitated, not wanting to insult the man, but Ciarán's expression was sharp, glinting with mischief, which was a bad sign. "Kilbane is an excellent player, Louis, and whilst I mean no disrespect, if you rarely play, it might not be wise. The game is for high stakes and—"

Louis got to his feet. "Lead on," he said to the marquess, whose slow smile made Max's stomach drop. He turned to

Barnaby, who was looking just as alarmed, but there was damn all they could do to stop him now.

Barnaby got up and grasped Max's arm. "Come along, perhaps we can stop him from losing the shirt off his back," he muttered, and hurried after his friend.

26th May 1842, Church Street, Isleworth, London.

Kathy added up the long row of figures and smiled as she drew a line under the total. Perfect. It had taken her an entire afternoon of haggling with the cloth merchant and her head was still aching, but it had been worth it. She had saved twenty-five percent on the cost of the uniforms, without compromising the quality, and that extra money would go towards games for the children's recreation time. Added to the money she had saved on the bibles and prayer books—for some fool had ordered expensive copies with lots of gold and fancy bindings—she ought to have a decent budget for them now. There was still an unresolved matter concerning the deliveries of building materials, though, and the discrepancies in the quantities the site manager had showed her. She had an unpleasant nagging sensation in her gut about that, but she was reluctant to take it to Vane until she was certain. Yet, if she was right, he ought to know at once. Muttering crossly, she decided she had best see him first thing in the morning. Providing he knew it was only a suspicion, it ought to cause no harm. He seemed to be a fair man who was doing his best to do a good job and she did not believe he would dismiss anyone on the strength of suspicion alone. She wished that she could avoid him though, for she certainly had not planned on seeing him again so soon.

The man she had seen recently bore too much in common with the sleeping prince she had spun such romantic stories about. He was handsome and kind, funny too, but she was no longer a foolish child with fairy stories in her head. Now, she was an adult, and one who knew his pretty exterior could hide all manner of sins.

Kathy sighed as she remembered how she had imagined him waking up from his fever and falling head over heels in love with her at first sight. Somehow, he would know it had been Kathy tending him, she who had snatched him from the jaws of death and forced him to hold on to life. She had promised him his life would be good, that he was loved, and she wanted him to live, that she would be waiting for him. Kathy had begged him to stay, to stay with her, and he had. Except then he had revealed his debauchery in crude language that she'd barely understood, though she'd comprehended enough to understand this man was no prince, but a libertine who took his pleasure wherever he chose and damn the consequences.

Foolishness, she chided, shaking her head. He wasn't the devil any more than he was a saint. She had been at the receiving end of respectable gentlemen's opinions, those well-bred men who thought of her as something less than they, because she did not know her parents. Lord Vane had never treated her like that. He had never given her cause to believe he thought her blood tainted, that she was less than a lady. But many of those *gentlemen* had. Kathy knew she could never consider marrying a man she did not respect and admire as well as love. Though she had not discussed it with anyone else, she knew her best hope lay with the kind of man who would not be invited to any *ton* event. A man who worked for a living and shared her values. But she had a beautiful new wardrobe, and her mother was excited for her, and so she must go through the motions, for this season at least. She would not let her parents waste such ridiculous amounts of money on fripperies again. Not when it was all for naught.

Sighing, Kathy set her pen down and regarded her ink-stained fingers. Unbidden, Vane's handsome face returned to her mind, along with the soft look he'd had in his eyes when he'd assured her he'd been offering her a compliment. He'd looked like the embodiment of her every dream, so handsome, his expression open and full of kindness and understanding. Her heart twisted with regret.

“Stop it,” she muttered, shoving the chair away from the desk.

The Earl of Vane was of no interest to her. No matter his attempt to be a better human being, their past would always stand between them. He was an earl, and she was simply someone who worked for him. She must put her foolishness behind her and not get drawn in by that handsome face again. Keeping her distance was for the best. Except she would need to speak to him first thing tomorrow morning. Muttering crossly under her breath, Kathy turned down the lamp and made her way up to bed.

26th May 1842, Grant’s, St James’, London.

Louis watched Kilbane as the marquess studied the shuffled cards with apparent nonchalance. He was good, as Max had said. Extremely good. Unfortunately for the marquess, that was not nearly good enough to beat Louis. Not even if he cheated, which Louis suspected he was contemplating doing now. Louis knew all the tricks, and could employ them too, if he chose, which he might just for the hell of it tonight. He was angry, a furious simmering anger which he had thought he’d rid himself of years ago. Whether or not it was rational, he could not shake the familiar sensation of being abandoned that had haunted his childhood. He wanted to destroy something, or someone, for no good reason other than that he was hurting, and he could not make it stop. This was what he had feared, the person he would become if he lost Evie. If he lost his grip on the good in the world, the darkness would swallow him up as it had tried to do so many times before. Except this time, he would not bother fighting it.

Kilbane dealt the cards, and Louis noted the sleight of hand as he dealt from the bottom of the deck. It was neatly done, and he doubted anyone else would have spotted it. He smiled, holding the marquess’ gaze as he took his hand, which was predictably poor. Well, two could play at that game. Louis allowed Kilbane to win the set, and took the cards back to shuffle, making a grand show of it as the cards flew between his hands. Murmurs rippled around the room as it became clear Louis was no ordinary card player. Kilbane laughed, clearly delighted, as he sat back and watched with appreciation.

"You are the very devil, *monsieur*," he said, grinning.

Louis' mouth twisted into a grim smile. "You have no idea," he murmured.

Waving a hand at a passing waiter, Louis ordered another bottle of wine. He could sense the tension among those watching the game. Barnaby and Max had folded after the first hand but kept their places at the table. Systematically, Louis had taken each of the remaining four players with ease, until only Kilbane remained, though they too had stayed to watch. The pot in the middle of the table held a staggering six thousand pounds, and the tension in the room was electric. Louis felt certain Kilbane knew he was toying with him simply because it amused him to do so. He thought perhaps the marquess was enjoying himself, even though he was about to lose an obscene amount of money. If the rumours were true, he could well afford it.

A disturbance at the door had Louis glancing up, and he experienced a pang of guilt and regret as he saw his brother standing there, glaring at him. Louis returned his gaze and gave a slight shrug. What did it matter now?

Nic had forbidden him to play when they'd come to England. He had not wanted Louis to remind everyone that he had been just as involved in their scandalous nightclub in Paris. They had fed the *ton* the lie that the nightclub was entirely Nic's affair, but that was far from true. Louis had run it with him, and it was his devilish luck with the cards, alongside robbing many of their patrons, that had earned them the money to make it into the exclusive place it was now. Rouge et Noir had made them wealthy beyond their wildest dreams, but Nic had wanted more for Louis. He'd wanted him to retake his place in society, to earn the respect of his peers by marrying well. And where had that got him, exactly? The only woman he wanted was being wooed by a strapping Scot in the wilds of some godforsaken land, and he was here, alone. He no longer gave a damn what the *ton* thought. He had no doubt that Gabriel Knight had been behind the man prying and asking questions in Paris. Evie's father was shrewd enough to know he'd only discovered the half of it when Nic had married Eliza. By now he'd have a full report on exactly who the Comte de Villen was, and any chance he had with Evie was doomed.

Not that he was giving up. Not yet. Not for anything.

He laid his cards on the table.

"Monsieur le Comte, you really do have the devil's own luck," Kilbane said, throwing his cards down with a laugh, as the men around the table murmured with shock. His violet eyes glittered. "You must tell me your secret," he added, lowering his voice.

"Which one?" Louis replied dryly.

Kilbane smiled, a slow smile that put Louis in mind of hungry things with teeth. "I find you quite intriguing. You must have spent rather more time in your brother's club than we have been led to believe. Exactly why have you kept such a formidable talent a secret?"

"My brother thought it bad manners to ruin our new friends and neighbours," Louis replied, aware of Nic's unhappy presence at his back.

"Time to go, Louis," Nic growled. "You've had your fun."

Kilbane shook his head. "But I haven't," he said to Nic, narrowing his eyes. "It's only polite to allow a fellow a chance to win back his losses."

Nic snorted. "If you've not realised by now, you've not got a hope in hell of beating him, but you are likely to lose everything you own. Believe me, I'm doing you a favour. Come along, Louis."

Nic's tone promised trouble if he didn't do as he was told, but Louis was feeling belligerent and unwilling to behave himself. He stared at Nic, unmoving, and instead picked up his glass and took a large swallow. The room had fallen silent, everyone aware of his volatile mood and agog to see what would happen next.

"I say, Louis, that was remarkable. Now, I'm glad you never played cards with me, or I'd be up the River Tick without a paddle. Never seen anything like it. Got any tips you can pass on? Reckon I need the help," Barnaby said cheerfully, though he did not fool Louis, who was well aware he was being managed. "Why don't we toddle back to your flat, and you can see if I'm beyond help, eh?"

Louis turned his furious gaze upon Barnaby, who quailed but held his ground, returning an anxious smile.

"Might be best, old man," he added softly, so only Louis could hear.

For a moment Louis toyed with the idea of telling him to go to hell, but found he couldn't do it. Barnaby had a kind heart, and he was a good friend, and Louis didn't have so many of those that he could afford to lose one.

"As you wish, Barnaby. I will behave myself for your sake," he added, glaring at his brother, which he knew was unfair, but he was spoiling for a fight and Nic at least knew what he'd be getting into.

"I'll come round in the morning, then, and settle up," Kilbane said as Louis stood.

Louis turned around and waved this idea away. "Not tomorrow. I'm away for a week or so. I'll call on you when I return. There's no hurry."

Kilbane inclined his head. "As you wish. Goodnight, monsieur, and thank you for an entertaining evening."

Louis bowed and took himself off with Nic, Barnaby, and Max hurrying after him.

Chapter 7

Dear Kathleen,

Are you going to Lady St Clair's Spring Ball? I hope to see you there.

Do you think Ashburton will attend? It seems such a long time since I have seen him. Have you had any news? Even Jules doesn't seem to know where he is.

—Excerpt of a letter from Lady Rosamund Adolphus (daughter of their Graces, Robert and Prunella Adolphus, The Duke and Duchess of Bedwin) to Miss Kathleen De Beauvoir (daughter of Mrs Minerva and Mr Inigo de Beauvoir).

27th May 1842, Vane Hall, Chiswick, London.

Max shrugged into his coat and tried not to fidget as his valet insisted on smoothing the lapels and adjusting his cravat. The old Max would have snapped with impatience and stalked off, but this new version of himself had become aware Hewitt took a deal of pride in his work. To dismiss him out of hand would be to treat him with a lack of respect and hurt the fellow's feelings. Max wondered how he'd been so blind not to have noticed such things before, but he'd been spoiled and indulged his entire life, and no one had ever suggested he care about his servants. Now, the realisation of his past selfishness made him squirm inwardly, but the past was gone, and he could not change it. He could, however, feign patience when he was desperate to get downstairs and discover the reason for his early morning visitor. Miss de Beauvoir had demanded his attention and his heart had given a little skip of anticipation when his butler had informed him of her arrival.

Hewitt finally deemed him worthy of public viewing, so Maxwell hurried downstairs, reminding himself sternly that he was a grown man and an earl, and that running would be ridiculous. He *was* ridiculous; he reminded himself, because Miss de Beauvoir would rather hit him over the head with a heavy object than kiss him, and so her arrival was work-related, and he was a fool to hope otherwise. Still, a fool he was because he could not shake the little burst of happiness fizzing in his chest at her unexpected arrival.

"Miss de Beauvoir, forgive me for keeping you waiting," he said, taking in the sight of her standing by the window in his study.

His breath caught as she turned, and the sunlight highlighted her elegant profile. She wore a high-necked gown of soft dove grey, trimmed with pink velvet. A dusky pink underskirt peeped between the open skirts, and the tight bodice emphasised her slender waist. Her blonde hair, arranged in a simple chignon, complimented the severity of the dress and accentuated her long neck. She looked cool, disdainful and utterly untouchable, which naturally only made him quite desperate to do so.

"It's of no matter. I admit I forgot men of fashion rarely rise before noon," she added apologetically, though her discomfort with the idea of spending half the day abed whilst most people worked for a living was audible.

Max's lips twitched. "Actually, I was swimming. I'm usually up by six at the latest."

“Swimming?” she asked, her surprise melting the stern expression she’d adopted upon seeing him enter the room. “But where?”

“There’s a small lake upon the estate,” he informed her, enjoying overturning her preconceptions about the kind of man he was now. Of course, not so long ago, she would have been entirely right. He’d likely not have surfaced until late in the afternoon to ready himself for another night of wickedness.

“Isn’t it cold?” she asked, glancing out the window at a spring day which was sunny but far from warm.

“Freezing, actually, but it gets the blood moving.”

“I’m surprised it doesn’t give you pneumonia.”

“I’m assured by my physician that it is good for the constitution. You ought to try it. I should be happy to give you the use of the lake whenever you desire,” he added, unable to resist. “It’s wonderfully invigorating.”

“I can’t swim,” she said, staring at him with open curiosity.

“I’d be happy to teach you.” He ought not to have said such a scandalous thing, he knew, but she was irresistible.

“N-no, thank you.”

Max found himself delighted by the breathless quality of her reply, more so as she blushed, her fair skin tinting a delicious shade of pink. He wondered what other parts of her were pink too, before scolding himself and getting the conversation back on track.

“You wanted to see me?”

“I did,” she said, and her stern façade slid firmly back into place. “I had an interesting conversation with the site manager, Mr Rogers, onsite yesterday morning. He assures me four cart loads of brick arrived yesterday morning as usual, the same the day before, but that they are running short of supply.”

"Oh. Well, can we get more? I don't want any delay to the build. I thought they had arranged a delivery schedule that suited Rogers. At least, he approved it, as I remember."

"There was, and he did, which would suggest an error of some description."

"Did you check with the supplier?"

"I did. Four deliveries were ordered and supplied. In fact, I saw the carriages as they passed our house on their way to the site."

"Well, if Rogers arranged the quantity delivered, and that quantity arrived, why is there a shortfall, unless he miscalculated?"

"Exactly," she said, her lush mouth setting into a stern line and her eyebrows slanting down.

She was so dreadfully fierce. Max wished he might kiss her, might soften all those hard edges until she was pliant and sighing in his arms, but as he liked his private parts where they were and in one piece, he kept to the matter in hand.

"You don't think he miscalculated."

"No," she replied.

Max sighed. "You suspect someone is stealing," he guessed, realising this was what was making her so anxious.

She threw up her hands in agitation and started pacing. "Yes! Which is awful. I've spoken to most of the men on site and, though they hardly like a woman sticking her nose in, they've all been polite enough and seem to work hard. I do not want to be the one to discover that someone is robbing you, but I can find no other explanation."

Max watched, entranced by the way her skirts whooshed and swished as she paced, and the mesmerising sway of her hips. Yet she was upset, and with good reason. He tore his gaze away from the delicious picture she made and cudgelled his brain into making an appropriate response.

"Well, if you think something is amiss, I had better investigate."

"You can't!" she said, irritated. "Not if you want to keep your involvement a secret. No, I shall have to deal with this. It's my job to do so, only I did not like to act without informing you first."

"You most certainly will not deal with it," Max objected.

Her grey eyes flashed, lightning behind stormy skies. "Whyever not? It is a part of my job to ensure your money is being spent wisely, not wasted. Missing materials must then fall within my purview. Is that not so? I take it if I were a man, you'd consider my interference welcome?"

Max hesitated a moment too long as he tried to find a tactful answer, and she carried on.

"Well, materials *are* missing. I need to discover where from and who is responsible, and I intend to do so."

"You will *not* confront a lot of blasted workmen and accuse them of stealing!" Max retorted, going hot and cold at the idea.

"*Will* not?" she exclaimed, and Max knew at once he had made an error of judgement.

He backtracked wildly.

"I beg your pardon, Miss de Beauvoir. I do not mean to give you instruction on how to do your job, but I believe you might be acting somewhat rashly," he tried, which was as diplomatic as he could manage with his pulse speeding up as it was.

She rolled her eyes at him in a manner that suggested she was used to dealing with intractable men. "I was not suggesting that I accuse them to their faces. I'm not a complete idiot, my lord, no matter what you may think."

"I don't think I ever suggested anything of the kind. I only worry that a female, alone on a building site, might put herself in a precarious situation if she discovers there are indeed men guilty of stealing. That would make them criminals, and likely to be dangerous. Do you think it would please them if you uncovered their little scheme?"

"No," she allowed. "I do not. But as I mentioned, I am not a fool. I was not considering going unchaperoned and neither was I intending to crash about like a bull in a china shop, issuing accusations. That might be the male method of getting things done, but I was thinking of something a tad subtler."

Her eyebrows had a most intriguing slant to them, which somehow emphasised the slightly feline cast to her eyes. After delivering her little set down, one eyebrow quirked, daring him to issue another challenge. Sadly, Max had never resisted a dare in his life. He assured himself this was not behaving badly, however, for he was only doing it to keep her safe, therefore his intentions were entirely honourable.

"I can be subtle," he said, taking a step closer to her. "You could introduce me and imply that I'm a difficult neighbour, one who is anxious about having a school for disreputable elements on his doorstep. It *is* on my doorstep, after all."

She frowned at that, looking at him with an expression of such puzzlement he could not help but smile. Miss de Beauvoir was quite enchanting, and that the poor girl did not know what to make of him only made him adore her all the more. He wanted quite desperately for her to like him, though he knew it was a forlorn hope. Still, a fellow ought to have goals.

"You would let people think badly of you, just so you can accompany me?" she asked sceptically.

Max laughed. "My dear young woman, most people do think badly of me, and with good reason. I thought we'd already covered this?"

"I am not your *dear*," she said, bristling a little, but then her expression softened a degree. "But if you will present yourself in such an unflattering light, I will accept your chaperonage. I admit I am somewhat anxious, for I have no desire to make unfounded allegations or get anyone into trouble. Come along, then. If we leave now, we should arrive in time for this morning's delivery."

She was very managing, he noted, and realised he might rather enjoy being managed by such a female. Max moved towards the study door and opened it for her. "I am at your disposal, and you are entirely fair-minded, Miss de Beauvoir. That speaks well of you and gives me a glimmer of hope that you might not despise me for all eternity," he said, employing what he knew was his most charming smile. Predictably, it fell on stony ground.

"I do not despise you, my lord," she replied, her tone conciliatory. "I simply do not think of you at all."

She sent him a dazzling smile.

"Ouch!" Max spluttered, holding her gaze. He leaned in then, lowering his voice. "And yet I do not think that entirely true. Are you prone to fibbing, Miss de Beauvoir?"

"I am not, and you may think what you like!" she said, looking pink and marvellously flustered before putting up her chin and stalking past him out the door.

But Max had seen that tell-tale blush again, and he didn't believe her.

27th May 1842, Lower Square, Isleworth, London.

The journey to the school was a short but uncomfortable ride for Kathleen. Lord Vane had insisted one of his maids travel with them for propriety, which was thoughtful of him, but she still spent the entire ride sat upon thorns. She could feel his gaze upon her, though whenever she glanced up she found him staring out of the window, looking as if butter wouldn't melt in his mouth. Well, she knew that was far from the truth. The wretch looked far too pleased with himself. He hadn't believed her when she'd denied ever thinking about him. That much was obvious. Drat the man. Yet it wasn't as though she was thinking romantic thoughts. It was only that the man was such a puzzle, *and* he was her employer, so it was only natural that he was on her mind a good deal. She fidgeted uncomfortably as a little voice suggested she was being deliberately obtuse. Oh, it wasn't fair. It was diabolical of him to be so kind and thoughtful. If only he weren't so handsome and… and *male*, things would be a good deal simpler. It was extremely hard to disregard the fact of all that rampant masculinity, however, when it was sitting directly in front of you.

He'd crossed his arms, and the fabric pulled tight over his biceps and broad shoulders, highlighting the physic of an active man. His long legs stretched out between the seats of the carriage, crossed at the ankles, and his breeches hugged muscular thighs. Annoyingly, it was proving the devil's own job not to sit and gawk at him. She thought perhaps he had put on weight and bulk since she had tended to his wounds. He'd been beautiful then, but leaner, more boyish. There was nothing the least bit boyish about him now.

The knowledge that she had put her hands on his naked skin, and he didn't know it was at once disturbing and indecently erotic, stirring disconcerting sensations deep inside her that left her restless and uncomfortable, as though her skin no longer fit her. She could not help but remember how it had felt to touch him, the silk of his body beneath her hands, the little mole beside his left nipple, and that they were a dark pink. There was hair on his chest, a shade of darker gold than that on his head, and it led a trail down his abdomen which was taut and defined. She felt the blush steel up her chest and throat and stared determinedly out of the window. If she caught his gaze now, he'd know she was thinking about him. Thinking lewd thoughts about him. Oh, good Lord!

There was a part of her that felt she ought to confess, for it seemed wrong to have such intimate knowledge of him when he was unaware of the fact, and yet wild horses could not have dragged the words from her. If she confessed, he would guess why she'd said nothing, that he affected her far more than she wished him to know, and there was no point in continuing to deny the fact. She was too honest not to admit that much. And why ought she deny it? He was a fine specimen of male beauty, and there was no shame in enjoying the view. Though she ought not to dream about him at night—not that she did it on purpose. More than just looking or dreaming was an exercise in stupidity, however, and Kathleen was not stupid. Vane may have changed but he was still an aristocratic male with no use for the likes of her, and she wasn't about to forget that.

"At last," she said with relief as the carriage halted in the muddy lane beside the school building site.

Vane simply smiled and climbed down from the carriage, turning to offer her his hand. Kathleen almost refused, not wanting to get that close to him, but that was silly. Still, his touch was unsettling, even through their gloves, and she snatched her hand back as quickly as she could. He made no comment, though he must have noticed, and Kathy hurried across to where she could see the carts trundling down the temporary driveway to the building to be unloaded.

"Who would usually be in charge of unloading?" Vane asked, his long strides keeping pace with hers.

"I don't know. Perhaps if we don't make our interest in the delivery obvious, they'll carry on as usual."

He nodded, accepting this, and offered her his arm. She frowned at him, and he raised his eyebrows. "You are supposed to be in the business of charming me—dissolute and ramshackle fellow that I am—into accepting this offending building, may I remind you? You do know how to charm a fellow, don't you Miss de Beauvoir?" he asked, all innocence, the dreadful man. As if she didn't know he was flirting with her.

Kathy narrowed her eyes at him. "You said your reputation preceded you, so there is no need to engage in amateur dramatics."

"I beg to disagree," he murmured, his keen gaze sweeping the building site.

Kathy followed his gaze, pleased to see the site was as busy and orderly as she'd noted on previous visits. Mr Rogers seemed a decent, hardworking sort and she very much hoped he was not involved in stealing from the site. She thought it unlikely, for it was Mr Rogers who had brought the discrepancy to her attention.

"Have you never met Mr Rogers before, then?" Kathy whispered, aware of the man himself moving to greet them.

"No. I've never spoken to anyone on site. I was trying to be discreet," Vane said, taking her hand and placing it firmly upon his sleeve.

Kathy bit her lip against an irritated exclamation, aware the foreman was within earshot. She desperately wanted to pull her hand away, too aware of the muscular arm beneath it, but she dared not make a fuss.

"Good morning, Mr Rogers," she greeted him. "How do you do?"

"Mustn't grumble, miss," Rogers replied warily.

Though he had been polite, Kathy knew well that he disapproved of her presence on his site. The appearance of the finely dressed gentlemen at her side was no doubt ringing more alarm bells.

"My Lord Vane, may I present the site manager, Mr Rogers? Mr Rogers, the Earl of Vane is a near neighbour to the school. His lordship is rather troubled by our little enterprise here, I'm afraid, sir, and so I suggested a brief visit to put his mind at rest."

"I'm just in charge of putting the building up where I'm told, my lord," Rogers said, snatching off his cap and smoothing back his greying hair. "Further than that, 'tis Lady Elizabeth you need to speak to."

"I am aware," Vane drawled with a sigh. "I suppose the building looks well enough. What's visible, at least. Only I don't want Vane Hall besieged by cutthroats and villains. You do see, Miss de Beauvoir? It's not at all the thing. One might get murdered in one's bed by one of the little reprobates. Just *imagine*!" He tsked and shook his head, his expression mournful.

Kathy stared at him, aghast. Vane had turned into some swaggering dandy and the effect was unsettling. She hesitated, momentarily diverted by the twinkle in his eyes. The devil was enjoying himself.

"They're only children, my lord. Not hardened criminals," she said severely, belatedly remembering to play her part.

Vane waved a limp hand. "Tyburn blossoms," he pronounced airily. "What's in the carts?" he asked, apparently diverted by the delivery, which was still sitting unattended.

Kathy muttered a curse and hurried after him. Drat the man. They were supposed to wait and see who unloaded them, though no one had come to see so far and two of the drivers were looking decidedly shifty, their gazes darting about the site as if looking for someone.

"Just bricks, my lord," Rogers called after them with a sigh that spoke volumes on his opinion of the nobility sticking their oar in on his site.

"Bricks?" Vane repeated. "What kind of bricks?"

Rogers muttered something that sounded like *bricks as thick as your blasted head*, but she might have been mistaken. At any rate, the fellow followed them to the carts.

"They're London Stock bricks. Made local. Yellow clay, see. From the Thames basin," he said, sounding hopeful that he might educate them on this small point at least.

"How fascinating," Kathy said politely as Vane lifted a brick from the back of the cart and gazed at it as if the secrets of the universe were inscribed there.

"It *is* yellow," he exclaimed, grinning. "I have a yellow waistcoat," he offered no one in particular.

"How nice for you," Kathy said faintly, noting the two delivery drivers giving each other anxious glances.

Vane set the brick down on the ground at his feet and lifted another. "No. Actually, my waistcoat is more canary yellow. This is… This is…."

"Ochre?" Kathy suggested helpfully as he set this brick beside the first.

"Ochre!" he exclaimed. "On the nose, Miss de Beauvoir. Well done. Mind you, this one is darker. What would you call that?" he demanded, taking two more bricks from the cart and laying those atop the others.

"Um," Kathleen said, fidgeting as she noted one of the burly delivery drivers heading for them.

"'Ere,'" he said, his tone and stance aggressive. "Leave them bricks alone. They need unloading and accounting for."

Alarmed, Kathy hurried to intervene. "Oh, I think we may safely rely upon Lord Vane not to steal any of your bricks, sir. Please don't be anxious on that point."

Vane gave a bark of laughter. "Thinks I'm going to steal his bricks, does he? Ha! That's a good 'un."

Oh, lord.

"Where's Frank and Jo?" Mr Rogers grumbled, scratching the back of his neck and putting his cap back on. "They ought to be unloading these by now."

The belligerent driver folded his arms. "I dunno. Ain't seen them, but if they ain't 'ere, I'm taking my bricks back."

Mr Rogers glared at him. “Don’t be daft, man. Why do that? I’ll have a couple of the other men come and unload, though I’ll be docking wages for this, I can tell you.”

The driver did not look at all happy about this suggestion.

“Are Frank and Jo usually unreliable?” Kathy asked Mr Rogers.

The man made a noncommittal noise at the back of his throat but did not deign to answer further.

“I’ll unload ’em,” Vane said, setting to and chucking the bricks about him in such a bizarre manner that Kathy had to bite her lip to stop from laughing.

“Oi! Leave off. Put them back!” the driver yelled, rolling up his sleeves and stalking towards Vane, looking murderous.

“Oh, I say. There’s not so many as it seems,” Vane said, gesturing to the thin planks he’d exposed on top of the next layer. At once, Kathy understood what had happened. Somewhere between the yard and the site, the bricks in the centre of the cart were unloaded, the void covered with planks and more bricks stacked on top to hide what was missing. Which meant the drivers of the carts with missing bricks knew, as well as Frank and Jo, who would have unloaded them. She suspected they were running from the site as they spoke, which was frustrating.

“What the—” Mr Rogers moved to take another look before turning on the driver. “Why, you thieving—”

He didn’t manage the rest of the sentence as the driver hit him, sending him sprawling in the mud on his backside. Vane lunged, far quicker than Kathy would have credited, taking to his heels as the driver made a run for it. Turning, she saw the driver of the second cart had already made good his escape and was halfway across the field.

“Well, don’t just stand there!” she yelled at the workmen who had stopped to watch the kerfuffle. “Get after him!”

To their credit, they did just that, running hell for leather across the field. Kathy turned back to Vane, expecting to see that he'd given up the chase and instead saw him tackle the driver to the ground. She gasped as the two men began fighting in earnest and smothered a shriek of alarm as Vane's head snapped back with the force of a right hook that looked hard enough to break his neck. Vane must have been a deal tougher than his pretty face suggested, though, as he retaliated with enthusiasm. The two men wrestled together in the mud, Vane's elegant clothes quickly ruined beyond repair, though his clothes were the least of his worries when his opponent drove his fist into his belly. Vane turned a ghastly shade of white and, with a furious growl, kneed the fellow in his tender parts. The driver let out an ear-splitting shriek that must have been heard on the other side of the city. Glassy eyed with pain, the fellow put his hands about Vane's neck and squeezed.

"Oh!" Kathy exclaimed, truly concerned that the fool would get himself killed. She stared about for a weapon that might help, and her gaze landed on the planks atop the missing bricks. Snatching up the only one they'd yet uncovered, she discovered it was surprisingly heavy. Staggering slightly, she swung the plank with as much force as she could manage and winced as it connected with the driver's head. There was an unpleasant *thwack*, and the fellow dropped like a stone. Vane pushed the dead weight off him with a groan at the same time Kathy dropped the plank with a shriek of disgust. Sadly, it landed on Vane… somewhere unprotected.

"Christ!" he yelped, clutching his privates as his eyes watered. "You're supposed to be on my side!"

"I'm so sorry!" she said, mortified. "I was trying to help."

Vane groaned and closed his eyes. She suspected he was counting. When he finally opened them again, he let out an uneven breath of laughter.

"You did," he said, managing a pained grin. "He was trying to choke the life out of me."

"Oh, look at the state of you!" Kathy cried, furious with him now that the danger had passed. She hurried to offer him her hands, pulling him to his feet. "Good heavens. This is your idea of subtlety, is it? Well, I should be fascinated to know what a cruder approach would look like. You might have been murdered before my eyes! And poor Mr Rogers has a nosebleed, and… and you're all m-muddy and you've ripped your c-coat!"

Kathy snapped her mouth shut, aware she was babbling, but she only now realised how very frightened she'd been. To her horror, her throat grew tight, and she felt horribly close to tears.

Vane's expression softened, and he did not allow her to snatch her hands free, holding onto them tightly. "I'm all right, Miss de Beauvoir. No harm done. Just a few bruises, and I've a thick head, as I'm sure you know by now."

"You might have been killed!" The words burst from her without her approval, but it was too late now. Unbidden, the image of him dying in a dingy room came back to her, and she knew she wouldn't change anything. He'd not been the man she'd dreamed he was, but she was glad, glad he had lived and was here before her, flawed and wicked as he was. She was trembling and tears burned in her eyes. Vane let go of one hand, reaching instead to touch her cheek. Somewhere along the way, he'd lost his gloves and his hand was badly bruised, but his touch was careful.

"The devil won't have me," he whispered softly. "But I'm grateful for your concern all the same."

A tear slid down her cheek and Kathy swiped it away with irritation.

He regarded her for a long moment, his blue eyes filled with something that looked like regret before he dropped his hand.

"Well, it looks like you have your culprits and I doubt we'll see Frank and Jo within five miles of here any time soon." He gestured across the field to where the workmen were marching the second driver back towards them. "I suspect Mr Rogers can deal with this now. You've done what you needed to do. I really ought never to have involved you at all, but you were marvellous all the same. Thank you."

Kathy held her tongue lest she say anything else she ought not. She was feeling wholly befuddled, and she held Vane entirely accountable. Terror at seeing him in danger warred with impatience that this ridiculous scene had erupted at all and with the dawning realisation that she would have been devastated if anything had happened to him. The truth was, she cared. She cared far too much about this imperfect, infuriating man. Damn Lord blasted Vane, for the truth was upsetting and maddening, and she needed to keep her distance, because being close to this man posed a greater danger to her than she could ever have realised. She knew what manner of man he was, knew the kind of life he'd led, and yet… and yet she was a fool because her heart simply did not care about his past, only for him.

"Allow me to escort you home, Miss de Beauvoir," Vane said, speaking to her gently, as though soothing some skittish horse, but there was no way on earth she was getting back into that carriage with him, maid or no maid.

"No, thank you," she said, relieved that her voice had stopped trembling, and she sounded cool and composed. "My home is a short walk from here. Don't trouble yourself."

"It's no—"

"Good day to you, my lord," she said curtly, and took herself off back across the field before he could stop her.

Chapter 8

Yes, Ozzie, dear, I shall be at Lady St Clair's Spring Ball. Heaven help me. I rely on you to keep my spirits up. I have a gorgeous dress, at least. It's such a glorious shade of blue, though that feels small comfort when I must pretend not to hear the insults about my dubious bloodline. Ah well, all the usual kindly friends and relatives will seek me out for dances and for that I am grateful. It might be a good deal worse.

Darling, I hardly move in the same circles as Montagu's sons, but as it happens, I overheard Mama talking to Aunt Prue the other day. Pip's father had words with him recently and he took it badly, I think. The marquess reprimanded him for spending too much time with demireps and opera singers and not in society. Though you know how he loathes the ton and one can hardly blame him when females are forever laying traps for him. No doubt it's a relief to avoid it. He had a narrow escape recently; I believe. Still, I think after his father's words; he is likely to attend rather than face the consequences. I know I would. Montagu is rather terrifying.

—Excerpt of a letter from Miss Kathleen De Beauvoir (daughter of Mrs Minerva and Mr Inigo de Beauvoir) to Lady Rosamund Adolphus (daughter of their Graces, Robert and Prunella Adolphus, The Duke and Duchess of Bedwin).

27th May 1842, Vane Hall, Chiswick, London.

Max eased his bruised frame into the hot water with a sigh of relief. His eye had swollen shut and was throbbing like the devil, but it had been worth it.

Miss de Beauvoir didn't hate him.

In fact, she'd had cried. A single tear, yes, but she had been visibly upset. Though he was sorry she'd been frightened, her concern had eased something jagged and anxious inside him. He realised now that he had wondered if anyone could ever care about him, even a little. Though he was under no illusion that she *liked* him. His parents had indulged his every whim, and he'd only need to mention that he wanted something before they gave it to him. Yet they'd not liked him much, either, or so it had seemed so to him. Like most aristocratic children, a parade of nannies and tutors had attended to him with varying degrees of kindness and attention. No one had ever seemed terribly interested in him beyond ensuring that he learned his lessons, dressed well, and knew how to speak to his betters. It had been lonely; he acknowledged now, though he'd never put it into words before, even to himself. He'd been an only child, with any other siblings stillborn or dying before their first year. His mother had not been strong and had become obsessed with her own health, forever trying some new cure or remedy. Ironically, she had outlived his robust father by ten years and had died of influenza the week after someone had tried to take Max's life, too. Perhaps it had been the shock of his disappearance that had made her so ill? Perhaps, but somehow, he doubted it.

It was a strange notion, to be grateful to the person who had caused you such pain by trying to end your life, but it was true. It was like being reborn with the scales fallen from his eyes. Everything was so clear to him now when before he'd been utterly blind, not only to his own vileness but to how easily he could have made life happier for himself and those around him. A kind word might change everything, giving a moment of your time or saying yes when it was easier to refuse could make a difference. Small gestures counted as much as grand ones, he knew now. They might not change the world, but perhaps they might help someone get through the day, someone who might return the favour when you were alone and wretched.

Looking back at who he'd been was a peculiar sensation, like looking at a stranger. He'd not realised how desperately unhappy he'd been, how empty his life. His own fault, he saw now. Life had given him opportunities for happiness, and he'd run from them, seeing only a trap. Nausea roiled in his guts as he remembered words he could never take back, actions that had consequences he must live with for the rest of his days.

Max closed his eyes and remembered how it had felt to wake in Burt's dark rooms.

Two and a half years earlier…

20th July 1839, Covent Garden. Parish of St Giles.

The pain was dizzying. Max licked his lips, finding them papery and dry, his throat parched.

"Here, lad," said a raspy voice as a tin cup was placed to his lips. Lukewarm weak tea was not a drink Max would have thought he could enjoy, but at this moment, it tasted like nectar from the gods. "Woah, slow down, else you'll choke. That's it, easy like."

The voice was wrong, Max thought anxiously. It wasn't the one he wanted. There had been another, sweeter voice, the one he'd stayed for. He'd held on through the fiery pain and the endless misery just to cling to the sound of that voice, needing to put a face to it. She'd sounded like an angel.

He jolted away, eyes flying open, and tried to sit up, immediately reprimanded by the lancing pain in his side. He cried out and stared around, panting with terror, expecting to see flames and the devil himself come to mete out punishment to one of his greatest sinners.

"Easy, there," counselled that same scratchy voice, and Max turned towards it to see a thin whip of an old man watching him with interest. "There ain't no need to look so afeared. We kept you safe and tended you this long. Ain't no reason to do you in now, is there, eh?"

Max stared at him, waiting anxiously to see if it was a trick, if horns would sprout from his greying temples and his eyes glow red. But the old man just smiled placidly and reached out, ruffling Max's hair.

"S'all right, lad. You had a close shave and no mistake, but you'll be well again soon."

"Where is she?" he demanded, needing the girl, she'd promised to be here when he woke.

"Where's who? Ain't no girls here, son. You must have dreamed her."

"A dream?" he repeated, his heart aching. *No.* No, not a dream, *please*. She had promised to save him, to be here and he… But that was foolishness. He didn't deserve anyone who was that kind, that sweet.

He was alive, he realised, as a fine tremor began in his bones and would not stop. Some beneficent deity had given him a second chance just as he'd prayed for, a chance to do better and make amends for all he'd done wrong. To his consternation, he felt hot tears sliding down his cheeks, unstoppable, and a sob rose in this throat. He turned his face away, ashamed to be seen crying like a baby, but the old man only patted his shoulder and left him alone to weep with relief, misery, and gratitude until he was exhausted and slept once more.

When he next woke, there was a boy watching him.

"Blimey, you don't half sleep a lot," he said, a complaining note to the observation. "Burt said I had to keep you company, but it's a dull job when you just lay there. At least before when you was off ye head, you was more entertaining."

"Sorry," Max offered cautiously, biting back the instinctive desire to tell him to go to the devil. He would not be that man again, he reminded himself. His head was pounding, and everything hurt, but this lad had been watching over him, no matter how ungraciously.

"S'all right," the boy said with a gap-toothed grin. "You're awake now. So, what's your name, then?"

Max went to answer, only to find a blank. He frowned, a panicky sensation flitting around in his chest.

"Don't remember?"

Max shook his head.

The boy sighed. "Ah well. We'll call you Valentine. That's what old Mrs Wilkes called you, on account of you being so pretty, she said. Burt said you might not remember stuff. Said when you get a big fright like you did, it can addle your brain box."

"It can?" Max asked, casting around his beleaguered mind to remember what else he knew of himself.

"Oh, yes," the boy said, with all the assurance of a small boy who knows everything. "It'll come back, don't fret."

Max nodded, deciding he was too exhausted to worry, anyway. This was his second chance, that much he remembered clearly. There was likely a reason he was here, a reason his memory was gone, so he may as well let things play out. Looking around at the room, with plaster falling off the walls and an unpleasant mouldy stain decorating the ceiling in the corner, he knew one thing with certainty. He'd never been in a room like this in his life. His world had been one of privilege and ease.

"My things?" he asked the boy, who was watching him avidly.

"Well, they robbed anything valuable afore we got to you, save for your boots. They're here. I polished 'em for you. Must have cost a bleedin' fortune. Your clothes were here too, but they're so bloody and messed up they're no good for you now. Burt sold 'em because some of the material was good. Expensive cloth."

"He sold my clothes?" Max asked, taken aback.

"Yeah. Only to buy you new ones." The boy glared at him. "We ain't thieves here."

"I beg your pardon," Max said at once, aware he'd caused offense. This boy and his father had cared for him when they could barely care for themselves. "I meant no insult to you or your father. I'm most grateful to you."

"Cor, don't you talk funny? You a lord or summat?"

A lord? Max turned the notion about in his head. "Yes," he said slowly. "I… I think I might be."

"That explains it, then. You sound like a toff." The boy nodded, satisfied with this explanation. "Burt's not my pa, anyhow. He just took me in when no one else wanted me. Why'd someone try to snabble you, then?"

Max shrugged and then sucked in a sharp breath as the motion tugged at the wound in his side. "Any number of reasons," he replied on a gasp, knowing that much was true, which was a sorry indictment of his character, when he could remember that much and not his own name.

"A bad 'un are ye, then?" There was no judgement in the boy's eyes, only curiosity, so Max nodded.

"Yes. I was, anyway. I've decided I shan't be bad anymore."

"That's good. Burt says wicked fellows go to hell. He reckons it's good to help people out. Like takin' me in. I ain't the first, neither. Do good things and good things come back to you. That's what Burt says."

Max smiled. "Burt sounds like a wise fellow. Do you think he could teach me to be good?"

The boy considered this for a moment and then gave a decisive nod.

"Reckon," he said.

Present Day…

27th May 1842, Church Street, Isleworth, London..

Kathy poured herself a small glass of brandy and took a hesitant sip. Screwing up her face, she winced as she swallowed. Well, it was medicine, she supposed. At least, Mama always said it was medicinal when she had a glass after a difficult day. She swore it soothed the nerves. As a pleasant glow of warmth bloomed in her stomach, Kathy realised she might have a point. Taking her glass with her, she made her way to her brother's greenhouse. Hart wasn't here today, which meant she had the place to herself. She let herself in and took a deep breath, inhaling the warm damp air with a sigh of relief. It was strange, as she'd never been overly fond of the countryside, preferring the life and bustle of the city, but there was something about the greenhouse that quieted her, and she always felt better here.

She took a seat on the high stool by the workbench, and a larger swallow of the brandy, forcing it down. The next swallow was rather easier, and she felt the tension in her shoulders unknot a fraction. She could not get the image of that big, ugly brute trying to strangle the life out of Lord Vane from her mind. Somehow it got tangled up with the image of him years ago, fighting for his life on that meagre little bed in that dreadful building in the Dials. Emotion snarled in her chest, making her breathless, and she took another sip of brandy, blinking back tears. She did not want to feel this way. Oh, why had she crossed paths with him after all this time? And why had she been so stupid as to guilt him into giving her this job? Though the job was everything she wanted, there was no avoiding being in his company and, the more time she spent with him, the worse this would become. He was just so likeable, and wasn't that just typical? Why was a man who was a womaniser and libertine not as ugly as his actions? But then he'd not have much success at being a libertine, would he? Kathy groaned and put her head in her hands.

"What the bloody hell are you playing at, you little dimwit?"

Kathy jolted, almost toppling from her stool as her brother's voice.

"What?" she squeaked, alarmed. "I didn't touch anything. I'm just sitting here!"

Hart muttered a rude word under his breath and strode in. "I mean, what's this I hear about your new job? Mama said you're working for Lord Vane. Are you out of your tiny mind? Or are they for allowing it? I thought you said you were working with Eliza."

"Oh, that," she said, relaxing. She'd wondered how long it would take for him to find out. "It's a wonderful opportunity. For you too, if you design the gardens."

"He's not fit company for you," Hart growled. "Has he made any advances? Said anything he ought not? Because if he has—"

Kathy smiled at her brother's fierce countenance, even though his overprotectiveness was often irritating.

"No, no, nothing of the sort. He's turned over a new leaf. That's the whole point of this project with the school. He's trying to mend his ways. He's been a perfect gentleman."

It was true, she realised, and half the reason for her current turmoil. If he'd only made inappropriate advances or acted like a wicked seducer, she'd not be in half as much trouble. Not that she was about to tell her brother that.

Hart gave a snort of disgust. "Likely biding his time. A leopard doesn't change his spots, Kathy."

She rolled her eyes. "Oh, give over. Mama trusts me not to get myself into trouble, so you ought to do likewise."

"From what Pa has told me about how Mama pursued him, I'm not certain that's the least bit comforting," he grumbled, folding his arms.

Kathy laughed and went to pick up her glass again, but Hart snatched it, taking a sniff.

"Brandy?" he exclaimed, glaring at her. "In the middle of the day? What did he *do*?" he demanded, his eyes flashing dangerously.

Kathy sighed. "He tackled a thief at the building site. The man had been stealing materials and was about to abscond. Lord Vane stopped him, but the big brute put up one hell of a fight. I'm just a little shaken, that's all."

"What kind of job is it that has you witnessing a brawl, for the love of God? That's it. I'm telling Papa. He'll put a stop to this nonsense."

"Hart!" Kathy jumped off the stool and ran after him, clutching at his arm and tugging. Hart stopped, which was just as well, for he could have dragged her halfway around Isleworth without batting an eyelid if he chose to. "Don't you dare snitch on me."

Hart's expression softened, and he let out a sigh. "Sis, be reasonable. You remember what you were like before over this wretched tosspot? You cried for days, and it was my fault for allowing it. I had to cover that up and keep it from Ma and Pa, and

I've never forgiven myself for letting you get involved. And now you're *working* for him?"

"It's different now," Kathy insisted, praying he'd listen to her.

He looked disgusted by this suggestion, his lip curling. "What? Now he's a good man because he's throwing his money at some charitable project and getting pats on the back for being so generous, is that it?"

"No!" she exclaimed with a huff. "For one thing, no one knows. He's keeping it a secret."

"*You* know," he said dryly.

Kathy tutted. "I found out by accident, but that's not the point. Back then, I was a silly little girl with a tendre for a man that didn't exist. It all seemed very romantic to me, nursing a dying young man back to life. But I'm not a child anymore, Hart, nor a fool. I know him for what he is, and I have no interest in him. I'll take no silly risks with my person or my reputation, I promise you. And if he offers me the slightest insult, I'll let you pound him. How's that?"

She looked up at him hopefully. Hart's thick eyebrows drew together. He didn't look happy, but Kathy could usually wrap him around her finger if she tried hard enough.

"You swear it?" he asked, scowling.

Kathy nodded.

He blew out a breath and raked a hand through his hair. "Fine," he said, sounding displeased. "But if he so much as looks at you the wrong way, you tell me, and I'll wring the devil's neck. Got it?"

"Got it," Kathy agreed, nodding.

"Right you are, then, but I don't like it."

"You don't like anything that isn't green with roots," Kathy remarked.

"True. They don't cause me any trouble," he muttered. "And keep the door closed properly. Orchids—"

"Don't like draughts, yes, I know," Kathy said.

"Hmmm," Hart replied, before finishing her brandy in one swallow, handing her the empty glass back and stalking out again.

Kathy sighed. Well, she'd convinced her overprotective brother that she was in no danger.

Now she had only to convince herself.

Chapter 9

Dearest Matilda,

Thank you for your letter. It was so lovely to hear from you. Believe me, I understand how troublesome sons can be. I would not be without my boys for the world, and they have become fine young men, yet sometimes I could merrily lock them in the cellar and take myself off to Bedlam for a bit of peace. They are the most ridiculous creatures on occasion, and I despair of them. I shall be relieved when they are all safely married off and their wives have the managing of them.

Yes, it is wonderful to have Helena come to stay, though Gabriel is returning to London for a couple of weeks. That terrible train crash in France earlier this month has made his investors jittery, and he must return to soothe their nerves. Such a tragedy makes your heart bleed. It quite makes one anxious about stepping foot on a train again, though naturally I did not voice such a concern to Gabriel.

Things seem to be going well with Evie. She's a delightful girl and has fitted in wonderfully well as we knew she would. Helena and I are hoping one of the boys catches her eye, and vice versa. She seems to have taken to Muir and the two of them are as thick as thieves, but I'm uncertain if there is a romance there yet. I think Muir will offer for her, for he knows a good thing when he sees it. Yet sometimes when no one is observing her, she seems rather melancholy, and I wonder if she is not just doing her best to make everyone else happy. I hope not, but I cannot shake the feeling something is troubling her.

—Excerpt of a letter from Ruth Anderson, Countess of Morven to Matilda Barrington, Marchioness of Montagu.

3rd June 1842, On the road to Wick, The Highlands, Scotland.

"Barnaby." Louis gave his friend a little shake as the carriage rolled to a halt. They were finally on the last leg of this interminable journey, but he suspected Barnaby would appreciate a hot meal before they went any farther. He'd been snoring soundly for the past hour, which was not entirely soothing, but as the journey was being undertaken for Louis' sake, he hardly felt in a position to complain.

"Wha' what's that?" Barnaby mumbled sleepily before focusing on Louis. "Are we there?" he asked hopefully, rubbing a weary hand over his face.

"Not yet, but the inn looks decent. I thought you might want a meal."

"Lord, yes. My belly thinks my throat's been cut," Barnaby said, stretching in his seat.

"Well, let's hope they've got something edible," Louis murmured, not holding out much hope after the horror of the stuffed sheep's stomach last night. Why anybody would want to do such a thing was incomprehensible to him.

"You're not still upset about the haggis?" Barnaby asked him with amusement.

"I shall go to my grave upset about the haggis," Louis retorted darkly.

Barnaby sniggered.

Louis got down from the carriage and stretched out his spine with a groan. "Did people really undertake this journey before the train arrived?"

"Yes. Did myself a few times. Bloody awful it was, too," Barnaby said with a grimace.

It had taken them a day and a half to make a little under half the journey by taking the train from Euston to Birmingham, and then on to Manchester. From Manchester they could get as far as Preston, but then they were back to a carriage journey over indifferent roads and increasingly difficult terrain for the last four hundred odd miles. After the speedy train journey, it felt like crawling. It was taking days, and Louis was beyond impatient.

They ate a decent if hurried meal at the Sutherland Arms in Golspie, which was thankfully free of haggis or anything else he couldn't identify, before climbing back into the carriage again. With luck, they'd arrive in Wick late that evening.

As the carriage moved on once more, Louis glanced across the carriage at Barnaby, who was looking out of the window at the countryside. He'd never once complained about the tedious journey or in any way made Louis feel beholden to him for doing him this favour. He was a rare friend, and Louis knew it.

"Thank you, Barnaby," he said, needing the man to know he appreciated what he was doing for him a great deal.

Barnaby turned back to him, surprised. "Eh? What for?"

"For everything. For being my friend, for bearing with me along this trip, and not thinking me a fool."

"Oh, that's nothing. Happy to do it. Anybody would be," Barnaby said with a cheerful smile, waving this away.

Louis shook his head, determined that Barnaby realise how much he appreciated him. *"Non, mon ami.* Everyone would not. In my experience, people who go out of their way to help others are uncommon. At least there are few who have ever helped me or been kind without expecting something in return. You are a good man, and a wonderful friend. I wish for you to know this."

Barnaby blushed and mumbled something incomprehensible, which made Louis smile, but he was clearly pleased by the comment, so that was what mattered.

They sat in silence for a bit, with Barnaby smiling to himself. He turned back to Louis. "You help people, though, Louis. Helped me, didn't you? And Miss Aggie, the little minx. Where would she be without you, eh? What goes around comes around, I reckon."

Louis frowned. "That's what worries me," he murmured.

Barnaby chuckled, thinking he was joking, which he wasn't. He was certain Gabriel Knight was the one asking questions in Paris, but until he'd left London, he still hadn't shaken off the crawling sensation that he was being watched. Perhaps this business with Evie was truly making him lose his mind. He felt a little unhinged without her, adrift, as if they had taken his anchor away and he was all at sea. Perhaps paranoia was a part of it. Or perhaps ghosts were not as implausible as he'd always believed, and a dead man had tracked him down to make his life hell all over again. A shiver of fear and distaste rolled down his spine.

He looked up as Barnaby spoke again, relieved to be distracted from such disturbing thoughts. "You understand, though, Louis," Barnaby said, his expression grave, "I can't guarantee you'll see her, or even hear news of her. I'll try my best, but—"

"I understand," Louis said, though the knowledge sat in his chest like a lead weight. "I do not expect miracles, and I would never hold you responsible if this is all for naught. I'd rather take this journey ten times over than be miles away from her in London, wondering if I've lost her for good. Do you think me ridiculous? I should not blame you."

Barnaby shook his head. "No, I don't think that. It's romantic, ain't it? To try everything. To grab at every chance for happiness. I'm no good with poetry or pretty words, as you well know, but it feels like doing something important. You and that young woman ought to be together, if I know anything. Perhaps she don't see it yet, but I reckon she will. Blimey, half the world seems to be in love with you. Dashed fond of you myself. Surely she'll fall too, in the end."

Louis snorted and shook his head. "The world does not know me. Not really. They see only a pretty face and don't bother with the rest. Even Evie doesn't know me as she ought, not well enough to make such a momentous decision. If she did, she'd probably run a mile. Even so, she knows me better than most anyone, outside of two men I count as family, and you, now, Barnaby," he added with a smile. "I rather hope she does not discover the rest before I can persuade her to marry me, and I know that is a wicked thing to say."

"What would she discover that's so dreadful?" Barnaby asked cautiously.

Louis lay his head back against the squabs with a sigh. "I sometimes feel I have lived a hundred lives. And each time I move on, I try to shed the old skin and all that went with it, but it does not work that way. We carry the past with us." He turned back to Barnaby, holding his gaze. "You cannot imagine the life I have lived. I truly wish I could not either. I ask you, what kind of aristocrat has a tattoo like that across his back? Do you think it will horrify her?"

Barnaby shifted uncomfortably in his seat. "Honestly, it's rather beautiful, though I cannot imagine how or why you got it, but I reckon there was a good reason at the time and… and if she loves you, she won't care about such things, past wanting to know why too, I imagine."

"If she loves me," Louis repeated, turning to stare out of the window but not really seeing the passing scenery. He nodded, his stomach twisting with anxiety. "*If* she loves me."

3rd June 1842, The Countess St Clair's Spring Ball, St James's, London.

Max tugged at his waistcoat, trying not to feel too conspicuous. He would have avoided this kind of event like the plague in times past. Polite society, polite conversation, and a lot of marriage hungry young women out to snare a husband. Back then, he'd have far rather been indulging in more decadent pleasures at the notorious Orchid House or gambling in one of the infamous hells to be found in the city. He and Kilbane had cut a swathe through London, pandering to their baser desires, each egging the other on. Partners in crime. They had seen each other at their worst, and he knew that was why he did not want the man around. Kilbane was a reminder of his past and his darker self.

Max turned his gold signet ring around and around on his finger. It had become a nervous habit, ever since Humphrey Price had returned it to him. He'd not known the young man well, but he'd been drinking in The Crown that fateful night, too. He'd seen Max leave, following about twenty minutes later. It had been Price who'd found his signet ring in a pool of blood and raised the alarm, not that Max had known it.

Burt and Pike had, though they'd held their tongues, both to the police and to Max himself. Burt later explained he'd figured it best for him to keep out of sight if someone wanted him dead. Let them think they'd done the job thoroughly. Until he was well again, at least. Burt had been of a mind that it was better for his memory to return without being forced, too. Max suspected that was not entirely true. He believed Burt had heard who he was, heard the kind of man he'd been, and wanted the chance to help Max remake himself before his old life caught up with him again. He'd done it, too. For that alone, Max would be eternally grateful.

He sighed, wishing Barnaby and Louis had not taken themselves off to Scotland on whatever family call of duty they had forced Barnaby to take. Though why Louis was accompanying him, he couldn't fathom. Except that the two of them seemed fast friends these days. Max smothered an unwelcome niggle of jealousy and told himself he was being ridiculous. Friends took time, that was all. He'd see them both when they returned, but for now he ought to make new friends among those people around him. The idea was remarkably daunting. He'd never troubled himself to make friends before, he realised, and he wasn't certain how to go about it. Drinking cronies and men who indulged in the same vices as he'd enjoyed were easy. Friends, decent men and women with more on their minds than the next pleasure to be had were another matter entirely.

Such concerns fled, however, as he glimpsed a familiar face in the crowd and a thrill of excitement fizzed in his blood.

Max hurried closer, muttering abject apologies as he bumped into an elderly dowager in his haste and received an arctic glare in return. Wincing, he returned his attention to his quarry. God, but she was lovely. Dressed in a gown of pale blue, Miss de Beauvoir looked like an ice queen from a fairy story, her cool expression distant and rather daunting. Frowning, he realised she was alone and, beneath the formidable expression, she seemed as awkward as he'd been feeling. It occurred to him to wonder what an event must be like for her. He knew she'd been adopted from a foundling home and could only guess at the treatment she must receive from the judgemental *ton*. He hoped she had friends here, for he knew how cruel society could be and he doubted they'd been kind to her.

"Miss de Beauvoir."

She gave a little start of surprise and stared up at him, her grey eyes wide and startled. "Oh! I beg your pardon, Lord Vane. I'm afraid I was wool gathering. How do you do?"

"Very well, thank you. I did not expect to see you here. Are you enjoying yourself?"

"Oh, yes, of course, thank you," she said automatically.

Max quirked an eyebrow at her and she sighed.

"No, actually. If you must know, I'm bored stiff."

Max returned a sympathetic smile. "But you have friends here, surely?"

"I do," she admitted. "And they're very kind. That's Lady Rosamund over there, dancing with Mr Anson. She would have sat out to keep me company, but I told her not to. My friends are most attentive, my lord. They are always rallying around and making certain I have dance partners among their brothers and their other friends. It's never the same when someone is dancing with you out of kindness, though, is it?" she added with a sigh.

Max frowned, shaking his head. "I cannot believe the men here are so foolish as not to ask you to dance."

"Not all of them, but I've become cautious who I accept, which doesn't help." She looked away from him, and Max wondered what she meant.

"You don't mean to say…. Has anyone insulted you?" he asked, taken aback by the surge of rage he felt.

Her colour rose, but she turned back and held his gaze. "Oh, come now. Don't tell me you're surprised," she said, laughing a little. "You know as well as I that I'm unlikely to marry anyone here, not when my blood is an unknown quantity. My actual mother might have been a prostitute, my father a criminal. It's hardly astonishing some men think I'd accept a carte blanche, is it?"

Her words were hard and candid, and yet he heard the vulnerability beneath her bravado, and he wanted to hit something.

"Who?" he asked through gritted teeth. "Who dared ask you such a thing?"

She stared at him for a long moment, her expression unreadable. "Don't fret about it so, my lord. I assure you, I know my own worth. And be honest, might you not have made the same offer not so long ago? I do not think it fair to ask you to play knight in shining armour in the circumstances."

A sickly sensation of guilt uncoiled in his guts, cold and slithery and disgusting. She was right, of course. He'd been just such a man, and he'd have not thought twice. He wanted her now. The old Max would have desired her too, and he'd have tried everything to get her.

"I beg your pardon," he managed, unable to meet her eyes now as shame and remorse overwhelmed him. God, how she must despise him, and with good reason. "I'm so sorry, I…forgive me."

He fled, his chest tight with regret, unable to breathe as he made his way to the doors. Escape was the only thing he could think of, getting away from her, for she ought not have to suffer his company. If only he could escape himself, shed his skin and leave the old Max behind, but there was no escaping the man he'd been. That was his punishment, and he must stand it. He'd changed, but that change came at a price. Realising now what it took to be a decent human being meant forever knowing just how far from decent he'd been.

He burst out onto the terrace and took a deep breath, praying he'd not throw up and make a spectacle of himself. To his relief, the terrace was empty, and he made his way to the balustrade, leaning on it to steady himself. His hands were shaking, he realised, and he closed his eyes.

"God forgive me," he whispered.

"My lord?"

The softly spoken words made all the hairs on the back of his neck rise, his heart thudding with hope as he recognised the voice that had brought him back from the dead. He spun around and for a moment he could not understand why Miss de Beauvoir was standing before him. She reached out and placed a tentative hand on his arm.

"I'm sorry," she said, her beautiful eyes awash with tears. "That was a vile thing to say. Please forgive me."

He shook his head, uncomprehending why she of all people would seek his forgiveness. She should loath him as much as he loathed himself.

"I deserved it," he replied, his voice unsteady. "You were absolutely right, and I deserve far, far worse, believe me."

"Perhaps, but it is not for me to judge you, and certainly not to make nasty comments at your expense. I promise you I feel horribly ashamed of myself for doing so. It's not like I'm perfect, or anyone else in that room. We're all flawed and… and perhaps that makes you better than most. Because you know the things you did were wrong, and you are making amends."

"I'm trying," he said, wanting her to know that much.

She nodded. "I know," she said, the understanding in her eyes making him want to fall to his knees in gratitude for not reviling him.

"What if it isn't enough?" he asked, staring at her in bewilderment.

It was her. He was certain of it. This was the voice of the woman he'd lived for, the one who had promised to be there when he woke but had never shown herself.

"I don't know," she said, her honesty razor sharp. "But I think if you keep trying, maybe it will be, one day."

"You do?"

She nodded then, giving him the ghost of a smile. "I do."

He let out a breath of relief. If she thought he could do it, maybe there was hope for him. Maybe there was hope that she might consider him worth knowing, worth liking, a little at least. He desperately wanted to ask her why, why had she not been there when he'd woken? Why had she been there in the first place? Why had she given him those tender words and then broken her promise? And why had Burt and Pike denied her existence? He couldn't, though. The memories were still hazy, but he remembered the feeling her voice had evoked, remembered the tone of her words, the intimacy of it. If she knew he'd remembered, the knowledge would embarrass her and drive another wedge between them when she had just offered the first tentative step closer to him. He did not want that.

"You'd best go in, Miss de Beauvoir. It will do your reputation no good to be found alone with me."

She nodded, and he suspected the regret flickering in her eyes was wishful thinking on his part. He watched as she turned away, wishing he could keep her with him longer without causing her harm, but that was not possible. The moonlight silvered her hair, casting her in an ethereal light that gave the entire interlude a dreamlike quality that made him doubt it was even real. If she were a dream, she would turn and kiss him, he thought wildly, and then she did turn, and his heart gave an extraordinary kick in his chest as hope rioted through him.

"W-Would you like to dance with me?" she asked, the words bursting out of her so fast he knew she had not thought it through.

She looked startled by her own audacity. Max felt a smile tug at his mouth, realising with chagrin that he was not so reformed as to let her retract the offer. Her hands were twisting together, and she was breathing very hard. It was impossible not to note the rapid rise and fall of her breasts against the neckline of her gown, but he tried his damndest to be a gentleman and kept his gaze upon her face.

"I would like that above all things," he said, meaning it.

"Oh." She dithered, looking like she did not know whether to stay or run, or whether she'd done something exceedingly reckless. "W-Well, good. I'll save you a—"

"A waltz, if you have one. Please," he added, hoping he wasn't pushing his luck.

She nodded, her hands reaching to smooth her hair and then her skirts, as though she did not quite know what to do with them. Nervous, he realised with a rush of tenderness. She was nervous.

"I only have the midnight waltz left. You'll have to take me into dinner, too," she said, chin up, as if she thought he might change his mind if he had to sit with her. Foolish creature.

"Perfect," he said. "I'll come and find you."

"Fine." She nodded again. "Good. I… I'd better…."

She made a gesture towards the doors and began to walk away, thought better of it, turned and dipped an awkward curtsey and then fled.

Max let out a ragged laugh, wondering how it was possible to go from the depths of despair to experiencing something that felt very much like it might be happiness, in such a short space of time.

Chapter 10

Dearest Ozzie,

I'm so sorry not to be at the St Clair ball with you, though I am certain you will have a splendid time without me. You'll have Kathy with you after all, though, do keep an eye on her. You promised to keep the toads away, remember, and don't let her forget to ask Pip to dance with you. Don't pretend you don't want him to, either.

I am having a wonderful time here in Scotland for everyone has been so very kind and welcoming, but I do miss you all, and the season. It feels like being on the other side of the world, like I've stepped out of my own life for a time, and it is an odd sensation. Though it has given me time to think. The trouble is, the more I think, the more confused I get.

Why is life so complicated?

Tell me everything that happens at the ball, what everyone is wearing and all the scandal. Was Monsieur Le Comte there with all the ladies swooning about him? Has he a new mistress yet? Please, give me all the latest gossip.

—Excerpt of a letter from Miss Evie Knight (daughter of Lady Helena and Mr Gabriel Knight) to Lady Rosamund Adolphus (daughter of Their Graces, Robert and Prunella Adolphus, the Duke and Duchess of Bedwin).

3rd June 1842, The Countess St Clair's Spring Ball, St James's, London.

Rosamund felt her heart flutter as she saw a familiar ice-blond head of hair. He was here.

Surreptitiously, she bit her lips and pinched her cheeks, hoping The Earl of Ashburton might look her way. Kathy had promised to ask him to dance with her this evening, for Ashburton—or Pip, as his close friends knew him—was protective of Kathy. He always danced with her, treating her with the same fond impatience he bestowed on his little sister, Cat. Rosamund always found herself torn between envy and relief. She wished he would give her more attention, but she certainly did not wish to be regarded as his sister. He hardly noticed her at all, though. She was his friend's little sister no more. Just another one of Jules' many siblings. Kathy had disappeared whilst Rosamund was dancing with Ashton Anson, though, and she'd not seen her since.

She stood on her tiptoes, craning her neck to get a better view and for a moment, she thought he was coming towards her. Yes. Yes, he was! Rosamund smiled, her heart thudding uncomfortably as she wished she'd not pinched her cheeks so hard for now it felt as though they were glowing. Except then Pip walked past her, and she realised he'd not been looking at her at all. He'd not noticed her. Mortified, she spun away and walked directly into a solid mass.

She gasped and then gave a little squeal as chilled champagne splashed her chest and funnelled into her décolletage.

"My lady!" said a deep voice, sounding utterly horrified. "I beg your pardon."

"Oh!" she exclaimed, wondering if the evening could possibly get any worse. She looked up, and then up rather more, and stared into eyes the colour of gingerbread, flecked with cinnamon. "Oh," she said again, shivering against the sensation of champagne trickling between her breasts and the way the man's eyes darkened as they lingered on her neckline. He tore his eyes back to hers.

"Forgive me. I'm not usually such a clumsy oaf," he said.

"It wasn't your fault," she managed, realising that if he'd been standing that close, he may well have witnessed her humiliation. "It was entirely m-mine, and I suspect you know it."

His expression softened, which was somehow worse. Just what she needed, a handsome man's pity. "He's a fool not to have noticed you."

Rosamund let out a little groan of misery. *Kill me now*, she begged no one in particular.

"Let me introduce myself, at least, Lady Rosamund," the fellow said. "I'm Hargreaves."

"Viscount Hargreaves?" she asked, staring at him in surprise. He gave a crooked smile and nodded. "Yes, *that* one. So you've no need to feel the least bit embarrassed, you see."

There was a wealth of meaning in his tone and the smile and she felt a rush of sympathy for him. His beautiful wife had caused a dreadful scandal by having a very public affair with an artist. She had made something of a spectacle of herself and her husband, and Hargreaves had taken her to France with him to let the dust settle. Though Rosamund did not know all the details, she knew her father had sympathised with the viscount.

"You know who I am?" Rosamund asked in surprise, and then blushed, wishing she hadn't.

"Of course," he said with a warm smile. "A fellow always knows the names of the prettiest girls even if he hasn't the opportunity to speak with them."

She stared at him curiously but found only friendly admiration in his gaze and a little twinkle of amusement. Rosamund relaxed, recognising a good-natured soul who was endeavouring to put her at ease.

"Why, Lord Hargreaves, you are trying to charm me," she said, finding his attempt had worked, and she did not feel so dreadfully foolish after all.

"I am. I'm hoping you'll forgive me for throwing champagne at you. Is it working?" he added in an undertone.

"It might be," she replied.

"Would you do me the honour of taking a turn about the room with me then? I promise not to spill anything else on you." He made a great show of setting his champagne glass down and taking a step away from it, holding his hands up in a defenceless gesture.

She smiled, enjoying his silliness, and nodded. "I would be pleased to," she said, taking the arm he offered.

They strolled about a little, with Rosamund stopping now and then to speak to people she knew. Everyone greeted him with pleasure, though she saw pity in some of their eyes, which he must find hard to bear. Yet he showed no sign of it and conversed politely and with ease. He was a very comfortable man to spend time with, perhaps because he was married and therefore she did not need to worry about trying to impress or please him. It was rather liberating.

"You know, he did not ignore you. He simply hasn't noticed you yet. I find it inconceivable personally, but some men need to be hit on the head with a fact before it sinks in."

Rosamund stared up at him, blushing as she realised he was speaking of Pip.

"Oh, no, but I… I'm not…."

"You're head over ears in love with him," he said, though not unkindly. He sighed and shook his head. "I remember the sensation, though it seems a very long time ago."

Rosamund stared at him, wondering if he realised he'd said that last bit aloud. She thought not as he cleared his throat, looking awkward, and hurried on.

"You've got to put yourself in his way," he said, his tone more decisive now. "Ashburton is chased about by women left and right, so one can't blame him for being a bit icy on occasions like this. No, we need to find a way to put you in front of him without it seeming as if you're interested."

"We?" Rosamund echoed in astonishment.

He nodded. "I must make amends for the dousing with champagne."

"Oh, don't be silly. There's no need—"

"Don't look a gift horse in the mouth, my lady," he said, wagging a finger at her. "I happen to know Montagu quite well, and Philip a little too. I'm sure I can manage something."

"But what?"

"Well, give a fellow a chance to think," he said indignantly.

Rosamund giggled, rather entertained by him.

"How well do you know the man?"

"Montagu?" she queried.

He tsked at her.

Raising an eyebrow at his imperiousness, she could not help laughing. "Oh, Pip. Well, he's my older brother's friend. We grew up together."

"Ah, that explains it. He thinks of you as a childhood annoyance, I'll bet. One who tried to spoil their games, I don't doubt. He has yet to notice you've blossomed into a beautiful woman. Right, then. We need something to stir his protective instincts."

Rosamund stared at him, dubious as to his intentions. "We do?"

"Undoubtedly. We need an unsuitable fellow to show an interest in you, but that could be dangerous. Can't have you putting your reputation at risk by encouraging some loose screw." He frowned at that, pondering the idea.

"No, I'd rather not," she agreed hurriedly.

"No. Someone who can be relied upon to play a part without putting you in a difficult position. After all, Pip just needs to *believe* a wicked fellow has set his sights on seducing you. A little word in his ear might be enough."

"But whoever it was might risk getting into a dreadful scrape. Jules—my brother, that is—says Pip is not the sort of man one gets into a fight with. He boxes and fences and he's awfully clever too. If he set out to take revenge… well, I should hate for anyone to get hurt on my account," Rosamund said anxiously.

He waved this away. "It need not go that far. He just needs a little push in the right direction. He'll get the picture quick enough."

Rosamund looked sceptical. "I cannot imagine who would risk offending Pip on my behalf. They'd be mad to do so. What if Montagu got involved?" she added, horrified at the prospect.

He considered this. "Well… I could do it."

"*You*?" she asked, clearly looking sceptical enough to insult him.

"I'm not that old and decrepit, am I?" To her amusement, he looked genuinely concerned. "Is the notion of me having designs on you *that* repulsive?"

"*No*!" she said at once, not wanting to offend the poor man when his wife's flighty behaviour must have done nothing to bolster his confidence. "No, you're very handsome and… and not that old."

"Not *that* old," he repeated doubtfully, though amusement shone in his eyes.

"Well, how old are you?" she demanded, and then rushed to apologise. "I beg your pardon, I ought not…."

"No, no," he waved this away. "I'm ancient, as must be obvious. To you, any fellow over two and twenty must seem ancient at any rate. *Almost* thirty might as well be a hundred and fifty to a young woman, I suppose," he said sadly.

Rosamund giggled. "Almost," she repeated mischievously.

"I'll be thirty next year," he said, looking a bit put out.

"Methuselah," she murmured, her voice trembling with amusement, and rather surprised at herself for being so cheeky.

"You," he said severely, "are not half so sweet as you look. Methuselah, indeed!"

She bit her lip, and he sent her a crooked grin. "Well, we have the beginnings of a plan, Lady Rosamund. Let's see what else we can come up with, eh?"

3rd June 1842, The Countess St Clair's Spring Ball, St James's, London.

"Well, he's very handsome. Rather dashing, actually," Kathy said, regarding the Viscount Hargreaves, who was speaking with Rosamund's father. Her friend seemed taken with the man who had clearly made an impression.

"He's a lot of fun, too. Very charming."

"Yes, he's well liked. That's why it was such a dreadful scandal, of course, with his wife, I mean."

"Where is she?" Rosamund asked, obviously dying to know what the woman looked like.

Kathy craned her neck but found no sign of her. "I don't know. I wouldn't trouble yourself to meet her, though. She was frightfully rude to Mama, you know."

"No! Why?" Rosamund asked, looking horrified.

"Because Papa isn't a gentleman and because Hart and I were foundling children. She made some rude comment within Mama's hearing. On purpose, I might add. She's a spiteful cat."

"Oh," Rosamund said, appearing crestfallen to know her new friend was married to someone so unkind.

Kathy nodded, grimacing. "I'm only repeating gossip, of course, which I ought not. But they married very young. A whirlwind romance, apparently. My father said his parents ought to have been shot for letting it go ahead, because everyone could see they were ill matched. He was only eighteen and head over ears. She's actually a little older, I think. Only a year or two, not much, but Hart said she was a flirt even then."

"Hartley knows her?"

Kathy pulled a face and nodded. "I think that's why she was rude to Mama, between you and me. She…." Kathy lowered her voice. "She tried to seduce him, but Hart refused her. She's hated him ever since."

"Oh, poor Lord Hargreaves."

Kathy patted Rosamund's hand. The poor girl looked stricken on the man's account, not that Kathy blamed her. It was a tragic story. The idea of being trapped in a marriage with a wife that not only did not love you but continued to make a fool of you in public must be beyond bearing.

"Yes, that's what people always say. 'Poor Lord Hargreaves.' Can you imagine how that makes him feel?"

Rosamund shook her head. "It's a wonder he's not a bitter, angry man. I think I would feel angry."

"Oh, he's had his moments. According to the scandal sheets, at least, but I think perhaps he's past caring now. That's what people say, anyway. Oh, my…." Kathy's stomach dropped as she saw Lord Vane crossing the ballroom. She spun around to face Rosamund. "Is my hair still neat or is it a mess? Do I look fine? I look fine, don't I?"

"It's lovely. You look lovely," Rosamund said, frowning.

Kathy glanced down and smoothed her skirts out and then cursed herself. She was acting like a prize ninny. What was wrong with her? Her heart was racing, her skin prickling with the anticipation of being in his arms. *Foolish creature, stop being so silly!* She could have no romantic interest in the man, she reminded herself severely.

"Miss de Beauvoir?"

She turned, doing her utmost to paste a calm smile to her mouth when her insides had decided to dance a mad jig and she had a terrible desire to giggle for no reason. Good Lord, but this man turned her into such a twit.

"My lord, is it that time already?"

"Already?" he repeated with a smile. "It seemed an eternity to me. Shall we?"

He offered his arm to her, and Kathy took it, glancing at Rosamund, who was waggling her eyebrows at her in encouragement. Oh, dear. What on earth had possessed her to offer him a dance? *And the supper waltz, no less*, she wailed inwardly. He'd have to take her into dinner. They'd have to sit together throughout the meal. She'd have to *talk* to him. Kathy was increasingly aware that talking to Lord Vane was a dangerous exercise. It made her want to like him, like him even more than she already did. Worse than that, it made her want to trust him, and that was very bad. Very. Bad. She sounded the words out in her head in capital letters and then spelled them for good measure.

"Bad, bad, bad," she muttered.

"I'm sorry?"

Good heavens, had she said that out loud? She was losing her mind.

"Nothing!" she said brightly. "I was just wondering what was for dinner. I'm famished."

"You're not going to faint from hunger, are you?" he asked, eyeing her with concern.

"I've never fainted in my life!" she retorted, a little indignant.

He grinned then, and Kathy tried to bury the giddy sensation that erupted in her belly. The jig her insides were performing was becoming increasingly energetic. And then he took her in his arms for the waltz, and any remaining good sense flew out the window. It felt like flying. A magical sensation, all fizzing excitement and something joyous like champagne bubbles was rushing through her veins. This was why dancing with friends and relatives was not the same thing at all, she realised. She closed her eyes and told herself not to be foolish. It was just a dance, and he was just a man, a beautiful but flawed, unhappy man who had lived selfishly for most of his life. He might return to his old ways at any time, no matter how he appeared now. A leopard didn't change his spots, as Hart had counselled her. Being good was likely dull, after living such an indulgent and exciting life as he had… and yet….

And yet, the way he'd looked when she'd suggested he would have offered her the same insult and asked to make her his mistress. All the colour had drained from his face, and she'd wondered if he might be ill. He'd been truly distressed. Surely that could not be feigned? That had to be genuine, did it not? Even so, she'd be foolish to trust him, especially as she was so susceptible to him, and he could have no interest in her past a dalliance. He was an earl, for heaven's sake, and if he ever married, it would be to one of his own kind. No. She needed to keep this professional. He was her employer, nothing more.

She made the mistake of glancing up at him. He was watching her, a soft look in his eyes that made her heart flutter. Kathy looked away, taking a deep breath, but that didn't help either, as the intoxicating scent of him wrapped about her. She could smell sandalwood and something woodsy and warm, spicy like cloves. She could smell *him*, indefinable but unmistakably masculine. To her alarm she realised too late she had leaned in, chasing the scent of his skin, the intimate musky scent of a man that made her want to do something appallingly rash.

His eyes darkened, his hold on her tightening imperceptibly and her breath caught. She tore her gaze away, trying to put more distance between them, though every instinct demanded she get closer. Madness, she told herself firmly. This was why he'd been the man he was, because he was to a woman like catnip to a feline. He was dangerous, whether or not he was reformed. She w*anted* him to act badly, and was horribly tempted to encourage him to do so.

"Miss de Beauvoir?"

"Yes?" she said, too aware her voice was an octave higher than usual. *Stop it. Stop it this instant*, she scolded herself.

"You dance beautifully."

"Thank you. So do you," she replied at once, polite small talk a safe retreat.

It was true, though, and she did not wish for the dance to end with the same fervent desire she wished it had never begun. His powerful body was too close, the heat of him seeping into her bones and stealing what remained of good sense. He made her weak, and she hated that, hated him for his ability to do it. She was better than this, and she had things to do. Being another of his conquests was not something she would wish to be remembered for. Her life had more value than that, and she meant to achieve something worthwhile. She had sworn to make a difference, to help those who had not been given the remarkable chance that she and her brother had. Besides, it wasn't as if he had given her any reason to believe he was pursuing her. He'd been a perfect gentleman, and she did him a disservice by imagining he felt the same mind-numbing attraction that was provoking such a ridiculous riot of conflicting emotions in her breast.

She let out a ragged sigh of relief when the dance finally ended, wishing she could go home instead of taking his arm, but there was supper to sit through now. An endless supply of lavish dishes and meaningless chatter to endure, and his company too. Lord Vane at her side, being charming and funny and making her want to like him. Making her *want* him.

"I don't feel very well." The words were out before she could think better of it. She looked up at him and felt certain he knew she was lying. Too late now. "I… I don't think I could face eating anything."

She sensed rather than felt the way his body grew taut, the way he withdrew, shutting himself off.

"I am so sorry to hear that," he said.

There was a politely distant expression on his face now; she knew she had hurt him. He knew she was making excuses to be out of his company, and a large part of her wanted to explain that it wasn't for the reasons he believed, but self-preservation came first. There would be time enough for encouraging him on his path to redemption, for letting him know she admired him for it. But the ugly truth was she did not entirely trust him. Worse, she did not trust herself to be around him.

"Allow me to escort you to your mother," he said, deftly threading his way through the crowd.

She followed him blindly, too aware of the rigidity in the muscular arm beneath her hand. The memory of his distress earlier that evening returned to her, the misery she'd seen in his eyes, and she wanted to cry with frustration for having made him unhappy again. Suddenly, the lie was no lie at all, for she felt ill, and her head was pounding.

"Kathleen?" Mama asked, her sharp gaze moving between Kathy and Lord Vane.

"It's nothing, Mama. Just rather a headache. I think I should like to go home."

Mama slipped an arm about her waist as Lord Vane took a step back. "I do hope you feel better soon, Miss de Beauvoir. Thank you kindly for the dance. Good evening to you."

Kathy nodded and opened her mouth to say something, *anything*, but he had turned and walked away.

Chapter 11

Dearest Kathy,

Enclosed is the list of books you asked Sterling for. What is this new project of yours? Do write and explain. I know you are working on the new school Eliza is building, but in what capacity? You always were clever, so am I not surprised at you taking on such a challenge? I admire you greatly, you know, for going out into the world men keep closed to women and working among them. I should never have the nerve to do such a bold thing. Do they treat you with respect? I hope they do not cause you any difficulties. I know you are a sensible woman, far more than I ever was, but do be careful, won't you? I worry for you.

—Excerpt of a letter from Mrs Grace Oak (daughter of Jemima and Solomon Weston, Baron and Lady Rothborn) to Miss Kathleen de Beauvoir (daughter of Mrs Minerva and Mr Inigo de Beauvoir)

Two years earlier…

23rd February 1840, Covent Garden. Parish of St Giles.

“Here, let me do that,” Max said, getting up to help Burt with the heavy box he was carrying in. “I take it you got a good price for them?”

“I did,” Burt said, grinning broadly.

Max set the box on the rickety table and peered in. Fresh bread, tea, potatoes, rice, bacon, even a bit of butter and a packet of sugar. Well, they’d have a fine feast tonight. “I’m glad.”

“It was good of you to donate them, lad. A fine pair of boots, they were. You’re not sorry?”

Max shook his head, frowning. “Of course not. Good Lord, Burt, you think a pair of boots can come anywhere close to repaying you for all you’ve done for me.”

Burt waved this off, looking vaguely irritated. “I didn’t do it for no reward,” he grumbled.

Max smiled, knowing this was true. Burt did nothing for reward or favours; he was simply a good man. Max had known no one like him before, had not known that such people really existed outside of books and bible stories. The good Samaritan, that was Burt. Except this was not some moral lecture trotted out by rote by some smug priest on a Sunday morning. This was real. This was charity and goodwill to all men from a pure soul who truly believed in the principle.

Burt bustled off to wash his hands—cleanliness was next to godliness—and Max sat down at the table, considering the box before him. He’d remembered who he was weeks ago, and he’d been here for over six months now. Everyone must believe him dead. It was a strange notion, but liberating. He liked being dead. The realisation that no one would care much, except for those people who’d be dancing on his grave, if he had one, made him want to stay dead and never go back.

Yet the meagre haul that Burt had just carried in, he could buy with pocket change if he went back. Lord, the lowliest servant on one of his many estates would think it slim pickings. Max didn’t want to leave. He'd not told Burt and Pike about who he was, or that he remembered. If they knew, they might despise him, and he couldn't bear that. They *liked* him. They thought he was good and kind, and he wasn't ready to let that go. Selfish bastard, as always. He could have bought them food and clothes, given them a decent place to live, though Max knew instinctively they wouldn't accept it. Burt would say he didn't need such fine things, that he was happy as he was. The sale of a fine pair of boots in lieu of bed and board was one thing, a gift from a man who could afford to buy them a mansion in the heart of fashionable London, quite another.

The rest was still a hazy muddle. He remembered his home, Vane Hall in Chiswick, a vast mausoleum of a place. He remembered his mother and had read of her death in the papers with sadness, but it was more a vague sense of losing something he'd never really had than the grief of losing a parent. The faces of people he knew slipped in and out of his mind, but much of it was indistinct, and Max liked it that way. He did not want to remember. His mind shied away whenever something stirred a memory of the past, because he knew too well what he'd discover. He'd been a villain. Not the theatrical kind who twirled a moustache and robbed old ladies, but a villain nonetheless. He'd been cruel, needlessly cruel, and selfish, and so damned arrogant.

When he was feeling at his most pathetic, he tried to make excuses for himself. What chance had he had, after all? No one had ever taught him to think of others, showed him it was just as easy to be kind, to offer help instead of turning away. Burt had showed him, though. A man whose clothes were patched and worn, and who owned little more than a few shabby bits of furniture and tin crockery, had shown him such generosity he still found it hard to fathom. And he was happy. That was the strangest thing of all to reconcile. Maxwell Drake, the Earl of Vane—who'd had everything, wealth, a title, good health and a life of ease, every advantage a man could possibly want—had been miserable, lonely, and utterly wretched, and Burt, who had nothing, was perfectly content.

Max had determined to learn the trick of it, only to discover there *was* no trick. It was simply that Burt was at peace with himself, and helping others made him happy.

He had a job now, and that amused him more than anything. It was a labouring job that Burt had found for him. He hauled boxes and crates, loading and unloading wagons, and he kept his mouth shut as Burt had told him to. Burt had explained to the boss that Max was none too bright and talked little, rather than let them hear his cut glass accent and begin asking questions. He communicated with a series of grunts and nods, mostly, which suited Max… or Valentine, as everyone round here knew him. He didn't want to talk to anyone, content to work hard for the meagre wages he took home and gave to Burt and Pike to put towards his keep.

It couldn't last. He knew that. But he was afraid to go back to his own life, afraid of what he might remember, and that he might go back to being the man he'd been before.

Burt came back and nodded his approval as he noted Max had unpacked the food and put it away, and was now washing the dirt off the potatoes. Another new skill he'd never expected to learn.

Burt grinned at him and smacked his lips. "Bacon and fried potatoes," he said with such anticipation that Max laughed.

"Sounds good."

Burt chopped the potatoes into little cubes as Max passed them to him, but he felt the old man's gaze upon him, watching.

"Where's Pike?" he asked, unnerved by the quality of the man's gaze.

"He'll be along presently. Mother Brown had a few errands for him to run for the girls."

Max nodded. Mother Brown owned a brothel a few doors down, but Burt judged no one. Mother Brown was better than most, as abbesses went, and the girls had few other options to earn their living.

"You ever going to tell me your name, then?" Burt asked, not looking at him.

Max stilled for a moment before scrubbing the last grainy bits of mud from the potato he held and passing it to Burt to chop up. His stomach dropped.

"You mean to say you don't know it?" he asked, realising in that moment that Burt had known for some time.

Burt looked up and grinned, showing an uneven assortment of teeth. "P'raps I'd rather you told me."

Max snorted and wiped his hands on the tea towel beside him. "Perhaps that man is better left where he fell. Dead in a filthy alley."

"You're that man, Valentine. We've all got our demons, lad. Pretending they ain't there won't work."

"What if… what if it was a mistake? What if I should have died, because of everything I did?" Max looked up, discovering his heart was beating very hard and he felt clammy, hot and cold all at once. "I don't want to be him again, Burt. I'd rather stay here. If I go back, I might fail, I might forget all this, I might—"

"Valentine, listen to me. Staying here would be failing. This ain't who you are, any more than the man we dragged out of a filthy alley is who you are now. You ain't no saint, but you're not the devil neither. None of us is perfect, none of us goes through life without making mistakes. P'raps, you'll make a few more. Who can say, but if you don't try, you might as well 'ave died, and that's a damn shame."

Max looked at him, something close to anger raging in his chest. There was a part of him that wanted to shout at the old man and tell him it wasn't fair, but that was childish and cowardly. Besides, it wasn't anger. Not really.

"I'm afraid," he said, the words nearly choking him, but it was a relief all the same, to say it out loud. "I'm afraid to go back.

Afraid to remember who I was, what I did. People despise me, Burt, and with good reason."

"Then you'll have to try real hard to change their minds. Sounds like the kind of challenge a young man ought to be able to face. In order to make amends for the past. Eh?" Burt's leathery old face creased in a smile, his bright little eyes compassionate and filled with hope.

Max let out an uneven breath, trying to find the courage to take the first step towards the future, because Burt was right: staying here would not make him worthy of redemption, it was merely hiding from the truth. He wasn't ready to face it yet, either the past or the future, but he would be. He must be, and soon. A man of his means, with his power and wealth, he could change the lives of so many people. He could do some good in the world, and perhaps that would allow him to sleep at night once he reclaimed his true identity. He held out his hand to Burt, meeting his eyes.

"Maxwell Drake, seventh Earl of Vane. Pleased to make your acquaintance, Burt."

Present day …

15th June 1842, Vane Hall, Chiswick, London.

"The roof is coming on at a terrific pace, so it seems as if we are only a week or two behind schedule, which is good news." Kathy said, ticking off another item on her notes. "Did you see the draft plans my brother sent over for you? He's open to making changes, obviously. In fact, he asked you to provide a list of any requirements. Anything you wish to include that he has not thought to provide, that is."

Lord Vane shook his head. "It's an excellent plan. I've little knowledge of gardening or home farms, and I can see a recreational area has been set aside. I am happy to approve it and any changes you see fit to make. I leave it entirely in your hands,

Miss de Beauvoir, providing Lady Elizabeth is in accord, obviously."

Kathy looked up and nodded before turning her gaze back to the list.

"The uniforms are ready, if you'd like to look at them?"

"That won't be necessary. You had the ordering of them and if you're content, I know they're just as they ought to be."

"Very well." Kathy chewed her lip. Her stomach was in a knot, and it was getting worse. *He* was getting worse. Or at least, not worse, but… he was unhappy. She had done that. No, that was hubris, surely, to think she might be responsible for the light going out of him. Yet it had been two weeks since the ball and she'd not seen him smile once. He never sought out her company or teased her. He worked all hours, according to his staff, whom she was getting to know rather well now. "I hear you've joined Mr Pelham Villiers in working to repeal the Corn Laws."

"Yes," he said, closing the ledger books on his desk and stacking them neatly to one side.

"I imagine that raised a few eyebrows," she suggested with a smile, which was a vast understatement, and they both knew it.

"You imagine right," he replied with a quirk of his lips, which might have qualified as a smile, except it didn't reach his eyes.

He must have been the subject of a great deal of ill will from some of his peers. Landowners all over the country had a vested interest in keeping the prices high and forbidding access to cheap imports. If they repealed the Corn Laws, they'd lose money—significant amounts of money—but the prices would drop, and the poor might be able to afford to eat. For the moment, the numbers against the repeal were far too high for it to happen, but with high-ranking nobles like the Earl of Vane weighing in behind a Liberal Whig like Pelham Villiers, there was a chance for change.

"You're doing a good thing," she said, hoping he heard the approval in her voice, and not just about the Corn Laws.

He made a dismissive sound, and she could stand it no longer.

"Stop it!" she said, springing to her feet. The notepad she'd been holding slipped to the floor with a flurry of paper, but she ignored it, staring at him.

Lord Vane looked back at her in surprise. "Stop what?"

"This… whatever it is. I'm sorry. I'm sorry I didn't stay for supper, but… but it wasn't your fault."

He stared at her for a long moment and then snorted in disgust, shaking his head. "Of course it was. I scared you off. I don't blame you, by the way. You did right. And it's I that should apologise."

"What for?" she asked, bewildered.

"For the dance," he said, raking a hand through his hair.

When she continued to stare at him in obvious confusion, he let out a harsh breath. "Oh, come now, Miss de Beauvoir. I might not have offered you an insult, but I don't doubt you became aware of… of my…."

Kathy blinked, feeling heat suffuse her from head to toe. "Your…?" she pressed, holding her breath.

"My… desire for you," he bit out. "I don't blame you for running away. I ought never to have forced you to dance with me."

"You didn't force me. I asked you," she said faintly. He desired her. He desired *her.*

"Yes, and immediately regretted it," he snapped. "That much was obvious. I ought to have refused and let you go, but as usual I put my own bloody wants first, disregarding what was best for you. So for that, I apologise. Please, assure yourself that I shan't take advantage again."

"You won't?" she said, realising too late that she sounded rather crestfallen. "You won't," she said again, nodding vigorously. This was good, she reminded herself. Her own desire for him was undermining her, making her want to give into temptation, but she needed to feel safe around him and if he was determined to behave himself, she had half a chance. If he could behave, then she certainly could. But there was no need for him to keep feeling guilty and wretched when there was no reason for it.

"Do you forgive me?" he asked stiffly, not looking at her, clearly expecting an answer he wouldn't like.

"I do," she said softly. She did not dare tell him there was nothing to forgive, that she had been in a far worse state than he. Oh, no. Too dangerous for them both.

His gaze snapped to hers, his expression so relieved she felt her throat tighten. "You do?"

She nodded, smiling at him. "I really did have a headache, and… and I should like to call a truce."

"A truce?"

"Yes," she said, laughing. "And do stop repeating everything I say."

To her surprise, he coloured a little, but held his tongue.

"I think I have been rather hard on you, Lord Vane, and I should like it very much if we might consider ourselves… allies."

"Allies," he murmured, staring at her. "Dash it, I did it again, didn't I?"

Kathy giggled.

He grinned at her, and her heart turned over.

"I should like that," he said. "Thank you."

Chapter 12

Dearest Aggie,

It was so lovely to have you stay with us these past two weeks. I was sorry you had to return to school, and miss you already. I hope you'll come again soon. For the next holiday, perhaps?

I am so pleased you heard from your guardian. I know you have been worrying about him, and the presents he sent sound delicious. I'm sure the other girls must have been fighting to be friends with you. Not that they should do anything else. You are the very best of friends. I cannot wait for us to make our come out together. Monsieur Le Comte intends for you to come out in society, doesn't he? We shall set the ton on their ears!

You'll never guess what. You remember I told you the mysterious author of The Ghosts of Castle Madruzzo has published a new book? Well, Thorn was home at the weekend, and he left a copy behind, for which I shall write and tell him he is the very best of brothers. But not before I've read it, because I very much doubt he did it on purpose. He'll be bound to tell

> *Papa to confiscate it at once because it's very dreadful. It's called The Devil and the Maiden and it's about an impoverished young woman who lives with her aunt on a neglected estate. Everyone believes the lord of the manor is mad and living abroad until he returns out of the blue! Oh, Aggie, it's marvellous, and the wicked nobleman quite puts me in mind of Lord Kilbane, all that brooding menace and dark good looks. I cannot wait to see how it ends.*
>
> ***—Excerpt of a letter from Lady Catherine 'Cat' Barrington (daughter of Lucian and Matilda Barrington, The Most Hon'ble Marquess and Marchioness of Montagu) to Miss Agatha Smith (Ward of Louis César de Montluc, Comte de Villen).***

18th June 1842, Wick, The Highlands, Scotland.

"I'm so sorry it's been a waste of time. I did warn you," Barnaby said, watching Louis as he stared out of the window at a day that had begun with fog and was now progressing through various stages of mizzle, drizzle, showers, and the occasional downpour. Thank God they were leaving tomorrow.

Louis glanced back at him and smiled. "So you did."

The smile did not fool Barnaby. The poor devil was wretched, and who could blame him? They had made a few excursions to places it was likely Evie might visit during her stay here, but luck had not been with them. And now the weather, which had been unsettled the entire time but not so terribly dismal, must do this. Why his Great-Aunt Hester persisted in living here in this godforsaken place, especially when it must aggravate her rheumatism, was beyond him. But then she had been madly in love with her husband, Lord Balderston, if family history was to be believed. She had defied everyone to marry him, a rough about the edges Scottish lord with little to recommend him, according to Barnaby's mother. Hester had mourned the loss of him these past twenty years, rarely venturing far from the castle where they'd been so happy. The family had all tried to persuade her to return to London, but she was as stubborn as she'd always been and wouldn't budge. The only good thing about being here was that Louis' presence seemed to have brightened the wicked creature up considerably.

"Ah, there you are," said the lady herself, appearing in the doorway. "Moping still, are you?"

"My lady," Louis said, giving the old woman a polite bow.

"Morning, Aunt Hester," Barnaby said, moving closer to give her a dutiful kiss on the cheek.

"Hmph." She tapped her walking stick on the stone floor. "This won't do. I can't have you two underfoot like sulky boys the entire day. Not with him looking like some brooding poet." She waved an arthritic hand at Louis. "Far too distracting. I've called the carriage."

"Whatever for?" Barnaby demanded, eyeing the deluge outside the castle walls with consternation.

"Well, if I must have this beautiful creature under my roof, I may as well have some fun. You're leaving anyway, so I'm going with you to Fort William. Not been there in a decade or more. About time I did some shopping, I reckon. Monsieur can give me the benefit of his exquisite eye, as he seems to have made a gentleman of you at long last, Barnaby. If he can manage such Herculean feats, he can choose me some new outfits for a summer wardrobe in town. Then we shall see. At the very least, it should set a few tongues wagging," she said, her expression bright with mischief.

"I should be honoured to assist you, my lady," Louis replied.

"Just so," Aunt Hester said thoughtfully, watching Louis with a frown. "Perhaps then I'll get to the bottom of why you're really here. I suspect a woman. Escaping a bloodthirsty husband, are we? A duel?"

"Nothing so exciting, I assure you," Louis replied, lips quirking a little.

The old woman narrowed her eyes, looking unconvinced. "Hmm. I smell a scandal brewing, and I mean to know what's going on. We'll eat in The Prince's House."

Barnaby saw Louis' startled expression and grinned. "It's just a coaching inn, named for the Bonnie Prince Charlie."

"Ah," Louis said with polite interest. "I understand."

"We'll bring our own bonnie comte instead," Aunt Hester said with a cackle of laughter. "Come along then. I've told that valet of yours to get cracking and pack so you'll be free tomorrow, monsieur. We'll leave first thing in the morning.

She stalked out again, imperious as ever.

"Sorry," Barnaby said, wincing.

Louis waved this away. "One more day is of no matter. She has been hospitable when she'd no need to be. If this amuses her, I am happy to oblige."

"Hospitable," Barnaby murmured faintly. "Is that what's she's been? Ah, well."

18th June 1842, Church Street, Isleworth, London.

"Miss de Beauvoir, there's a gentleman to see you."

Kathy looked up, hearing the excitedly flustered note in the maid's voice, and instantly knew who it was. Jenny was pink-cheeked, her eyes alight with exhilaration.

"Lord Vane, I collect," she said, setting down her quill.

Jenny gave a nod and stifled a giggle. Kathy sighed, but could hardly blame the girl, who was young and had a romantic streak a mile wide. A man like Lord Vane appearing on the doorstep was the beginning of any young girl's wildest dreams.

"Well, ask him to come in then, please."

"Ought I stay with you, for propriety?" the girl asked hopefully.

Kathy narrowed her eyes at the maid. "That won't be necessary, thank you. It is a business matter, and I shall leave the door ajar."

Jenny bobbed a curtsey and hurried away. Kathy tidied her papers and got up, too aware of the ink on her hands and her hair escaping its pins. She had a bad habit of putting her fingers through it and disarranging it when she was thinking. Still, she smoothed her skirts and stood, waiting for his lordship to enter.

Though she'd had a moment to ready herself, it had not prepared her to see him in her home. His imposing frame filled the doorway, making the room seem suddenly far smaller than it had just seconds before. She was used to seeing him out of doors, or among the vast proportions of Vane Hall, or in a lavish ballroom. Though her parents' home was everything that was elegant and modern, it was far from a palace. He seemed wildly out of place here, and her breath caught, her heart skittering in her chest.

"My lord, this is an unexpected pleasure," she said, aware she sounded breathless and praying he did not realise how nervous he made her.

"I hope I am not disturbing you," he said, turning his hat in his hands, which Jenny had forgotten to take from him, Kathy noted with irritation.

"Not at all. Here, let me take that," she said, hurrying to retrieve it and his gloves and set them aside. "May I offer you some tea?"

"Oh, no. I don't wish to take up too much of your time, only…. You mentioned the workhouse here in Isleworth. The conditions are not satisfactory, you said. I was wondering if I might help? If we might do something about that?"

Kathy stared at him and her already over-excited heart fluttered in the way romantic poems and stories always described. Perhaps it was the 'we' that did it. It was ridiculous, and she knew it. But there he was, standing there looking so handsome and earnest, and remembering her rant about the conditions in the workhouse when she had been so dreadfully rude to him, and offering to help anyway. It was a wonder she didn't swoon. She almost wanted to hit him, or swear, because really, what chance did a girl have when he went about looking like that and being all noble and kind? What was the point of even trying not to fall in love with him? It was hopeless.

"What did you have in mind?"

He shrugged, looking sheepish. "I'm not sure, really. No doubt there are a board of governors or a charitable trust to be appeased if we do things properly. But I thought perhaps we could begin with a visit. If I stomp about the place and make loud noises of displeasure, as I am a near neighbour, that might be a start, mightn't it? There are benefits to being an earl, you see. People don't like to say no to me. You could take notes, obvious areas for improvement, and… and we'll go from there."

"Oh." Her hand went to her mouth, and she thought she might cry.

"Miss de Beauvoir!" he said in alarm, moving closer to her, one arm outstretched. "I had no desire to upset you. Please forgive me, if—"

"No!" she said, laughing now and shaking her head even as tears pricked at her eyes. He was standing very close, and the deliciously dizzying scent of him made her foolish. She reached out and placed her hand on his arm. "No, I am only overwhelmed with relief. If you knew how many letters I have written, how many times they have turned me away, refusing to give me a meeting. But they'll not turn you away, I think."

He gave a rueful smile. "It's unlikely," he admitted. "And I shall chastise them in the strongest terms for not heeding you sooner."

Oh, Lord, she really would swoon if he kept this up.

His gaze fell to her ink-stained hand, resting on his sleeve, and Kathy blushed, snatching it back, reminding herself sternly that they were merely allies, nothing more.

"Thank you," she said, hoping he could hear the sincere gratitude in her voice. "Thank you so much."

He shook his head. "It's me that ought to thank you. I have had my eyes opened to many things in the past few years, but you are helping me to see with greater clarity. You are helping me ensure the practical work gets done properly, to make change happen in the way it ought. You're a marvel."

Her mouth opened in a little 'o' of surprise, robbed of speech. It was a good job her brother was not here to see it. He'd consider it a miracle. Mind you, he'd also scold her from now until doomsday for being alone with this man.

"I'm really not," she managed, once the surprise of his compliment wore off enough for her to remember words and how to employ them.

"I beg to differ. Here I see the unmistakable proof that you work ridiculously hard for me. He reached out and took her hand in his, turning it to display her inky fingers. "You must do, for everything you've accomplished in such a short period is nothing short of astonishing. I hope I am not taking advantage of your charitable nature. I should not like you to faint with fatigue."

Well, she might well faint, but it wouldn't be from fatigue, she thought ruefully. Kathy swallowed, vibratingly aware of his hands holding hers, his thumb moving gently back and forth over the stained indent in her finger where she'd held the quill pen all morning. A strange, unnerving fizzing sensation stirred inside, her nerves all leaping to attention. She wondered if he knew what he was doing to her, for he was staring at her now, his blue eyes intent.

"I should not like you to wear yourself to a thread," he murmured, his thumb still caressing her finger. The most peculiar ache bloomed inside her, a flickering of… of something insistent and elusive that began where he was touching her and shot straight between her thighs. Unnerved, she sucked in a breath, heat flooding her cheeks, but did not pull her hand free.

Abruptly, Lord Vane took a step back, dropping his hold on her as if she'd scalded him.

"Forgive me," he said, looking hazy and appalled, and rather like he had woken from a dream. She knew just how he felt, for she almost followed him, demanding he not stop, and that could *not* happen in real life. "The workhouse," he said firmly, the words a little too loud against the quiet room.

"Y-Yes," she agreed, nodding, though she wasn't certain that had been a question.

"A visit, then?"

"Indeed."

"When?"

Kathy considered this, considered the sense of getting out of his company before she did something stupid. Then she considered the poor wretches in the workhouse, and changed her mind. Strike while the iron was hot.

"Now. If that suits you, my lord?"

His eyes widened, but he looked pleased by the prospect. "It does."

Kathy nodded. "I'll fetch my coat and hat."

18th June 1842, The Workhouse, Isleworth, London.

It was worse than Max had imagined and, having had some first-hand experience of living in poverty for a short while, he'd thought he had a fair idea of how bad it might be. He'd been wrong.

"The problem with the reforms to the Poor Law in the 1830s was that it forced anyone unable to support themselves to enter a workhouse. But the government's fear of supporting the lazy and unemployable drives them to make the places so appalling that any able-bodied pauper would do just about anything but end up here. The people who do come here are truly desperate," Miss de Beauvoir said, and he heard the tremble in her voice. "And this is how they are treated, worse than animals."

"Miss de Beauvoir!" boomed Mr Higgs, the day manager, who had condescended to give them a tour of the building only after Max had put his foot down and demanded it. Mr Higgs had been furious and unhappy, but there were benefits to being an earl. It was difficult for such a man to deny him. "These people are treated with decency and charity. They have a safe place to sleep, clean clothes, and regular meals."

"They have shapeless rags, thin pallets on the floor, and gruel if they are lucky. When was the last time they ate fresh meat or vegetables? When was the last time they were able to wash their clothes?" she demanded with fury.

Mr Higgs turned purple but did not reply, which was answer enough.

The building followed a familiar design, in common with many such buildings. It was cruciform, with four wings, each wing completed by a yard, surrounded by high walls. She had been right, of course. From the street side, the side that anyone driving past would see, it was a grand edifice, if forbidding. Once inside, it was a prison. It would certainly act as a deterrent to the workshy. Max could not imagine just how desperate a person might need to be to step through the gates of such a place, but even considering it made his guts roil. Worse still, they separated inmates by gender. So they separated husbands and wives, and kept women apart from their sons, and fathers from daughters. Max found he could not bear to meet the eyes of the inmates he saw, all of them set apart by a bland uniform of rough, ill-made fabric that loudly announced these people were the lowest of the low. And then there was the stench, not just of dreadful sanitary conditions, unwashed bodies and disease but… hopelessness. You could smell it, the scent of despair so tangible he could taste it too, lingering on his tongue like sour milk.

"I've seen enough," he said, needing to escape, needing to get out and see the sky above him and breathe clean air. That was his right and his privilege. A privilege not available to all. "Mr Higgs, this place is a disgrace. That you have wilfully ignored every one of this young woman's pleas to make conditions better for those poor devils who have no choice but to come here is beyond belief. We *will* do something about it."

Mr Higgs spluttered and made noises of outrage, but Max ignored him.

"Miss de Beauvoir." He turned to her and offered her his arm, unwilling to go another step without being certain she was beside him, wanting the reassurance of her close to him, knowing she was safe.

They exited the building and the immense doors slammed shut behind them. Max turned to stare at her.

"My God," he said, letting out a shuddering breath. "My God."

Burt might have ended in a place like that, when he was too old and ill to work any longer, or Pike, if anything happened to

Burt before he was old enough to look out for himself. Max closed his eyes for a moment. No. He would never let that happen. They were safe. He'd see to that.

Max opened his eyes with a start as something caressed his face. Miss de Beauvoir was staring up at him, her gloved hand touching his cheek.

"Are you well, my lord?" she asked gently, her wide grey eyes full of concern.

Something shifted in his heart, the giving way of some defensive structure, brittle with age and cynicism. The floodgates opened, longing sweeping through him like an incoming tide. It washed away everything in its path. Old hurts and resentments, fears and doubts, and when they were gone, there was nothing but her, the nearness of her, and the realisation of how very much he wanted her beside him, always.

He stared, knowing he would never be as certain of anything as he was of her, seeing before him the embodiment of his every dream, and knowing she was out of his reach. She would never consider a man like him. She'd made that very clear. Unless… Unless he could prove to her he was worthy. It would be a lie, of course. No man could ever be worthy of such a woman, but perhaps if he proved it every day for the rest of his days, he might make it true. He'd do it too, for her.

Max shook his head, unable to find words.

"You're very pale," she observed anxiously. "Do you need to sit down?"

He gave a startled laugh, fighting to find his tongue. "I think I ought to be more concerned about your tender sensibilities, Miss de Beauvoir. I should never have asked you to accompany me. It was selfish and—"

"And if you had gone without me, I should never have forgiven you," she said, her voice tart. "Besides, which you ought to know by now, I have no tender sensibilities."

"I beg to differ," he said, feeling something close to anguish as she withdrew her hand.

The desire to pull her into his arms was an ache beneath his skin, but he resisted the urge. How, he did not know, when he had spent his entire life giving into temptation at every turn, and he wanted her beyond anything, beyond reason. Instinctively, he felt she would keep him on the right path. This woman would never let him get away with anything, never let him slip and be anything other than his best self, and he would never slip, for he would never want to disappoint her.

"A cup of tea," she said decisively. "A cup of tea and some cake."

Max nodded. "Would you mind awfully if I put a tot of brandy in the tea?"

She frowned at him. "Only if you neglect to put any in mine."

He laughed then, and she smiled at him. The expression sliced through his heart like a blade. Oh, lord. He was in deep trouble, and it was nothing less than he deserved. How many women had believed themselves in love with him, and he'd laughed in their faces? Abruptly, a particular young woman's face came to mind, her beautiful eyes filled with tears, as she pleaded with him to help her, and he —

The memory lanced through him and shattered his newly vulnerable heart. If Miss de Beauvoir knew what he'd done—if she ever discovered *that*—she'd despise him for all eternity, and rightly so.

"My lord?"

He stared at her, shaken to the core. "Yes. Come, let me take you back to the carriage and away from this dismal place," he said, pasting a false smile to his face.

There was no future for them. Not in this lifetime. Not even if he lived as a saint for the rest of his days. He knew that. As much as he wanted to leave the past behind, he could not. He had burned his bridges, given up any chance for happiness because of his loathsome behaviour. His own fault. His own damn bloody selfish fault.

Reap what you sow. That was it, wasn't it? Well, he might have a second chance at life, a chance to make amends, but no one had said he had a right to be happy, had they? No. This was retribution for his sins, to fall in love at last and know he could never declare himself, never be worthy. For some sins were unforgivable.

Chapter 13

Thorn,

I am in a world of trouble. For God's sake, come to the address below before the 25th, and bring as much money as you can lay your hands on. I am being blackmailed and I need to silence the devil quickly. You see, there's a child. Her happiness is too important to risk ~~and…~~ Hell, I can't explain this now. Don't, whatever you do, breathe a word to a soul. If our father gets wind of this – Christ, I can't bear to think of it. Damn me, but I am a thousand times a fool. But it will not only be me who suffers for my selfishness and lack of foresight.

I do not know what to do, who to turn to, and I know I am a wretched fellow for dragging you into my mess and asking you to bear the burden of such a secret, but I do not know where else to turn.

Please come. Pip x.

—Excerpt of a letter from The Hon'ble Philip Barrington, The Earl of Ashburton (eldest son of The Most Hon'ble Lucian and Matilda Barrington, Marquess and

*Marchioness of Montagu) to his brother,
The Hon'ble Mr Thomas Barrington.*

18th June 1842, Wildsyde Castle, Caithness, Scotland.

Evie stood on the headland, the wind buffeting her face and tugging at her cloak. She pulled the material closer about her, lest it become a sail and have her flying off the edge of the cliff. The ruins of Bucholie Castle stood before her, and she knew better than to get any closer, having been warned of the dangers, but it was a romantic ruin and a beautiful if melancholy place. It drew her back over and over again.

"Here ye are!" called a cheery voice from behind her.

Evie turned to see Muir Anderson striding through the long grass. He looked like a great Scottish lion in a kilt, with his tawny hair blown about by the wind and his clothes all rumpled. He generally appeared somewhat dishevelled, as if he'd been wrestling some great beast. He was wild and untamed himself, and yet she sensed a gentle soul in him. He also had a dreadful sense of humour and made her laugh a good deal.

"I've been searching for ye this age," he said, coming to stand beside her.

He stared down at her and she saw his eyes were tawny too, flecked with gold. She turned away, staring out at the sea, a vivid, almost painful blue that made something in her heart twist.

"You like it here, aye?"

She nodded, brushing the hair from her eyes and staring out at the sun glinting on the sea, so bright it made her eyes water. "I do."

He leaned down then and kissed her, so swiftly she'd not known it was coming. It only lasted a moment, enough for her to tell that his lips were soft, and he smelled like heather and fresh air.

"D'ye mind?" he asked, drawing away a little.

Evie stared at him, wanting to cry. "N-No," she stammered, not wanting to hurt his feelings, and she didn't *mind.* She just wasn't certain she wanted him to do it again.

"You're not mad about the idea, though, eh?" he suggested, grinning.

To her relief, there was no trace of embarrassment or resentment in his open face.

"I—" she began, not having the first idea how to answer that question. The trouble was, she liked him. She liked him very much. Worse, she could imagine being married to him, and the life they would share. A good, steady life, filled with children and laughter, just as she had wanted, but….

But.

Oh, what was she to do?

"Aye, reckoned you'd not fallen arse over apex for my charm and good looks," he said wryly.

Despite everything, Evie giggled.

He winked at her and offered her his arm. "Come along. I'll escort ye back to the castle like a proper gent. I do ken how, ye know."

"I know," she said, smiling at him.

"Evie," he said, lowering his voice and her heart beat faster as her anxiety returned. "I know ye are not in love with me. The truth is, I'm nae in love with you either, but I like ye a good deal. I think love could come, for we're friends already. I think we suit, and I reckon we could be happy together, if ye gave me a chance. I'll nae ask ye the question now, for I know you've doubts. 'Tis only natural. But I will ask ye, and soon. So, I'd like ye to have a think about it. A very serious think about it."

He drew out the 'r' in 'very,' and she realised she liked his accent a good deal. It was rough, warm, and charming. So very different from another man, another accent. *His* words would be clever and seductive, so dreadfully sophisticated. Far more knowing and worldly than she could ever hope to be. She could handle Muir, she knew where she stood with him, and what to expect. He was not an unknown quantity, did not have secrets and a past which haunted him. He would be simple and direct and so much easier.

"Will ye do that for me, Evie, love?"

Evie, love. Would that be his endearment for her? Would he call her that with affection and a warm look in his eyes? *Ma petite.* Muir did not love her, and she did not love him. The trouble was, she did not know if anyone else loved her, or why on earth they wanted her, or if she had a chance of holding onto a man like that, because who *could* hold him? No one she'd ever seen. Beautiful women had come and gone, far more beautiful than her, and he'd never cared, not for one of them.

She blinked hard.

"Evie? Have I made ye cry?"

She shook her head, swallowing hard. "No. No, of course not. I… I am very honoured, Muir, and I shall think about it seriously, I promise. Very seriously indeed. You have my word."

Evening of the 18th of June 1842, The Hanover Square Rooms, London.

The concert was an excellent one. Herr Thalberg was a master of his art, and his hands flew over the piano in a mesmerising blur. Yet Kathy could not focus on the beautiful music. Lord Vane sat on the other side of the aisle in the front row, and she found she could do nothing but stare at the back of his head, his golden hair glinting in the candlelight.

It was a warm evening, and the concert rooms were stuffy. Kathy shifted in her seat. Her bottom was feeling decidedly numb and, as wonderful as the music was, she was rather longing for the interval. Stretching her legs and a glass of cold lemonade or fruit punch sounded like a wonderful idea, and perhaps there was the possibility of a word with his lordship.

She had not realised he was coming tonight, except perhaps she should have, for it was a charitable event to raise money for widows and orphans. Unwillingly, her gaze returned to him. He had turned his head, revealing his strong profile as he spoke to Humphrey Price who sat beside him. Mr Price had escorted Miss Morcombe, a friend of Rosamund's and the girl turned, noticed Kathy staring, and waved at her. Lord Vane did not. Kathy stifled a sigh and had to concede the truth she had been trying to smother for some time now. She was in a very bad way. Lud, but she was a fool. He might desire her, but he was an earl, and she… she didn't know who she was. No, she scolded herself, that was not true. She was Kathleen de Beauvoir, and she was an educated woman with a brain in her head … but no matter how accomplished she was, she was no countess. It was a ridiculous idea. Besides, he might well desire her, but desire was not love, not regard, not a basis for anything real and long-lasting.

Except there had been a moment, on the steps of that awful building, when she had touched his cheek. She had understood his distress for the poor devils within the workhouse for she had felt it too, but to realise that he really cared, really, honestly wanted to help these people had soothed any last doubts about him. He had appeared to need her, to want her with him. It had made her believe he wanted her by his side always. Not just in whatever professional capacity she worked for him, but something more than that. Her heart had leapt at the possibility.

Not to mention the fact he'd said, '*we* will do something about it.'

Well, she'd been done for.

And then he had opened his eyes and the naked longing she had seen in his expression had stolen her breath. But she had been mistaken. She must have been, for she had seen no evidence of it since. He was as charming as ever, and so very appreciative of all she did, but politely distant. She had imagined it then. No doubt her own silly fantasies at work once more. Would she never learn?

She had spun her romantic dreams about a dying man, imbuing him with all manner of heroic attributes he had no claim to, and that had not been his fault. He was just a man. And now that man was trying to remake himself, and what had she to do but fall into the same silly trap all over again?

"Kathy, do get up, there's a dear. I am parched and shall do murder if I cannot have a glass of something chilled."

Kathy tore herself out of her distraction to regard the Duchess of Bedwin, or Aunt Prue as she called her, though she was not truly her aunt at all. But Prue had a tendency to adopt people she liked as family, and she *was* Mama's cousin, after all. Kathy had come with Aunt Prue and her daughter Rosamund, all of them escorted by Rosamund's older brother, Jules, Marquess of Blackstone.

"Sorry, Aunt Prue, of course." She got to her feet, stepping out into the aisle and instantly colliding with Lord Vane.

"Oh!" she said, mortified, as he reached out to steady her. "I beg your pardon."

The warmth of his hands sank into the thin silk of her sleeves and shivers raced over her skin, a deliciously distracting reminder of that moment in her front parlour, when he had taken her hand in his.

"Miss de Beauvoir! The fault was mine, I assure you. Are you hurt?"

Kathy shook her head, too stunned to say anything.

"Vane, have a care. The ladies are under my escort this evening, and his grace will be tetchy if I return them with bruises." Jules drawled from behind her.

"Blackstone," Lord Vane replied, his tone polite but cautious as he released his hold on her. "I beg your pardon."

"It was my fault," Kathy said at once. Well, it was true, but Jules had moved closer, placing her hand firmly upon his arm, his posture somewhat protective.

"Come along, ladies," Jules said, moving her along, away from Lord Vane.

Rather to her own surprise, Kathy planted her feet.

"Jules," she said under her breath. "You're being rude."

But Lord Vane had already taken the hint.

"Forgive me, Miss de Beauvoir, Blackstone. I believe I see someone I must speak with," he said, bowing to them both before hurrying away.

Kathy glared up at Jules, who shrugged.

"Working for the man is one thing," he said, his tone dark. "Socialising with him, quite another. He eats little girls like you for breakfast."

"In the first place, I am not a little girl," Kathy said, stiff with indignation. "And in the second, he's changed."

Jules snorted, and Kathy was tempted to kick him.

"He has!" she insisted, "And I'm not your little sister, I might remind you. You are not my guardian."

"I'm escorting you tonight, and I'm in enough awe of your brother's fists to do a decent job of it," Jules retorted.

Kathy harrumphed. *Brothers.* They were all as irritating as each other, whether or not they belonged to you. "And I suppose you are all sweetness and light, and never put a foot wrong? Hmmm?"

Jules' expression darkened for a moment. "No man is sweetness and light, and no one ever gets through life without putting a foot wrong, but I'm a better man than him, and I assure you that's not saying much."

Kathy snatched her hand back, a wash of anger heating her skin. "I don't doubt that was true once, Jules, but no longer. You don't know. You don't know him."

"Neither do you, Kathy. Not really. And I pray you don't do something foolish like fall in love with him, for you'll—" He broke off, staring at her and muttered under his breath. *"Christ."*

The heat had become a furnace, her cheeks aglow, and she wanted to leave, to run away from his too knowing gaze, and all his reminders of the kind of man Vane had been. Instead, she put up her chin, defiant.

"Kathy," Jules said with a sigh. She saw only sorrow and kindness in his eyes, and that made her want to cry. He shook his head, his expression angry now. "Bloody hell."

Bloody hell. Yes, that was an excellent expression. She wanted to say it out loud instead of having it bottled up inside her. No, she wanted to shout it, to drown out the hum of chatter about her and scream it because it wasn't fair. It wasn't fair.

Bloody hell!

19th June 1842, Fort William, The Highlands, Scotland.

After a considerable perusal of all the fabrics on offer, Louis selected three different swatches—royal blue, fuchsia, and a deep, lush purple—and presented them to Lady Balderston, who looked at them with an expression that dithered between avaricious desire and doubt.

"They're rather bright," she said, and Louis heard the quaver of vulnerability. "I never wear bright colours anymore."

"I know," Louis replied, watching her steadily. She had worn nothing but dull greys and the occasional greyish lilac since he'd arrived. He placed her somewhere about seventy years, but she was still a handsome woman, straight and proud, with a slender frame and thick white hair. She'd been a beauty once, until life had ripped the heart from her. "But if your husband loved you as much as you loved him, he would want you to celebrate life, to show the world the beautiful and formidable woman who loved him so well, in all her glory. He would be proud of that, I think. *I* would be."

She blinked hard and sucked in a sharp breath.

"Well," she said, her voice unsteady. "Whoever the young woman is you are pursuing stands little chance, I think. You, monsieur, are quite deadly."

He smiled then, wishing that was true. *"Non*, only honest. You had something strong and true, and you mourn the loss of it. Your pain is tangible even after all this time, and yet I envy you."

There was silence as she studied him.

"She won't have you?" she asked, sounding astonished.

Louis shrugged. "I do not know. Her family has taken her away from me and put her in the proximity of gentlemen who are more suitable prospects. Far younger and far more innocent," he added with a huff of laughter at her enquiring expression.

"And did you take action to secure her regard before she left?"

"I did not know she was leaving, and she is very young, and very naïve, and I am afraid to taint that, to move too quickly and give her a disgust of me. I am her friend," he said helplessly, wondering if there were four more cutting words in the English language.

"Monsieur," Lady Balderston said, drawing herself up straight and fixing him with a steely gaze. "Whilst I do not doubt for a moment that you are far from innocent—no man who looked like you could be—I know a good man when I see one. Your charms, however, are beyond compare and I suggest you employ them at the first chance you get. The girl would be a ninny to let you escape."

Louis reached out and took the lady's hand, raising to his lips and kissing her fingers. She blushed and her eyes grew a little misty. "She would be a greater one to accept me. I am not an easy man, my lady. I have a past, and I suspect I will be the very devil of a husband, but I love her, with all my heart, and I would never betray her."

"Then I stand by my comment," she said, tightening her fingers about his for a moment. "My husband was rather a devil. He had a past too, a rather dreadful one, but I never had cause to doubt his feelings for me, and I never once regretted our marriage, even though it was not an easy one. I'd marry a faithful, loving devil over any good, dull, *easy* man in a heartbeat. So there, young man. The next chance you get, kiss the girl. Employ all your wicked wiles and leave her in no doubt of your feelings. Then there are only her own for her to wrestle with."

Louis watched as she stalked away from him, with a genuine smile on his face for the first time since he'd discovered Evie was gone.

"I want these colours," Lady Balderston's imperious voice demanded of the modiste as she thrust the three colour swatches under her nose.

With a soft huff of laughter, Louis headed for the door. Once outside, he drew in a deep breath. It was cool and damp, but it had stopped raining, which was a mercy. Deciding to stretch his legs, as the lady would be busy with her fitting for some time yet, he strolled down the main street, considering what Lady Balderston had said to him. Kissing Evie would be an inevitability if only he could get anywhere near her. He was going out of his mind, and he doubted his iron self-control would be in evidence if he ever saw her again. That he might not was too painful to contemplate. No. He would not consider that. He would find her. Even if they took her to the end of the earth, he would find her, and….

A burst of laughter, light and musical, drifted from a shop doorway and Louis halted at the mouth to a small side street. His heart reacted to the sound, crashing about behind his ribs whilst his senses—so dull of late—all leapt to attention.

He drifted towards the sound, hardly daring to hope, peering in windows as he went. A milliner's shop, busy, but not with anyone he recognised, next a carpenter, though the shop was closed, a sign on the door announcing a return this afternoon. The carpenter's workshop was set a couple of foot back from the rest of the shop fronts and Louis moved past it, hardly able to breathe. He did not have time to see what the next shop sold as a bell tinkled and the door opened.

"I'll see you in the milliner's," called a familiar voice, and then everything stopped, the noise of the town about him, the sound of a dog barking farther down the street, his heart.

He stood there, staring, unable to move or speak, as she turned away from the door.

Evie.

She blinked, froze, her green eyes wide with shock. Then she flew at him, closing the short distance between them, throwing her arms about his neck and holding on tight.

"Louis!" she whispered, and for the first time in forever, he could breathe again.

Chapter 14

Dearest Grace,

Please forgive me for my tardy reply. So much is happening of late. The days fly past me.

Yes, I am working on the school Eliza is building, though it is being financed by an anonymous donor. In fact, it is he I am working for, and the job is challenging and surprising and very exciting. There are certainly troublesome men to deal with, but I am helping to build something wonderful with my employer's help, and not just with the school. He is quite a remarkable man. I confess I had grave doubts about him to begin with, for his reputation is not a good one, but he seems determined to make amends for his past and I can only admire him for it. I hold him in the highest regard.

Oh, I have so much to tell you. Will you be in town soon? I know Sterling cannot leave the farm often, but it has been so long since we have seen you and darling little Betty. She must be so grown up now. Surely you will come and visit your parents soon? Do let me know if you are and we shall arrange a visit.

> ***—Excerpt of a letter from Miss Kathleen de Beauvoir (adopted daughter of Mr Inigo and Mrs Minerva de Beauvoir) to Mrs Grace Oak (daughter of Solomon and Jemima Weston, Baron and Lady Rothborn).***

19th June 1842, Vane Hall, Chiswick, London.

Max stared down at the papers on his desk, but he didn't see them. Morning light was streaming in through the open windows, promising a bright day. With a sigh, he tried to wrestle his brain away from thoughts of Miss de Beauvoir at the concert last night. He ought to be working, he reminded himself, though he'd been working all night and had not actually been to bed at all. That was what he was here for, though, to make up for lost time and so very much wickedness. Work, yes. Get on with it.

He stared at the papers, but his eyes blurred with fatigue, and he rubbed them irritably.

There was a knock, which he ignored, and a moment later, Jarvis came in bearing a tray. His staff were becoming somewhat insubordinate of late, he noticed, for he'd specifically said he was not to be disturbed.

"I didn't order breakfast."

"Forgive me, my lord, but you've been working all night. The staff are worried for you, so I took the liberty."

Max stared at his starchy butler, too surprised to say a word. The man had never liked him, not that he'd cared before. He had never even noticed his staff; they were just there, doing things he needed done, and he'd believed he'd paid them well to do it. That had changed. He noticed them now. He'd noticed a good deal that was wrong in their world, too, and done his best to put things right, but he'd never expected appreciation. They ought not to have been living and working in such conditions in the first place. He had certainly never expected them to like him for it… or to *care*. His throat grew tight, and he had to clear it before he could speak.

"Thank you. All of you, that was most thoughtful. I could eat something," he lied.

The man nodded and carefully set the tray down. He prepared a cup of coffee for Max before straightening again.

Max smiled, something he would never have done before, let alone offer his thanks. You did *not* thank servants. "Thank you, Jarvis."

The butler hesitated and then spoke again. "I would like to say, on behalf of all the staff, that we are proud of everything you are doing. You have made changes for us that have not gone unrecognised. The building of the new school, your visit to the workhouse, these things we are not supposed to know about, but we do, and we are proud to work for you."

Max was speechless with surprise, but Jarvis simply bowed and strode out without saying a word.

He let out an unsteady laugh. Well, that… that was nice. Max wondered what Miss de Beauvoir would say about it, and then reminded himself he wasn't supposed to think about Miss de Beauvoir. He ought to find her another job, something as challenging as this, where she could put her talents to good use, but far away from him. It was the only way. He realised that now. It was impossible to be around her, to be close to her, and not take advantage. His dreams were heated visions of her slender naked body, his hands and mouth exploring her most secret places, teaching her to be as wicked as he knew how until she screamed his name, begging for more.

Max closed his eyes, forcing the images away as desire stirred in his blood. Miss de Beauvoir was innocent, and she would remain that way. He would not taint her with his touch, with his base desires. Yet if he was forever in her proximity, eventually, he would kiss her, and she was too sweet, too vulnerable. He would hurt her, because that was what he did, even when he didn't mean to do it, apparently. She had been hurt last night, on his account of all things, the foolish girl. He had seen the regret in her eyes, her annoyance with Blackstone for treating Max as he had. Not that he blamed the marquess in the least; Blackstone knew Max was a threat to her happiness and safety. Max had even been grateful to discover a powerful man looking out for her, because he could not protect her. Not from himself.

He set the coffee cup down, untouched, and stared into its depths, unseeing. Perhaps when he had finished with the school, he would go away. He'd make certain the changes were in progress to the workhouse first, but that project would be safe in Miss de Beauvoir's hands, and he would find good people to ensure her success. Yes, perhaps rather than moving Miss de Beauvoir, he would move himself. No doubt there were troubles enough on his estate in Warwickshire to deal with. Perhaps he could persuade Burt and Pike to go with him, so he did not feel so very alone. But no, that was selfishness. They had their lives, their friends, here in London, though he intended to persuade Burt to stop being so damned stubborn and get them into a better property, a safer place to live, perhaps with a garden. Burt would like that, he thought.

Another knock at the door sounded, and he didn't look up at once, assuming his butler had gone rogue and would come in by himself again.

"My lord."

His heart jolted in his chest, and his eyes flew to the young woman standing in the doorway, as though he had summoned her with the force of his longing. Max leapt to his feet, gazing at her in shock.

"I beg your pardon." Miss de Beauvoir gaped at him, wide-eyed. "Am I disturbing you?"

Max shook his head, belatedly realising why she was staring at him with such an astonished expression. Lord, but he was half dressed. He'd discarded his coat, waistcoat, and cravat last night. He looked about remembering too late he'd rid himself of them before entering his study. Max raked a hand through his hair and began rolling down his sleeves.

"Forgive me, Miss de Beauvoir, I was not expecting visitors."

"No, the fault is entirely mine for barging in on you. I'm afraid I persuaded Jarvis that it was a matter of great urgency. I think he's rather scandalised, but I confess I am relieved to see you looking less than perfect."

"You are?" he asked doubtfully, horribly aware of his untucked shirt and the fact he'd not shaved.

"Yes," she said, moving closer to him. "It's reassuring."

"Reassuring?" he repeated, too aware of her proximity. "I must look entirely disreputable."

She nodded, smiling, reaching up to touch the scruff on his jaw. Max froze, his breath catching in his throat. He ought to tell her not to do that, he thought wildly, but his body had taken control of his mind and no words came out.

"Where is your maid?" he demanded, noticing too late that his study door was closed where it was usually ajar, her maid sitting directly outside for propriety.

"Scratchy and soft," she said in wonder, ignoring his question, her grey eyes moving over his face as her fingers traced a line across his cheek to his lips. "I have wondered if your lips are soft, too."

Max groaned inwardly and closed his eyes as she sighed.

Don't react. Don't react. Don't you move a bloody muscle, you bastard.

"So soft," she whispered in satisfaction.

"Miss de Beauvoir," he managed, fisting his hands at his sides against the desire to take her in his arms and hold her to him. "You must not. I'm not… not a good man. Not good enough for you. You deserve—"

"I deserve to make my own decisions, Maxwell Drake. *My* decisions, not my parents', or my brother's, or Blackstone's. And my name is Kathleen. You may call me Kathy, if you wish."

For a moment he was too afraid to open his eyes, in case it was a dream, in case it was like waking from the fever and he would find she had disappeared all over again. He risked it, finding her lovely face so close to his, staring at him with such trust in her eyes. *No. Don't trust me. I'll let you down,* pleaded a terrified voice inside him. *I don't want you to hate me. Not you.*

He wanted to say her name, to call her Kathy, his Kathy, and to hear her call him Max, but that was selfishness, that was —

She leaned in and pressed her mouth to his, and he was lost. So soft, so soft. Impossibly sweet. How could such a delicate press of lips provoke such a maelstrom of emotion inside of him? Inexpertly, she moved her mouth over his, and he wanted to weep. The moment was so devastatingly lovely.

"Max," she said, and he stared down at her in shock, his name on her lips, spoken with such tenderness, beyond anything he had hoped for. "Max, I love you. Kiss me. *Please.*"

"Kathy," he said helplessly, astonished and overwhelmed, and determined not to mess this up, not to hurt this woman who had been foolish enough to care for him. "You don't know what you're asking. You don't know."

"I do," she whispered, pressing her mouth to his and speaking the words against his lips. "I do."

She didn't. He knew that she didn't, but he could not deny her. The enormity of her trust in him was dazzling, overwhelming, and he knew he did not deserve it, could *never* deserve it. But he cupped her beautiful face with his trembling hands, tilting it just so, and dared to press his mouth to hers. Just for a moment, he promised himself. He wouldn't take more than this, just this much. She sighed, leaning into him, clutching at his shirt, her soft breasts against his chest. Longing, desire, a sense of something so perfectly right, swept him up, and he knew, at last, this was what love felt like. He loved her, would do anything for her, anything to make her happy, to keep her safe. This woman, his heart sang. *This woman.*

The door flew open with a flurry of skirts and a feminine gasp of horror.

"Take your hands off her, you bloody villain!"

Max jolted, dropping his hands to his sides as Kathy gave a little shriek of alarm but did not let go, still clutching his shirt.

"Grace?" she said in surprise, a trace of startled amusement in her voice. "Whatever are you doing here?"

Oh, God.

Max staggered away from her, skewered by the look in Grace's eyes, by the accusation. She hurried across the room and took Kathy's arm, towing her towards the door. Kathy resisted, alarmed now.

"Grace, whatever is the matter? Honestly, I don't know why you are here, but Lord Vane did nothing wrong, I wanted him to kiss me, I—"

"Mama?"

Max's gaze flew to the door where a little girl stood, clutching a well-loved rag doll. She was sucking her thumb, looking anxiously at the adults in the room, before holding her free hand out to her mother. His heart exploded into pieces, and he clutched the desk to steady himself. Beatrice Oak was two and a half now, and unbearably beautiful, an arrow shaft to the heart. A halo of golden curls surrounded the sweetest face in all the world, and she stared at them with wide, blue eyes.

His eyes.

Grace hesitated before letting go of Kathy and running to her child, sweeping her up. She spoke as she lifted the little girl into her arms, her voice implacable. "Your mother told me you were here, and I came at once. Kathy, he is not to be trusted. Lord Vane has not a shred of honour. He'll use you and cast you aside."

He saw Kathy take it all in, watched her staring at Grace, at the little girl, and then back at him. Max saw the moment when she understood, when he broke her heart, felt the shock of it ripple through him.

"Come with me, love," Grace said, her voice gentle now as she held out a hand to her.

Kathy hesitated, her face ashen. She stared back at him, as if willing him to say something, *anything,* to explain. But there was nothing to say, no explanation he could give.

Guilty.

Guilty as charged.

Worthy of being left dead in a filthy alley in the Dials.

"Go home now?" the little girl asked her mother, casting him anxious glances from over her shoulder.

"Yes, my sweet. We'll go home and see Nana and Pops."

The child gave an excited wriggle before glancing back at Max again. She frowned, pointing at him. "Who is he?"

Grace looked back at him, expressionless, before answering. "That's no one, Betty, my love."

She took Kathy's hand and gave a tug.

Kathy was perfectly still except for the rapid rise and fall of her chest. She stared at the carpet, though Max willed her to look at him one last time. He knew he would never see her again, but she did not look up, and only followed Grace blindly from the door.

Chapter 15

Pip,

I'm coming, but you've a damned lot of explaining to do, brother.

Who the hell is the mother? Please don't tell me you've ruined some poor girl?

—Excerpt of a letter from The Lord Thomas Barrington to his elder brother, the Hon'ble Philip Barrington, Earl of Ashburton (Sons of Lucian and Matilda Barrington, The Most Hon'ble Marquess and Marchioness of Montagu).

19th June 1842, Fort William, The Highlands, Scotland.

It took a moment for Louis to come to his senses, to realise they were standing in a public street, embracing in broad daylight. He grasped Evie's hand and dragged her behind him into the carpenter's workshop. She gasped, but did not murmur a word of protest. The door was locked but flew opened with one hard kick. He entered and pulled Evie in behind him, slamming the door shut and pulling her into his embrace, holding on tight.

His heart was hammering so hard he felt giddy, but Evie was here, in his arms. It felt like a dream. Her head rested against his chest, her hands clutching at his lapels. There was a dull thud as her bonnet slid to the ground, but neither of them made a move to retrieve it. They just stood there, holding on tight, neither of them saying a word. Louis lowered his head, burying his face in her soft hair and closing his eyes, breathing in the scent of her. *Home*, his heart whispered. Though he had come in search of her, he had come home.

"Ma petite," he said, hardly recognising his own voice, thick with emotion.

"Your heart is beating very fast," she observed. She was trembling, he realised now, he could hear the quaver in her voice, the fine tremor running through her body, so close to his.

"My heart is beating for the first time since you left me alone," he replied, trying to mask the anger behind the words, the hurt. Not her fault, he reminded himself. She'd had no choice but to leave him. Yet the sense of abandonment remained.

She looked up at him then, meeting his gaze. "I didn't know until it was too late," she said, beseeching. "I could not stop them."

He cupped her face with his hand, his thumb stroking the satiny skin of her cheek. She was here. She was really here. "I know," he whispered.

"But why are you here?" She sounded awed that he was. Uncomprehending.

"You *know* why I'm here," he said, and that had sounded angry, brutal. She drew back a little, wide-eyed.

Louis swallowed down the emotion roiling inside him, reminding himself to step carefully, but he was all raw edges and exposed nerves. He had not felt this vulnerable and afraid since he was a child. He had sworn no one would ever have the power to hurt him again and yet, here he was, with his heart exposed.

"I'm sorry," he managed, drawing in a shaky breath. "I'm just… *Merde,* Evie. Do you have any idea how much I missed you?"

She stared up at him, utterly guileless. "No," she replied frankly. "I don't. Not really."

Voices sounded on the street outside the shop, and she tensed, turning her head to peer through the grubby window.

"That's Mama and Muir. They'll be worried when they discover I'm not in the milliners."

"Muir?" he repeated, his worst suspicions confirmed when she blushed. "One of Morven's sons, I collect. Your prospective husband, perhaps?"

She swallowed hard, and he sensed her anxiety. "He's not asked me yet."

Yet.

Louis felt sick. No. He felt savage and on the edge of violence, like slamming out of the dingy workshop and finding this Muir and explaining to him that Evie was *his* in terms that would leave no one in any doubt. *Get a grip, Louis,* he warned himself.

"And when he does ask you?" Louis asked, the words little more than a growl. He wasn't certain he wanted to hear the answer, but he had to. You could not win a battle if you did not know who you were fighting. And the battle for Evie's heart was one he had no intention of losing. She looked away from him and pain lanced through his chest.

"I d-don't know," she whispered, blinking back tears.

Tension simmered between them, but she did not let him go. Her body pressed close to his, her hands still clutching at his coat.

"I know," he said, sliding his hand behind her neck, into her hair, tugging gently and tilting her head back. "I know, because you are mine. We both know it, even if you have been running from the truth. You belong with me, *ma petite*. When he asks, your answer is no. Do you hear me, Evie?"

Somewhere in the back of his mind, a voice was screaming at him to stop. This was not the way. He had promised to give her time, to make her own choice, to come to him because she loved him. But time was running out, and he was too afraid of what he might do if she did not make that choice at all.

Diable.

Louis shuddered as the evil voice whispered in his ear. No. Not that. Not now. He would not heed that voice now after working so hard for so long to silence it. Not after all this time. He concentrated on Evie, on her response to his command.

She was breathing hard, her breath fluttering against his face, lips parted, her eyes dark. Was that fear or wanting he saw? She did not reply, did not let go of her hold on him.

Diable.

"Are you afraid of me?" he asked softly, his thumb stroking over the pulse point in her neck. It fluttered wildly under her skin, like a panicked bird.

"A-A little," she admitted, but she still did not let go. "I never was before, but now—"

She broke off, staring at him uncertainly, but still, she did not let go.

"I would never hurt you," he whispered, lowering his head to nuzzle that sweet spot beneath her ear where her blood thundered. Her breath caught, and she pressed closer to him as a shiver ran through her, which pleased him. He pressed a kiss there, nipped at her earlobe, moved his lips over her jaw as her breathing became erratic. "Has he kissed you?" he asked, wondering if he could stand to hear the answer.

Diable, mauvais esprit, démon, serpent dans le Jardin d'eden, whispered the insidious voice, reminding him his beauty was a snare for the innocent, a gift from the devil, that *he* was the serpent in the garden of Eden.

She licked her lips, and the sight sent a bolt of lust straight to his groin. Apparently, she could not speak the word aloud, however, so she nodded. Jealousy was a knife to his heart, a vile twisting in his guts.

"Did you like it?" he asked, his voice dangerously low.

She stared at him, her skin flushed pink, her eyes growing darker, her breasts rising and falling faster, pressing against his chest. "It w-was… nice," she said carefully, watching his reaction, her gaze upon him intent.

"Nice," he said in disgust, remembering her saying that to him once before. "My kisses are not nice, *mon amour.*"

Louis lowered his mouth to hers and she tensed, a startled gasp escaping her, allowing him entry. He took the opportunity she gave, as he would take this opportunity to make her see once and for all that she belonged with him. His tongue swept in, and he felt shock vibrate through her. To his relief, he discovered at once that she did not know how to kiss, so either this Muir was a damned fool, or he had not kissed her at all thoroughly. Louis taught her the way of it, gently teasing her response from her, triumphant when she followed his lead, sliding her tongue tentatively over his. Desire rioted through him. Control was slipping from his grasp, but for once, he found it hard to care. It had been a very long time since he'd had a woman, all because of her, because he felt as if he betrayed her every time he tried to take his pleasure elsewhere. He was a man with a ferocious libido and his frustration had tormented him to the point of madness. The darker side of his nature wanted her to understand that, to feel a little of his torment. So now, to have her in his arms… he was on the brink of behaving very badly indeed.

Carefully, he adjusted his hold on her lush curves, pulling her hard against him, so close she could not fail to feel his arousal, his need for her. He wondered if she would shy away. He was going too far, too fast, and he knew it, yet he could not make himself stop. But the tension left her body all at once and she melted into him, and he knew such overwhelming relief that he wanted to weep with gratitude and had to fight the temptation to take her to the filthy floor and make her his, once and for all. If he ruined her, she would have to marry him. The thought nagged at him, but he could not do that to her. There were limits to his bad behaviour, it seemed.

She pulled away with a gasp, staring at him with dark eyes as though she beheld the devil himself. *Ah, sweet Evie, how right you are.*

"Oh, you… you are very bad," she whispered, touching her fingers to her mouth and gazing at him in wonder.

"Evie," he murmured, nipping at her lips before tasting her again.

Dieu, but she was so sweet, so maddeningly divine, and he was beyond thought, beyond reason, lost in the feel of her. He turned them about so she bumped up against the wall and slid his hand over her delectable bottom to her thigh, catching her leg behind the knee and pulling it up around his hip. She made a startled sound as he moved into the cradle of her body, pressing his aching cock against her with a low groan. There were too many damn layers in the way and his control was fraying, but somehow he resisted ripping the damn skirts and petticoats away.

He canted his hips against hers and she cried out, clutching at his hair, burying her face against his neck, her breath hot and harsh against his skin. He sought her mouth, and she kissed him again, willingly, ardently, her innocent passion stirring his blood like nothing else had ever done. Louis broke the kiss, trailing his mouth over her cheek as she made a sound of protest, wanting more.

Diable! The devil sent you from hell to tempt the innocent to sin.

"Now do you see, my Evie? My little love."

He tipped her head back before she could answer. Her gown had a high neck, fastened with what seemed a thousand tiny buttons. One by one, he flicked them undone, kissing each newly revealed inch of flesh as she trembled in his arms. Down and down the buttons went, over her breasts to her waist.

"Louis," she whimpered, her hands clutching at his shoulders.

"Hush," he murmured, parting the material and staring with hazy desire at the generous swell of her luscious breasts. *"Je péris de tant vous désirer, mon amour."*

"What does that mean?" she asked, her words breathless.

He brushed his lips over the curve of her breast, close to the lace on her chemise, speaking against her skin. "I'm dying from wanting you so much, my love," he whispered.

"Oh." She swayed in his arms. "Louis, I—I can't stand, I—" she pleaded, so he lashed his arm tighter about her and released his hold on her thigh in favour of cupping her breast. He smiled as she curved her leg about his hip all on her own and rewarded her by pressing his cock against her sex until she moaned. Her blasted corset and too many layers were driving him to distraction, but her breast swelled above its confines as he squeezed and he licked the delicious mound, hearing her breath leave her in a shocked exhalation. Though he knew he was wicked, beyond the pale, he could not resist the temptation. He held her tighter as he ducked his head again and she gave a little cry of pain. Her hands tightened in his hair, pulling, holding on as he raised his head and looked with satisfaction at the mark he'd left on her breast. No matter if this Muir was in the same house as her, she would see that for days and remember him, remember his mouth upon her breast. He could not remember ever experiencing such a devastating need to possess, to claim. It was unlike him, but he could not deny the truth of it. She made him act like a madman, like some primitive version of himself he did not recognise. *He*, who had always prided himself on his self-control and sophistication, had become nothing but sensation and raw need, marking his place upon her body like a randy boy.

Though he knew he must stop this, *now,* for the love of God, he did not know how he could let her go. He raised his head, staring at her, knowing he must look wild, for he felt it to his bones.

"What will you say, Evie? When this… this *boy* asks you to be his wife. What will be your answer?"

Her eyes were hazy with lust, her lips red, still parted, her breath coming in harsh little gasps. She wanted him. At last. She wanted *him.* All the things he wanted crashed about inside him, the things he wanted to do to her, the ways he needed to love her. *Merde,* his sweet little innocent Evie, would be shocked to her bones if she knew the things he dreamed of.

"Evie!" He gave her a little shake, and she shook her head with a soft moan.

"H-How can I think when you do such… such… Oh, you are wicked," she protested weakly, one hand hitting his shoulder in frustration and then curling back about his lapel.

He would go mad. "Damn you, Evie. Do you not understand how I have suffered without you? I need you. Do you hear me? *I need you.*"

"Do you?" she asked, reaching up to touch his cheek. He closed his eyes and turned into her caress, kissing her palm.

"Oui," he moaned. "Don't make me suffer this any longer, *ma petite,* I beg you."

"I did not mean to make you suffer. I did not know," she replied, her expression pained, fear flickering in her eyes.

Louis saw her fear and understood that he was overwhelming her. He ought to have taken more care, used more finesse. But all his usual *wiles,* as Lady Balderston had called them, had deserted him the moment he had seen her. And then she had run into his arms, and nothing had mattered but that she belonged to him. He had been nothing but want and need and the anger of being left behind, which had taken him by surprise and unleashed his desires.

"I know," he said, gentling his voice. "And I know I… I ought to have been tender. I want to be, Evie, I *will* be, but I have been so wretched without you I have gone a little mad."

"Miss Evie?"

They both stilled as a voice called outside, close to the workshop.

"They're looking for me," Evie whispered urgently. "I must go, Louis. If they find you here. Oh, my word, there will be such a scene!"

She pushed him away.

"Wait," he pleaded, holding on and kissing her again. She resisted for a moment and then melted into him, pressing closer with enthusiasm, curving her arms about his neck. Louis plundered her mouth, dropping his hands to her bottom and hauling her hard against him. Her breath hitched, and he revelled in her submission to him, but even in his overheated state, he could not ignore the people outside, searching for her.

"Your kisses are *not* nice," she admitted breathlessly, as he finally consented to let her go.

"I am not nice, or good, or easy, *ma petite,"* he said, holding her gaze. "But I am entirely yours."

She swallowed, gazing up at him in wonder. The voice called her again, further down the street, and much as Louis wanted to consign the bastard to the devil, he knew he could not. With reluctance, he reached for the buttons on her dress and began setting her to rights.

"When are you coming home?" he demanded, too aware of the petulant quality of his voice. He sounded like a sulky boy, for the love of God.

"Soon, I think, but I don't know exactly," she replied, her eyes upon him as he worked at her buttons. The last one slid into place, and he settled his hands upon her hips, watching her. She avoided his gaze, stroking her hand over his chest, smoothing down his rumpled lapels.

"Did you miss me, at least?" he asked gruffly. "You didn't say."

Her face softened, and she looked up at him, her beautiful mouth curving. "Oh, Louis. How could you doubt it? Of course, I missed you. I missed you very much."

Something in his heart eased a little, and he let out a breath. "If I stay here, will you come again? I need to see you again."

She shook her head. "We're returning to Wildsyde first thing in the morning, and there's nowhere there I can meet you."

He wondered if he imagined the relief in her voice, but was too afraid to question her. There was one question he would have an answer to, though.

"When he asks you, you will say no?" he queried, needing to hear her say it.

She frowned, glancing away from him as shadows passed by the dirty windows outside. Her mother's voice spoke low, agitated, and then the figures hurried past.

"I must go," she said, pulling away from him.

Louis caught her hand, holding on tight. "Evie, please, love," he begged her, beyond pride, needing her reassurance.

"I won't accept anyone, Louis, you have my word." She leaned in and pressed a soft kiss to his mouth, snatched up her bonnet, and hurried out of the door.

Louis stood there, her kiss a burn against his lips, marking him as her property more tangibly than any brand she could have given him, and he realised… that had not been the answer he'd been seeking.

19th June 1842, Vane Hall, Chiswick, London.

Max stared at the door, though it had been closed for some time. He'd heard the front door shutting, too. They were gone.

This was why he'd not died in that alley, he realised now. It hadn't been the act of a merciful God, but a vengeful one. Dying would have been simple. This… This was retribution. It hurt worse than the knife had, he thought, a hand going to the scar on his side as though that might help ease the wound. But that wound had healed. This was fresh and raw, and it felt fatal, though he knew he'd not be that lucky. A part of him welcomed the pain. He'd long felt he had not been punished enough for his past, that he did not deserve to live in luxury, to never know hunger. It was part of the reason he'd stayed with Burt for so long.

He tried to move, and staggered, finding his legs felt weak, discovering he was shaking. Somehow, he made it to the chair behind his desk and sank into it. His breath was coming hard, in sharp little gasps, and he closed his eyes, pressing the heels of his hands against his eyes.

"You deserve it," he reminded himself. "You bloody deserve it."

Yet he was not so reformed that he could deny himself a little pity, as the enormity of all he had lost hit him all over again. Beatrice's beautiful little face, staring at him, Grace's eyes filled with disgust, and Kathy… *Kathy.* A sob rose in his throat, and he forced it back down again. He'd done this. If not for Sterling Oak, Grace's situation would have been very different. *I would have gone back, I would have married her*, he pleaded with his conscience, but he should have done that at once, should never have taken advantage of a girl's infatuation with him, should never… should never… should never….

Too late, chimed a spiteful voice in his head. *Too little, too late.*

He drew in a deep breath, trying to steady himself, and his gaze fell upon the brandy decanter. The desire to lose himself in drink was beyond tempting. No. That was the man he'd been, that had caused this bedamned mess in the first place. The man who had taken Grace's innocence and left her with a child would do that. He would drink and drink and return to his vile ways, and he would not be that man again.

He'd known he could not have Kathy. That she had come to him, that she had kissed him of her own free will, was a blessing. The memory of the way she had touched him, had spoken his name, he would hold in his heart until his dying day, because he loved her. And this time he understood what that meant, to love someone. It meant leaving them alone, even though it felt like dying, if that was what was best for them.

So, he would leave, go back to Warwickshire as he had planned to do before Kathy had arrived. He reached for a fresh sheet of paper, noticing his hand trembling as he did so. Quickly, he left written instructions to all relevant parties that Miss de Beauvoir was to have complete control of the school project and granted whatever help she needed for the workhouse renovations, plus access to any funds she required. She could draw upon his accounts without limit and make use of Vane Hall as she saw fit. The staff were to accommodate her in whatever way she required.

Once the letters were done, he felt a little steadier. Handing them to Jarvis', he left instructions that his valet was to pack for a long absence, snatched up his coat, and went out, tying the cravat haphazardly about his throat as he left the house.

He had one last call to make before he left.

19th June 1842, Albany Gardens, Piccadilly, London.

Kathy sat on the bed in Grace's old bedroom. She had visited here many times in the past when the Baron and Lady Rothborn were in town. Grace sat beside her, holding her hand.

"She's really his… his daughter," she said, still numb with shock.

Grace nodded. "I'm so sorry."

"Not your fault," Kathy replied, wondering why she was so calm, except… she had known this, hadn't she? Among the vile litany of his confessions when the fever had been raging, he had said as much. She'd perhaps not understood the words at the time, or… or perhaps she had just refused to understand them.

"He regrets it. What he did to you," Kathy said, feeling Grace stiffen beside her. She looked up, shaking her head. "I'm not… not defending him. It's only… he…."

She wanted to tell Grace that he'd changed, that he'd been working so hard to change, but how could she? Grace would not want to hear it. She was no longer certain she could bear to hear it herself. Perhaps some things were unforgivable?

"You understand why I had to come? Your mother must think me a madwoman, for I did not explain, just murmured an excuse about a forgotten appointment. But when she said you were there at that moment, working with *him*…. As soon as I realised that vile creature had inveigled himself into your life too, I knew I had to go to you, had to keep you safe. I'm so sorry to burden you with my secret, but it was the only way. I know how easy it is to believe in him, to imagine yourself in love with him, and that he loves you, but it's all lies, Kathy. You do see that?"

Grace's expression was full of sorrow and anxiety, and Kathy knew she was a true friend, one that had risked her own reputation and that of her child to ensure Kathy was safe.

"Yes," Kathy replied, nodding, though the word tasted bitter on her tongue. "Yes. I do see."

She got to her feet, needing to get away, to be alone with her thoughts, for she could not think at all with little Beatrice sitting in the corner of the room, playing with her wooden bricks. The child looked up as she rose, and Max's eyes looked back at her. She swallowed a sob and forced a smile to her lips.

"Goodbye, Grace. Thank you for what you did and don't worry about me. I'm fine, truly."

"No, you're not," Grace said softly, reaching out and taking her hand again. "But you will be. We're a lot stronger than we realise, you know. It took me some time to discover that, but you will too."

"I will," Kathy replied, leaning down to kiss her friend's cheek."

"You should take your dare," Grace said as she straightened. "Cat is in town with her parents. I'll ask her to send it to you. It will give you something else to focus on."

"My dare? *Oh*," Kathy said, realisation dawning. "Yes. Why not? Thank you."

"Goodbye, love. I'm staying for a few days if you want to talk again."

Kathy nodded, struggling to keep the smile fixed in place, it felt unnaturally stiff. "Yes. Thank you. Goodbye, Grace. Goodbye, B-Beatrice."

With that, she hurried to the door and left.

Chapter 16

Thorn,

I am a lot of things, but I don't touch innocent girls. Christ! If anyone else accused me of that, I'd break his bloody nose.

The child is Jenny's. I swear I did not know. As I told you, we parted company. It was months ago now and a mutual decision I had believed, for she implied she had another protector in mind, but now I doubt this was true. She was a good woman, a kind one, and she knew what trouble this baby would bring me. I think she hid the pregnancy from me. I had left her financially secure so she would have wanted for nothing, but she died, Thorn. Poor Jenny died bringing my child into the world and I shall never forgive myself.

And now I am stranded here, pretending to be a widower – Mr Russell, with a squalling infant I do not know what to do with and a blackmailer who will tell Father all if I don't pay him off. I know I can't keep it from them forever, but I can't confess yet. Father is already frustrated with me, and I dare not make things so much worse. You know how he feels about men who leave bastard children in their wake.

Thorn, I can't bear to see the disappointment in his and mother's eyes. I have let them down, but I cannot let this child down, this little girl. I have a daughter, God help me. And she's so tiny, so helpless and yet she makes me feel helpless too. I won't be though. I shall make this as right as I can, but I need time. I need your help. Please, brother.

—Excerpt of a letter from The Hon'ble Philip Barrington, Earl of Ashburton to his younger brother The Lord Thomas Barrington (Sons of Lucian and Matilda Barrington, The Most Hon'ble Marquess and Marchioness of Montagu).

19th June 1842, Covent Garden. Parish of St Giles.

"Valentine!" Burt exclaimed, his leathery face crinkling with pleasure at the sight of Max. His smile faded as he took in the sight before him, though. Max knew he must look a sight, in his rumpled clothes and unshaven, and with the heart having been ripped out of him. He assumed that was visible, too. Something that felt so catastrophic must leave some physical mark, surely.

"Come in, lad," Burt said, his voice kind as he stepped back and ushered Max inside.

Max went in and sat down at the table in his usual spot. A part of him wished he'd never left. He could still be Valentine, couldn't he? He was good at stacking boxes, loading and unloading carts. It didn't take brains, but it took muscle and stamina, and he'd gained both in the months after his recovery. As tempting as the idea was, he knew it would be cowardly. He'd promised to make amends, and just because it was hard, that was no reason to stop, but a reason to keep going. If he was truly repentant for his sins, he had to try harder than ever, not give in.

"What's wrong, lad?" Burt said, pulling up a chair beside him, his expression full of concern that Max did not deserve. "Tell old Burt what's happened to put that look on your face."

He realised absently that no one but Burt had ever asked him that before. As a child, his parents had seen him for an hour each day, during which he was neatly dressed and on his best behaviour. He would answer their questions, thank them for any present they gave him, and otherwise sit quietly whilst they spoke with each other and mostly ignored his presence. He could never remember them asking him what was wrong, or if he was happy, or sad, or… anything at all. Servants were there to clean up skinned knees and bloody noses, and besides, only girls cried, so that wasn't allowed. Then he'd been sent to school and barely saw them at all, thrust into the merciless world of Eton and bigger boys who'd thrash you for the fun of it.

He shook his head, trying to rid himself of the memories, and took a breath. Before he left, he must get Burt and Pike settled somewhere safe, persuade them to accept enough money to keep them that way and to help anyone else they chose to, and explain that he was going away. He opened his mouth, but no words came out. Turning to Burt, he tried again, but his eyes burned, and he snapped his mouth shut before he made a fool of himself. Burt reached out and placed a gnarled, arthritic hand on his shoulder.

"It's all right, Valentine. Take a deep breath and try again. A trouble shared is a trouble halved, eh? And there's no judgement here, you know that."

"Perhaps there ought to be," he managed. "Everything is such a mess, Burt. I ruined everything without even knowing what I was doing. I was such a cruel, selfish…."

He broke off and put his head in his hands.

“You’ve told me this, afore, lad. I know you behaved badly in the past, but you’ve been doing good things, making the world a better place. You seemed happier too. Why are you beating yourself with the same stick all over again?”

“Because someone ought to!” he exploded, wishing someone would beat him, beat the vileness out of him until he felt he could bear to wear his own skin. “Because I’ve no right to happiness and it’s all become so much worse. I’ve hurt someone else, someone I love, and… and I don’t know how to live with the fact that she hates me.”

“Tell me then,” Burt said, patient as ever.

And so he did.

Starting with Grace.

19th June 1842, Fort William, The Highlands, Scotland.

“I hope you’re not coming down with something.” Mama fretted as the carriage took them back to their hotel. “You still looked flushed, though you don’t seem to have a fever.”

“I’m sure it’s just a headache, Mama,” Evie assured her, avoiding her gaze and that of Muir, who was watching her with concern. “I just want to lie down in a dark room.”

For a very long time, she added to herself. She was still shaking. Her body was vibrating with shock and… and she was not certain what else. *Liar*. Oh dear. She did have a fever, and she knew who was to blame. Louis César. The place between her thighs throbbed uncomfortably and his touch still burned her skin, all the places where his mouth had been. Her hand went to her breast and covered the spot where he’d… heavens, what had he done? She’d felt the pull on her skin, a powerful sensation that had been as much pleasure as pain. Had he bitten her? It had not felt quite like a bite, but she did not know, had not dared look, but she felt his mark upon her like a brand, like ownership. Helpless delight and fear rippled through her at the thought, and she did not know which was the right one to heed.

When she had seen him standing there, in that narrow backstreet, she had thought she was dreaming. She *had* dreamt of him. When it had dawned on her he was real, she had felt nothing but a jolt of pure happiness and then… relief. It was like exhaling after weeks and weeks of holding her breath or living under a thick pall of cloud and suddenly seeing the sun come out. She knew then, in that moment, as she had never really understood before, the effect he had on others. She had loved him as her friend first, had not seen his beauty as others had seen it, for she'd been too young to be interested in him as a man. Not now, though. Oh, not now. Now she saw, and she understood, and she recognised the power he could wield over her with a tremor of fear.

As soon as they arrived back at their hotel, Evie made her excuses, dismissed her maid, and stood in the quiet of her room, breathing hard. Had all that really happened? Had he really been here, in Scotland? Had he come all this way, just for the chance of seeing her?

Evie moved to the full-length looking glass and stared at herself. She touched a finger to her lips and shivered. They felt sensitive still, and she remembered his teeth nipping at her, his tongue caressing. Heat surged through her, and the insistent throb he'd provoked between her thighs had not ceased with leaving him. It had followed her home and now became louder again, echoing her heartbeat, as if calling for him to come and finish what he'd begun. With trembling fingers, she undid the buttons on her gown, drawing the material aside to reveal the swell of her breast. A small but definite red oval marked her skin, and a jolt of possessive pleasure surged through her. She touched a finger to it, her breath hitching as she remembered his mouth upon her, the feel of his powerful, hard body against hers, his arousal pressed so intimately against her sex as his hands explored her. The dizzyingly expensive scent of him had intoxicated her mind until she had thought she would go mad with wanting him, needing him closer, needing more of him. She could smell him still, the heady, masculine scent of him lingering on her clothes and she breathed it in, giddy all over again. Her body had come alive in his arms, had demanded wicked things she had never realised she wanted. She was not ignorant of what happened between men and women, her mama had seen to that, but never had she understood the lengths people went to, the terrible risks they took to be with the one they desired. The words of poets and writers who described the madness and pain of wanting and needing and longing had never really made any sense to her. Evie understood them now.

She had wanted him beyond sanity, needed him to rid her of the hollow feeling that clamoured for him, for his body to fill hers, to take her and use her however he wished, so long as he made her his. She had been mad with it, out of control, willing to give him whatever he wanted because she wanted it too. He could have lifted her skirts and had her against the wall, and she'd not have stopped him, and that… that was terrifying.

Lord, but he was dangerous.

This… This was why his mistresses looked so smug, so pleased with themselves, why they were so eager to proclaim their place in his bed. *This* was why her father had packed the family up overnight and taken them away to Scotland. Now, finally, Evie understood his concern for her. Louis had warned her repeatedly what kind of man he was, but she'd not really heeded him, because he was safe, *her* Louis, her friend, but that wasn't true. Not anymore, at least. Good heavens, she had once been naked in the same room as him at Beverwyck when he had helped her with that awful dress, and she had never realised the danger she courted, though he had warned her. She'd realised it gradually over the months since, had sensed the change in him, the way he looked at her, touched her. The increasingly lavish gifts he gave ought to have been warning enough, never mind the things he had tried to say, and she had refused to let him, refused to hear him.

Why, though? Why her? Of all the women he could choose, why her? *Because you were the only one he could not have, you're a novelty,* whispered a spiteful voice in her head. But people grew tired of novelty. Novelty became dull in short order, and what then? Louis had loved no one in his life, save his brother and Aggie, and that was different. He'd never cared romantically for anyone. He left his mistresses without a backward glance and with his heart entirely untouched. And would his wife have to endure that constant parade of lovers?

He cares for you, she told herself, knowing it was true. Louis loved her, she could not fail to see that, but *how* did he love her? As a friend, as the woman who would be his wife, the mother of his children? And if so, how long would it last? If she put herself in his keeping, how long before he grew tired of her? He had never lied to her, and in this she trusted him still. She could not believe he would take a mistress behind her back, but would that mean he would tell the truth, that she wasn't enough for him, when he realised he'd made a mistake? Or would he simply endure and pretend he loved her still, all the while regretting his decision and resenting her?

No, they were friends, they would always be friends, but Louis was dangerous in ways she'd never truly contemplated. If she loved him, her life would be one of turmoil, for she could not imagine him sitting at home by the fireside with her and a parcel of children, and that was what she had always wanted. Safety, security, a loving home. She had never wanted adventure or excitement, but Louis would bring her that with his secrets and his dark past and all the things she did not know about him. She knew he was a good man, and he had told her she knew him better than anyone save his brother, but she did not know about his life before she'd met him other than that parts of it had been dark and he carried the shadows of it still.

She closed her eyes, wishing she could will away the desire thrumming under her skin, because she could not deny that she wanted him, or that she loved him as her dearest friend, but she was not at all certain she wanted the life he would offer her. Oh, dear. Whatever was she to do?

19th June 1842, Covent Garden. Parish of St Giles.

The words were bitter and so vile, Max wondered if even good-hearted Burt could forgive him, once he knew it all. Well, he was burning bridges left and right today, he may as well set light to the last one and be done with it.

"There was a girl. A beautiful girl. Innocent and utterly besotted with me. She used to trail after me like a lovelorn puppy. It was amusing, at the time, to let her think I felt the same way. To see her eyes light up when she saw me. She was so naïve she hid nothing of her feelings." He shook his head, disgusted with himself. "I knew better than to dally with a proper young lady. Even I, as wild as I was, knew that much, but she was kind and she made me feel like I was worth something. I never meant for it to be more than that, Burt. I swear that much is true. It was just a game, a cruel one, but one that would have bruised her heart, nothing more."

"Right," Burt said, nodding gravely. He looked unhappy, but Max thought he believed him, though the Lord knew why.

Max ran a hand through his hair, trying to marshal his thoughts. "My mother was never a strong woman. She always fancied herself unwell, and she suffered with her nerves. After father died, she worried that when I came of age, I would mismanage the estate, that we would be left in penury." He laughed at that, and Burt's mouth quirked. "She did not know what that meant, of course. Her idea of being poor would have been having to make do with buying one diamond necklace instead of three."

"It's a tough life," Burt said with a sigh, his eyes twinkling, but no trace of malice or disgust.

For a moment, Max felt it on his behalf, for the mother who was so damned frivolous and self-centred, but she had known no better either and he had learned to pity her too.

"I decided I must follow in my father's footsteps, and perhaps then she would stop worrying and see I was a son she could be proud of. So I spent time with the trustees, the estate manager, learning what my father had not bothered to teach me, if he knew himself. I learned how to manage and run the many estates. I worked hard until I understood and knew I could take care of it all without making a mess of things and that Mama and the rest of the extended family would be safe. I'd never really worked at anything before that, not with any dedication, but I worked at that for months."

Burt nodded his understanding, but said nothing, so he carried on.

"On my twenty-first birthday, I came into my majority, and everything became mine in full. Mother gave me this," he said, pulling out a heavy gold fob watch. He turned it in his hand, smoothing his thumb over the inscription which bore his title and his birthday. No personal message, of course. His parents did not approve of sentimentality. That was shockingly middle class. The upper orders did not have emotions. He'd always preferred his grandfather's watch, but someone had stolen that the night he'd been attacked.

"I knew she was anxious, worried I would make a mess of it, so I sat her down and explained what I had done, that I had learned how everything worked and I would not make a mess of it. Foolishly, I explained about our money, how we invested it to make it work for us, the interest we would gain that year, et cetera. I told myself I was putting her mind at rest, but I was showing off a little too, wanting her to realise that I was not a fool, that I had worked hard to educate myself. That I had done it for her."

"She didn't appreciate the effort?" Burt suggested, his voice gruff.

Max let out a little huff of laughter. "She did not. I was accused of behaving like an accountant—a grave insult, as far as she was concerned. Only the poor worried about money, a gentleman did not concern himself with it. I should leave all that in the hands of men who were paid to do it for me. We had a blazing row, both saying things we ought not."

Burt's gaze upon him was as perspicacious as always. "What did she say?"

Max shrugged. It didn't matter, he reminded himself. It hadn't mattered then, and it didn't matter now.

"The usual. I was useless, a disappointment to her. If only I'd died, and her other children had lived. It was nothing I had never heard before, but I could never understand why that was, why they were so disinterested in me. Then she told me. I was not really the earl, I was an imposter, another man's bastard, but father had accepted me because none of the others had lived. If one of her other male children had survived, they would have put me aside. As it was, they had no choice. Apparently, my real father was a duke. He was dead by then though, so…."

"Bloody hell," Burt said.

"Anyway," he said, clearing his throat. "I was upset and angry, so I did what I always did and went out and got drunk, and then… and then *she* was there."

"The girl?"

He nodded. "She ought not to have been, but she'd come to find me, to wish me a happy birthday, and she was so sweet, and I…" Max shook his head in disgust. "I persuaded her to give me something else for my birthday, something far more precious, though I didn't realise it then, not really. I took my pleasure, left, and went back to getting as drunk as I could get. Callous fool that I was, I forgot all about her, about what we'd done. What *I'd* done. I went back to town and didn't see her for weeks. When she came to tell me she was pregnant, I laughed in her face. I thought she was having me on. Then I was angry that she should try to trap me. I… was not kind. By the time I remembered the truth, she'd gone back to the countryside."

"And?" Burt prompted.

Max sighed. "And I thought I'd better bloody well marry her. I didn't want to, and I was damned angry about it, but I had to marry someone, and she was beautiful, respectable. And I… I didn't want my child to feel like… anyway, I went out that night to drown my sorrows, and… and that's the night we met."

"Ah," Burt said, understanding.

"I didn't remember, Burt," he said, his voice thick, turning to stare at the only man who had ever really seen him, who had taught him to be better than the spoilt, selfish child he'd been and wondering if he too would hate him now. "I swear I didn't remember. Not for a long time, but… but what kind of man forgets that he's made a child? By the time I remembered, she was married to someone else. I went to see her then, to check she was well and provided for, but… Well, she was hardly pleased to see me, as you can imagine."

"What did you say to her?"

Max stared at the scarred tabletop, tracing the surface where Pike had scored a large letter P in the wood. "I told her I was sorry, that if she ever needed anything, I would do whatever she needed to help her, or the baby. No matter what."

"That was the right thing to do," Burt said, nodding.

"Too little, too late," he murmured. "But now Kathy—Miss de Beauvoir—has discovered my secret. She's the young lady who nursed me when I was ill. That's right, isn't it?"

Burt frowned and then nodded. "Her brother made me swear never to tell ye, Valentine. I'm sorry."

Max shook his head. "Don't be. You did right. But now I must go away, because… because I love her, and she hates me, and as much as I know I deserve everything I get. I can’t bear that, Burt. I can’t bear to see her, to see the loathing and contempt for me in her eyes. So, I’m leaving.”

Chapter 17

Your Grace,

I hope you will forgive me for writing to you out of the blue. The last time I laid eyes on you was not long after you married your lovely duchess. I hope she and your splendid family are all well.

As I believe you know, your uncle, Baron Fitzwalter, was a dear friend of myself and my husband and often came to stay with us in Scotland. I wrote to Charles every week until his death, which saddened me greatly. Over the years, he implied, perhaps with too much kindness, that you remembered me fondly, and would welcome me if I ever returned to town. Well, recently I have been reminded that I am not dead yet, and so I am doing just that, rather unexpectedly, and there will not be time enough for my staff to put my London house in order after decades of neglect. Might I presume upon you for a little while until such time as the house is habitable?

—Excerpt of a letter from Hester Henley, Lady Balderston (Great Aunt to Barnaby

Godwin) to His Grace, Robert Adolphus, The Duke of Bedwin.

19th June 1842, Covent Garden. Parish of St Giles.

Kathy sat on her bed, staring at the battered old top hat in her lap. Cat had called on her earlier, full of life and chatter. Thankfully, it had been a brief visit, for Kathy was all out of good cheer, but Cat said she'd bumped into Grace, who ordered her to bring Kathy the hat 'at once.'

"So I knew it was urgent," Cat had said with a grin. "And here it is. Shall you take a dare now?" she'd asked eagerly.

To the girl's disappointment, Kathy had shaken her head, but she'd promised to write and let her know what dare she got once she'd done it.

Setting the hat aside, Kathy moved to the window and looked out. Over in that direction was the school. The school Max was building. And over that way was the workhouse, the one he had visited with her and promised to improve because she had asked him to. She tried to reconcile this man with the one who had seduced Grace and refused to marry her, leaving her and her baby to an uncertain future.

She remembered seeing him in that dreadful room in the Dials with a festering knife wound and a fever that was going to kill him. But he'd not died. She'd prayed to God and done everything in her limited power to see that he lived, and he had. He *had.*

Why? Why had he treated Grace so badly? What kind of wicked man had he been? She got up and paced her room. Why had he said nothing when Grace had confronted him? She remembered the look on his face when he'd seen his daughter, the grief and devastation there. Did he really regret it, or had it just been a performance for her sake, another lie? Yet he had never lied to her. He had told her not to kiss him, though she'd known he wanted her to. He'd wanted her badly. But he'd told her no, told her he was not a good man, not good enough for her, and she had ignored him and kissed him anyway because she'd wanted to. And oh, it had been so sweet, so perfect, and she….

Anger ripped through Kathy. Was that what Grace had felt, too?

"Oh!" she wailed, sinking her hands into her hair and tugging as if she could pull it out by the roots. Kathy stalked up and down the confines of her room like a caged tiger until she could bear it no longer. What was she to do?

Grace had told her to stay away from Max, and Kathy had agreed, but….

Her gaze fell on the hat. The beaver skin covering was worn and patchy and, as she picked it up, the dares all rustled together. Kathy stared at them. Well, why not? Perhaps it would take her mind off Max. Doubtful, but she'd try anything. Kathy peered into the hat, wrinkling her nose. It smelt musty, a bit like mothballs and old books. Carefully, she reached in and took out a dare. The thin slip of paper crackled as she opened it, and she saw it was one of the original dares, old and yellowing now.

Go somewhere you are not supposed to go.

Kathy stared at it in awe, a shiver rolling down her spine. That had been her mother's dare. She must have put it back in the hat. Mama had gone to Papa's house alone, though she had known it might end in her ruin. Papa had been rude and difficult and rather unkind, but Mama had believed in him. She had seen that he was a good man, a lonely man, who just needed to be loved, and so she had risked everything, and done just that.

"Oh," Kathy said, wondering if this was fate telling her to give Max another chance, or just her own foolish heart wanting to believe it.

There was one man who might know more about him, who might give her some insight into who Max really was, and she was going to see him. And it was definitely somewhere she was not supposed to go.

"Thank you, Burt. You've relieved my mind."

Burt shook his head, bewildered. "You're setting us up in a fancy new house with a garden and you're thankin' *me*? Touched in the upper works, that's your problem."

Max smiled. "No. I'm being selfish. It took me a long time to realise it, but you taught me we find the greatest happiness in making others happy. So, I'm doing it for me, really. And think of all the people you can help with a big comfortable place like that. You can fill all the bedrooms with the people who really need you, and there will be a kitchen and a cook, so you can feed them all up. You'll make it a wonderful, safe place to be, and when you retire, Pike will take it over and it will be his place."

Burt's eyes glittered, and he sniffed, shaking his head. "You're a good man, Maxwell Drake. Do you hear me? Because it's about time someone told you. You might have been a villain once, but that's done now. You're a good man, and I'm proud of you."

Maxwell swallowed hard. That was the first time Burt had called him by his real name, not Valentine. And those words, coming from him, eased the pain in his heart, just a little.

"Goodbye, Burt."

"Bye, lad. And don't forget, it's not just other people that need kindness. You be kind to yourself, eh?"

Max smiled and nodded, raising his hand in farewell before he turned and walked away, out into the melee of filth and vice that was the Seven Dials. Though Burt's words rang in his ears, bringing him a little comfort, he could not rid his mind of the way Kathy had looked in the last moments before she'd left his home, as if he had taken all the joy from her and shattered her dreams. His guts clenched, but he forced himself to look up and take stock of his surroundings. He'd learned his lesson about this place, and you never let down your guard. Pausing, he stopped, listening intently as the hairs on the back of his neck stood on end. The road was narrow, dingy, and disgusting, and no different from most roads in this part of London. It was not the alley he'd been attacked in, but suddenly it felt the same, or perhaps it was him who felt the same as a prickling sense of alarm skittered down his spine. Shaking it off, he turned and hurried on.

"Miss Kathy!" Burt exclaimed in horror. "Tell me your brother is with you?"

Kathleen shook her head and gestured to the side, towards two burly builders. She had borrowed them from the school building site with the promise of a large reward. They'd finished for the day in any case, so it wasn't as if she was delaying the build. "No. He'd murder me quicker than anyone in the Dials if he knew. But I'm not stupid. I know it's dangerous, so I brought Len and Paul with me."

The two men nodded at Burt, who sighed.

"Right, why don't you two have a pint in the Crown? I'll send my lad to fetch you when the lady is ready to leave."

The men nodded and ambled away, happy enough to comply with the instruction.

"Right, miss. You'd best come in and tell me what it is I can do for you, though I reckon I can guess."

Kathy stepped into the dark confines of Burt's home, turning back to him with a frown.

"You can?"

"Reckon so. Valentine—that is, Max—was here not long since. You've had a shock, eh?"

His intelligent gaze missed nothing. Kathy swallowed.

"Yes," she said, dismayed to hear her voice quaver. "Yes, I have. Do you know why, Burt?"

Burt nodded. "Happen I do. Come along, and I'll tell you what I know."

Sometime later, Kathy sat by the fire in Burt's kitchen, or the part of the main room that passed as a kitchen. He said they kept the fire going year-round, for the room was damp and cold even in summer. There was a healthy stack of fuel, courtesy of Max, and Burt had supplied her with a large mug of strong tea with a generous tot of brandy in it. She sipped the potent brew now, digesting what he'd told her, about Max, about Grace, and what had happened between them.

"He did a terrible thing. I ain't saying he didn't. He ruined that girl without a thought, but that's the thing, see? He didn't think. No one had ever taught him to think about others."

Kathy frowned, wondering if that was a good excuse.

"See that?"

She looked at Burt, who was holding out his hand to show her a deep scar on his thumb. "Is that—?"

"A bite? Aye, 'tis. Pike did that, little sod. First time I came across him he tried to rob me. I held him off and the little blighter bit me and kicked me in the shin. Wasn't none too pleased with that, I can tell ye."

"I should think not!" Kathy replied, appalled.

"But his da—miserable excuse for a man that he was—had taught him to do that, to rob and to fight, to lash out and to take what he wanted. When his father died and I got my hands on him, it took me an age to show him there was a better way."

Kathy nodded, impressed that Burt had persevered. "I see."

"Do ye? Because who was there to teach Max how to be kind, how to think of other people and not just take what he wanted?

Servants weren't people, they were no more to him than a piece of furniture, because that's what he'd been taught to think. All that money and the fine life he had, and yet he stayed here for months after he was stabbed. Did you know that? He didn't want to go back to his life because he was so damned unhappy. Imagine that, a rich, handsome young fellow wantin' to stay in the Dials because he's happier here!" Burt shook his head in wonder.

Kathy looked about her and could not understand it at all.

"Good people do bad things sometimes, and bad people can change, given the right circumstances. Max has changed. He's learned how to be kind, learned what's important and what ain't. He did a wicked thing, but the child and the mother are safe and happy. He's trying as hard as he can to be a good man, and I don't think he ought to be punished for the rest of his life for a mistake he made when he was little more than an ignorant boy himself."

"You don't?" Kathy asked, realising this was what she had wanted to hear. Someone else, besides herself, who wanted to forgive him when she could not trust her own judgement, because she was in love with him. Grace might never forgive her, she realised, but she would have to live with that and hope that one day she might understand.

"I don't, and that's a fact. He's in love with you, you know."

Kathy gasped, almost dropping the mug she held. "W-What?"

Burt laughed, shaking his head. "Ah, young people. You're all dicked in the nob. As if it ain't plain as a pikestaff."

"*Is* it?" she demanded, her heart suddenly beating madly in her chest.

"It is," Burt said, hauling himself to his feet. "And even if it weren't, he told me so. Right. I'll go fetch Pike and get him to bring those two big bruisers to escort you home, or perhaps… somewhere else, eh?"

He'd told him? He'd told Burt he loved her!

“Somewhere else,” Kathy agreed, breathless now. “Somewhere else I’m not supposed to go.”

Chapter 18

Dearest Ozzie,

I hope this letter finds you well. I know we shall see each other at the weekend but I did not think this could wait. Nic tells me he overheard gossip in the card room at last night's rout party. There is some speculation over your friendship with Lord Hargreaves, for it seems you have spent a deal of time in his company of late. I am so sorry, darling, to bring it to your attention but people will talk and make something out of nothing. I know he is a lovely man, but you must have a care for your reputation, and for his wife. She is the vindictive type, and I would not want her to cause you any distress. I am not suggesting you ignore your new friend, but perhaps try to give equal attention to all the other eager, unmarried men who would so dearly love to be the focus of your regard.

Your loving sister. E x.

—Excerpt of a letter from Lady Elizabeth Demarteau to her younger sister, Lady Rosamund Adolphus (daughters of their

Graces, Robert and Prunella Adolphus, The Duke and Duchess of Bedwin).

19th June 1842, Albany Gardens, Piccadilly, London

"Drat it, where is the thing?" Grace demanded as poor Betty wailed in misery. The staff were tearing apart her parent's town house for the sole purpose of finding her much beloved toy, the worn little rag doll she took everywhere with her.

"I reckon I've not seen it since you came back from visiting Mrs de Beauvoir," the nursemaid insisted, though she searched under the child's bed just in case.

"Oh, no." Grace's stomach dropped, finally having to accept the inevitable. Betty definitely had it in the carriage on the way to Vane Hall, unless…. "Have someone check the carriage," she ordered, though she already knew fate would not be that kind.

Fifteen minutes later, the nursemaid was back, with the unwelcome but not unexpected news that Betty's cloth dolly had not been seen anywhere. Not in the house, not in the garden, or in the carriage.

Grace swallowed a sigh, but she would not have Betty unhappy for any reason, and probably she would only need to speak to a footman or the butler at the door. Not *him*.

"Have the carriage readied for me," she asked the nursemaid. "I'm going out."

19th June 1842, Vane Hall, Chiswick, London.

Max arrived back at the Hall to discover a hive of activity as the staff readied the house for a long absence and his impending departure. He handed his hat and gloves into Jarvis' keeping and shrugged off his coat as he strode towards his office. As he walked, he noticed an odd little lump in a dark corner under the stairs.

Frowning, he walked to it and bent to pick it up. His heart turned over as he saw the frayed and faded doll. His daughter's. *No*. No, he must not think of her that way, for he'd lost the right to do so. She belonged to Grace and to Sterling Oak. Oak was her father, a good one too. A better one than him. A strong, honourable man who would do all in his power to see Beatrice was safe and happy, and that… that was a good thing.

Though he knew it was foolish, Max raised the doll to his nose and inhaled. A lump formed in his throat as the innocent scent brought his actions crashing down upon his head once more. He wasn't sorry, he reminded himself. They wouldn't have been happy together, he and Grace. They were not suited, but Kathy… Max, could have made her happy, could have made a life with her.

For a moment, he allowed himself the foolish and painful glimpse of a dream where Kathy was his wife and they had a family of their own, a daughter who would look at him and see something worthy of loving. But that was nonsense. He had rejected such a future with everything he'd done, and Kathy was lost to him. So he'd better get on with leaving London. Yet he couldn't breathe, and he needed to, needed to gulp down a lungful of clean air before he choked, so he could rid himself of the tightness in his chest. He hurried to the back of the house and out into the gardens, fighting to calm the rising misery that threatened to drag him under. His feet had taken him far from the house before he even realised he was still carrying the doll.

Damn. Beatrice would be distraught without it. He must give it to someone to return it discreetly to Grace's household. They could pretend they'd found it on the street outside her parents' house. That would do. Before he could turn back to the house, a voice hailed him.

"You're hard to kill, my lord."

Max froze, staring with shock at the intruder, who had emerged from behind a tree. He was a tall, wiry man, in his early forties, if he had to guess. A gentleman, going on the quality of his dress and his accent, though fallen on hard times, or perhaps too distraught to care about shaving or the fact his boots were scuffed and worn. There was fatigue in the man's expression, a determined glaze to his bloodshot eyes that did not bode well, though the knife in his hand was a rather more definite clue as to his intentions.

"It was you," Max said, discovering to his surprise that he was entirely calm, his overwhelming emotion only a deep curiosity, for he did not recognise the fellow at all.

The man shrugged, an almost apologetic gesture. "It was, and I made a mess of it. I was certain I had struck true, but that's life. The best laid plans of mice and men, et cetera, but I shall do the thing properly this time," he said, his voice pleasant, conversational.

Well, wasn't this nice? Two gentlemen having a little chat in the garden.

"Why?" Max asked, eyeing the knife. The scar on his side throbbed with remembered pain. He wasn't certain he cared so much about dying, not now, but he did not much relish the idea of enduring such agony again, and certainly not another damned fever. If he was going to die, he too hoped the fool would do it properly this time.

"*Why*?" The fellow laughed, shaking his head. "Because you took my life, my lord. You tupped my wife and turned her head until she didn't want me anymore. She got a taste for the high life and is some duke's plaything now. But you did that. You took a good girl and spoiled her, because you could, because that's what men like you do."

Max felt revulsion churn in his stomach. *Had* he done that?

"Who?" he asked, his heart thudding as he moved away, one slow step at a time. The man with the knife smiled and advanced, eating up the distance between them.

"Mrs Linda Franklin," he said, moving faster now, his determination to destroy Max a fanatical gleam in his eyes. "My wife."

Max thought fast, turning the name around in his mind.

"Don't remember, my lord? Must be difficult, what with all the wives and whores that have passed through your bed, eh? Let me help you. Linda is a pretty, plump little redhead, nice tits. Does that narrow the count a little?"

His mind was racing so hard it took Max a moment to realise. A redhead? No, wait. "It wasn't me," he said in relief. Redheads were Kilbane's weakness, not his. "It wasn't me."

"Oh, of course not. It was another fellow, I'm sure," Mr Franklin sneered. "Who would that be?"

Well, he could hardly set a madman on Kilbane and besides, he didn't think it much mattered to this man now. If he remembered rightly, Linda Franklin had offered her charms to half the damned *ton* with enthusiasm, and he very much doubted Kilbane had been the first. He certainly would not have needed to do much seducing, but Max did not think it was politic to mention that to the man with the knife.

"Don't lie to me. I know it was you, the Frenchman told me so. He saw you together."

The Frenchman? *Louis?*

"The comte saw us?" he asked in confusion.

Franklin snorted in disgust. "Not that pretty creature, no. He's not the only Frenchman in London you know, though you'd think it, the way people carry on over him. No, this Frenchman is grotesque. Burnt in a fire, I reckon, though even he seems obsessed with that handsome devil. Always wanting news of him." He shook his head, waving the knife in a dismissive gesture. "Never mind that. I'm not supposed to speak of him."

Max frowned, trying to puzzle out who he meant. What other Frenchman did he mean, and why was he obsessed with Louis César? And what the hell did this madman think this had to do with Max, anyway?

Belatedly, Max realised he was still carrying the doll and set it carefully down on the grass, moving away from it. This was going to get messy, and he'd not have the child's most precious possession damaged in the struggle.

The two men circled each other, Max finding he was strangely calm, a fatalistic sense of peace steeling over him. He did not intend to die today if he could help it, but if he did, ah, well….

From over his shoulder, Max heard shouts and the crash of doors slamming open as his staff noticed what was happening. He did not dare turn to look, but he heard people running, shouts of appalled concern. Mr Franklin stilled, his eyes growing wide.

"Damnation," he muttered, taking a step backwards. He glared at Max in fury. "This isn't over," he warned him, pointing the knife at him before turning to run.

Max followed, taking to his heels as the man ran flat out around the side of the house. Christ, he was fast, he'd give him that. The fellow hurtled through a gate and into the kitchen garden, knocking over a wheelbarrow and running heedlessly through neat rows of carrots and lettuce as a gardener bellowed with fury. Franklin didn't heed the shouting any more than Max did, following the madman's erratic path as he smashed into a trellis of sweet peas and brought the whole thing crashing down before stumbling to his feet again. Max lunged for him, but the bastard was light on his feet and took off, out of the gate that led onto the path to Vane Hall's grand entrance.

Franklin ran straight past the front of the house, heading towards the driveway on the far side, and skidded to a halt, deliberating as he regarded the waiting carriage he'd run past, and yet another coming up the drive, followed swiftly by a man on horseback. Max did not have time to wonder where all these people had come from, only to see the swift calculation in Franklin's eyes as he realised Max was too far away, and his staff were crowding behind him and fanning out across the entrance until his path to freedom was cut off. He was trapped, his plan to hurt Max beyond his reach. Then Max saw Grace hurrying down the front steps to the waiting carriage. She was between them, oblivious to the danger she was in. He saw the moment Franklin decided, believing Grace was important to him. Max had taken his woman, so—

"*No*!" Max shouted.

Both men moved, and it seemed to Max as if he were wading through a thick swamp. Though his chest heaved, and his heart felt it would explode with effort, he would be too slow, too late. He forced his body harder, faster, muscles straining. He had hurt Grace enough already, and he would not allow Beatrice to lose her mother. He caught Grace around the waist, turning her away from Franklin and taking her to the ground, covering her body with his own. He glanced back, seeing the man with the knife raised, coming for him, and braced for the sensation of that deadly, steel sinking into his exposed back. The sting of the blade was sharp, piercing through the silk of his waistcoat and the fine linen of his shirt to his flesh, and then Franklin jerked back, and another man was there, pulling him away. Franklin staggered, and the knife flashed, the man cursed, and Grace screamed.

"Sterling!"

Christ! *Her husband.*

Then everything happened in a blur, people everywhere, Grace struggling to get up, but where was Franklin?

"After him!"

Men's cries, the sharp sound of feet running over gravel as his staff chased Franklin as he tried to make his escape.

"Grace! Grace, are you hurt?" Her husband reached for her, blood trickling from a thin wound on his forearm.

Max winced, removing himself from Grace to allow her to get up. His back was throbbing, a trail of sticky warmth moving down to his waist.

"Max!"

He wasn't certain who called his name and tried to stand, but slipped on the gravel. A strong hand appeared before his face. The calloused hand of a working man. Max looked up, astonished to see the hard face of Grace's husband staring at him, his dark eyes intent. He grasped the man's hand and stood as pain speared his back, and then nearly fell on his arse again as Kathy barrelled into him, throwing her arms about him.

"Max, Max! Are you hurt? Oh, God. When I saw that man with the knife, he…." She paled and let go of him abruptly, stepping away and staring at her hand with horror. It was covered in blood.

She looked up at him, her beautiful eyes wide with terror.

"Just a scratch," Max said faintly, and decided he'd sit down again after all as his knees gave out. Grace and Sterling were staring at him still, Grace clinging to her husband's arm. Max swallowed uncomfortably and then realised why Grace had come. "Oh, you came for the doll. I left it in the garden. I was going to send someone back with it but my, er… *guest* detained me."

He laughed at that and all three of them stared. Well, it had been an eventful day, and he was feeling a little odd.

"Fetch a doctor!" Kathy screamed, falling to her knees beside him.

"Grace came to get Kathy earlier," Max said to her husband, not wanting him to have any doubts, though he realised that was stupid. This man trusted his wife, and with good reason. She'd not go near Max again if he were the last man on earth, and Sterling Oak knew it. "Rescued her," he added with a wry smile.

"Max, hush," Kathy said, sounding a bit exasperated with him.

So Max sat still as Kathy undid his waistcoat buttons, tugging it out of the way, and bit back a curse as she pulled at his shirt to inspect the wound.

"It's not deep, but you're bleeding like a stuck pig. We need to get you inside. Mr Oak…?"

She looked beseechingly at Grace's husband, who nodded and moved forward, bending down and hooking a muscular arm beneath Max's before he could protest.

It suffused him with mortification that *this* man, of all men, should stoop to help him when he ought to have been the one wielding the bloody knife. It was too much. "Really, Mr Oak, I can manage. I am most grateful, but—"

"You saved her life. That madman was going to kill her, and you put yourself in his way," Oak said gruffly.

"Yes, but… but it was my fault. He wanted to hurt me."

"Shut up," Oak snapped.

"Right. Will do," Max said, chastened. He glanced at Kathy, still bewildered why she was there. Grace had come for the doll, Mr Oak… he didn't know, perhaps he'd found out and come after her, but Kathy? Kathy hated him. Except she was crying and watching him with such worry. He did not know what to make of it. "Where's Franklin?" he demanded, craning his head around to look for him.

"He got away," Oak muttered. "Your people went after him."

"Warn Kilbane," Max said. His head was thudding dully now, and he was shaking, though he couldn't fathom why.

"The marquess?" Oak asked, frowning at him.

Max nodded. "Mr Franklin—that was Mr Franklin with the knife, by the way—had come to finish his handiwork, as he was the one who tried to kill me a few years ago. He thinks I—" He glanced at Kathy and sighed. Well, she could hardly think worse of him. "He thinks I had, er, relations with his wife. I didn't," he added hastily.

"But Kilbane did?" Oak guessed.

Max nodded. "Yes, so Kilbane had best know about him. Just in case he figures it out."

Mr Oak nodded. "Now shut up. You look like you're going to puke and, if you do it on me, I'll drop you and that's a promise."

Max swallowed, unable to argue the point, and held his tongue.

Chapter 19

Dearest Eliza,

I thank you kindly for your concern, but I shall not let gossips and tittle-tattle dictate who I may or may not be friends with. I promise you I shall behave with the utmost decorum, and no one will be able to reproach me for my behaviour, but Lord Hargreaves has been treated monstrously, and he needs a friend. I intend to stay right where I am.

Your loving sister. R x.

—Excerpt of a letter from Lady Rosamund Adolphus to her elder sister, Lady Elizabeth Demarteau (daughters of their Graces, Robert and Prunella Adolphus, The Duke and Duchess of Bedwin).

19th June 1842, Vane Hall, Chiswick, London.

Much to her disquiet, Kathy heard the news that the murderous Mr Franklin had got away, but Jarvis had arranged for the biggest, burliest footmen to stand guard at all entrances to the house, and said he would discuss a formal security arrangement with the earl at his first opportunity. For now, she had to be content with that and hope they apprehended the villain quickly. No one could persuade her to sit down and drink a cup of tea until after the doctor had seen Max. He stood before her now and pronounced it to be a shallow wound. His ribs had deflected the knife from inflicting any serious damage and Kathy knew he'd been incredibly lucky that Stirling had acted as fast as he had. Max was a little tired and sore, but providing they could stave off infection, he should recover quickly and with no long-lasting effects.

Kathy stared at the doctor and burst into tears.

"Oh, love," Grace said, hurrying to her and hugging her tight as Mr Oak showed the man out. "Come now, you heard the doctor. He's going to be fine. His staff will take good care of him. It's time for us to go now."

"No," she said stubbornly. "No. I'm not leaving him."

"Kathy." Grace took both her hands in her own, her lovely eyes grave and full of compassion. "I know you care for him, but you can't trust him, he's not—"

"No." Kathy withdrew her hands from Grace's and folded her arms. She took a deep breath. "I know you don't want to hear this, Grace, and I don't blame you. Not for a moment, but Max has changed. He did a terrible, terrible thing and treated you abominably. I know he did. But he's not that man anymore. I know he regrets it and wishes he could change it, but he can't and… and I'm in love with him. I'm sorry, Grace, but it's true and nothing you can say can change that. I'll understand if you don't want to see me again."

Kathy hugged her arms about herself and swallowed hard as more tears threatened. Grace stared at her, open-mouthed, took a deep breath, and Kathy knew she was going to try again.

"Kathleen," she said steadily, clearly holding onto her patience by a thread.

"Grace." A large hand rested on Grace's slender shoulder, and she turned to look up at her husband. "She doesn't want to listen to you. She's made up her mind, and though it pains me to admit it,

Vane was ready to die for you, love. I still despise the bastard and he'd better not come within fifty miles of you or Betty, but I think perhaps he's earned a second chance. If Miss de Beauvoir wants to give him that chance, that's her affair. Not ours."

"But, Sterling," she said, staring up at him and shaking her head.

He cupped her cheek and Kathy felt her heart ache at the love she saw in his eyes for his wife. "It's not our business, little wren, and it was you that taught me that people sometimes deserve another chance, even when they've hurt us deeply."

Kathy did not know to what he referred, but his words seemed to resonate with Grace, who gave a jerky nod. "Very well," she said, turning back to Kathy. "Only—"

"I know," Kathy said, moving quickly to hug her friend. "I'll be careful, I promise."

Grace nodded and took her husband's arm, and Kathy walked them to the front door. "You ought not be here alone, though, Kathy," Grace warned, anxiety flashing in her eyes. "Your reputation will suffer if anyone finds out."

"I work here," Kathy reminded her, though she forbore to mention she had not brought her maid with her this time. "But I shan't stay long," she said, adding to her lie, though only to put her friend's mind at rest.

"Very well. Goodbye, Kathy." Grace kissed her cheek, accepted the rag doll Jarvis held out to her on a silver platter, and took her husband's arm as he escorted her out to her carriage.

Once they were gone, Kathy hurried up the stairs to the room they'd helped Max to earlier. She glanced about, hoping that if anyone was watching, Max's staff were discreet enough and liked her well enough not to gossip.

She turned the doorknob silently in case he was sleeping, and slipped noiselessly inside the room, closing the door with a soft click.

"Jarvis, do stop fussing like a mama hen. I'm only in bed because of you fretting over me. I'm perfectly well, so there's no need to keep checking on me every…."

Max's impatient voice trailed off as she stepped farther into the room.

"Kathy," he whispered, and then roused himself, sitting up with a sharp intake of breath. "Go away!" he told her firmly, pointing at the door.

"No," she said, smiling at him and walking closer. Lord, he was gorgeous. He sat in bed, with the covers to his waist, the bandage about his middle visible. Golden hair glinted on his bare chest and Kathy drank in the sight of him.

"Miss de Beauvoir, if anyone sees you here, you'll be ruined. Now turn yourself around and—"

"No," she said again, shaking her head.

"Dammit, Kathy!" he growled, trying to get out of bed.

She ran to him and put her hands on his bare shoulders, forcing him to stop. He went still at the touch of her hands and Kathy blushed but did not remove them. His skin was hot, not with fever, but simply with vitality, with the energy that seemed always to radiate from him.

"Do you love me, Max?"

His eyes widened at her question, staring up at her as if he did not quite believe she was real.

"Yes," he said, his voice hoarse. "Yes, I do. With all my heart."

Kathy let out a shaky breath and smiled, feeling happiness bubble through her, fizzing in her blood.

Max huffed out a bitter laugh and shook his head. “I’ve no idea why that pleases you so much. Even if you were mad enough to want me after everything you know now, your father and brother would finish the job Franklin began before they’d let you marry me.”

“Marry you, Max?” she said, her heart beating harder and faster until she felt lightheaded. “Was that a proposal?”

Without taking his eyes from hers, he took her hand from his shoulder and kissed her palm, then closed his eyes as he turned into her hand, and she stroked his cheek. “I’d marry you in a heartbeat, Kathy. But why on earth would you want me, after everything I’ve done?”

“Because you’re not the man you were, Max. You’ve worked to change your life, and I know you’ll keep working, to make things better for other people, and I want to help you with that, with helping them, with helping you. But mostly I want to marry you because I’m hopelessly in love with you, and I don’t think anyone else will do.”

She saw hope and joy and then misery flicker in his eyes in quick succession, and then he shook his head. “I thought you’d understood, when Grace came here, when little Beatrice came in….”

“She’s your daughter. Yes, I know.”

He gaped at her.

“T-Then why? How can you think to… Grace would never forgive you, and she’d likely shoot me. I can’t let you turn your back on your friends for me, Kathy, you’ll—”

Kathy pressed a finger to his lips to silence him.

“She knows how I feel, and she understands. Well,” she said, frowning slightly. “Perhaps *understands* is overstating things, but she accepts my decision. Grace is one of the gentlest, most loving and forgiving people I’ve ever known, Max. She won’t turn away from me. Though you must stay far away from them. Beatrice has your eyes. She looks like you, and even if Sterling would allow it, which he won't, you two must never be seen together."

"I would do nothing to put her at risk. Not ever," he said urgently, his expression grave and sincere.

"I know that," she whispered, stroking his cheek with the backs of her fingers. "Now then, Maxwell Drake, are you going to propose to me or not?"

Hope glittered in his eyes, but caution tempered it still. He didn't dare believe this was what she wanted, that she understood what she was doing. "I want to, but, Kathy, are you sure? Have you really thought about it?"

She grinned at that. "I'm sure that seeing you sitting in this bed with next to nothing on is giving me ideas that suggest we'd better marry as soon as possible, and I can think of little else."

"Christ, Kathy. Don't say such things," he groaned, shaking his head.

Kathy stroked his hair, finding it soft and warm, sliding through her fingers like silk as an unpleasant idea stirred unwillingly in her mind.

"I love you, Max, and I want to be with you, but if it's because of my-my blood, my background. I suppose I never really considered it mattering with you, because you never made me feel anything less than a lady, but that's stupid, isn't it?" Her heart trembled as she wondered if this was the reason for his hesitation and he just didn't want to hurt her. Why hadn't she realised? She'd been a fool not to consider it. A stupid fool. She pulled away from him. "You're an earl, and I was born in the workhouse, and—"

She gasped as he reached up and slid a hand behind her neck, pulling her down to claim her mouth. The kiss was sweet and infinitely tender, and then he released her.

"I don't give a damn about any of that, Kathy. I cannot imagine anyone else as generous and loving as you in the entire world. You're all I dream of, all I want. That you know the worst of me and can still find something worth loving and putting your trust in is a blessing I never expected. I will never take that for granted. I love your energy and your determination to change the world, I love that you make me see things differently, and I love you. I do. Kathleen de Beauvoir, I want you to be with me always."

"Then let me," she whispered, cupping his face in her hands. "I forgive you for the past, Max, but I shan't forgive you if you don't let me share your future."

He took a deep breath. "I'll never betray you, Kathy, I swear upon my life. I shall be a good husband—or at least I'll try my best—but whatever stupid mistakes I make, that will never be one of them. I'll be faithful. You need never doubt me."

"I didn't, and I won't doubt you. So, ask me, Max. For heaven's sake!" she exclaimed, laughing now.

He laughed too then, and it was a joyous sound, filled with wonder and delight. "Kathleen, my love, would you do this flawed, dreadful mess of a man the very great honour of becoming my wife?"

Kathy gave a little shriek and climbed onto his lap. "Yes, Max! Yes, please."

And she kissed him.

19th June 1842, Vane Hall, Chiswick, London.

Max hardly knew whether he was dreaming or if the warm weight of Kathleen's body against his could possibly be real. It felt real, her soft mouth pressed against his so astonishing his entire body came alive with happiness, with longing for her.

"Kathy, stop," he said, breaking the kiss with a gasp. "We must see your parents. I must ask your father's permission. Do you think he'll allow it?"

The terror that he might get this close to the miracle of marrying the woman he loved, only to have her parents refuse him, was like feeling the knife sinking into him again… except this time his heart was the target.

"I don't think he'll be thrilled. Not at first, but he'll allow it. Eventually," she added with a shrug.

"Eventually?" Max repeated, alarmed.

Kathy shifted on his lap, distracting him as her hip pressed against his burgeoning arousal. He was far too aware of the fact he wore only his small clothes beneath the sheet covering him, and his body was primed for bad behaviour. Which would *not* be happening, he reminded himself severely.

She sighed, pursing her lips, which did not help, as her lush mouth was crying out to be kissed. "We'll have some persuading to do, though I suspect Hart will be the biggest problem. He's very protective."

"As he ought to be," Max said, catching hold of Kathy's questing hand as it coasted down over his chest. "As I must be," he added firmly.

Kathy frowned. "Do you mean it, then? We *will* get married?"

"Of course I mean it!" he exclaimed, a little hurt that she would doubt him, though he could not blame her for it.

"Then stop being so silly," she said, looking triumphant. "I want to touch you. Your skin is so warm, and so silky, too. I hadn't realised that, but the hair here is all coarse and wiry. I want to explore." With her free hand, she trailed her fingers through the hair on his chest. Max shivered with pleasure but caught hold of that hand, too.

"No," he said, shaking his head, as much for his own benefit as hers. "I'm not doing this with you until our wedding night."

She smiled up at him. "Not even a kiss," she asked, eyes wide and beguiling. "It will be a very long engagement if you won't even kiss me."

"A special licence," he murmured. "I'll have one by the end of the week."

"Promise?" she asked him.

Max nodded. He wasn't about to wait any longer if he could help it. Though her father might have other ideas. That thought, he kept to himself. He shifted on the bed and winced as the movement tugged at the cut on his back.

"Oh!" Kathy jumped up, her expression mortified. "I'm such a selfish wretch. Does it hurt, Max? Come, lay back against the pillows. How awful of me! Did I make it worse?"

Max chuckled as she fussed about him, revelling in her attention as she arranged his pillows before he laid back and then tugged his covers into place. "No, love. You make everything better."

"Will it hurt you if I lay down with you?" she asked, such a hopeful glint in her eyes Max did not like to refuse her, but for his own sanity it seemed best.

"No, but I think it best you don't—"

She climbed onto the bed.

"Is this what married life will be like? With you ignoring my every command?" he said, mouth quirking.

Kathy snorted. "If you're thinking to command me, yes," she said frankly. "But if you want to discuss, debate, or negotiate, I'm quite biddable," she added with a disarming smile.

"Little liar," he murmured, staring at her in wonder. Surely, he could not be this fortunate after everything he'd done?

She sighed, staring down at him.

"Don't look at me like that," he pleaded, the desire to touch and kiss her an insistent ache beneath his skin. "You make me want to do wicked things."

"Show me what it's like to be just a little wicked, Max," she whispered. "Just a taste."

"No, Kathy," he said, fear slithering in his gut at the idea.

Kathy stared at him, considering. "Would you ever force yourself on me?" she asked, the question startling him so much he almost shouted his response.

"No! Damn it, Kathy, how could you think it? Even at my worst, I would never have done that. *Never*!"

"*I* didn't think it," she replied, apparently unphased by his outburst. "But if I persuaded you to make love to me, would you refuse to marry me afterwards?"

Max stared at her in horror, crushed that she could ask him such a thing after everything. Though why should she not doubt him? After all, he'd done it before. But had he really changed so little? Did she think he was that same vile creature?

"No!" he said again, unable to keep the distress from his voice.

"And do you want to kiss me?"

"More than anything," he growled, growing frustrated now.

"And so why can you not take me in your arms and kiss me, Max? I know you would never hurt me or treat me with such disregard. I trust you. Why don't you trust yourself?"

He only saw the trap once he'd walked into it and sighed, a raw place in his heart healing over as he realised she'd been making a point. "I just… I want to treat you with respect. As you ought to be treated."

“Then perhaps,” she whispered, leaning into him, careful to remain on his good side, away from the knife wound. “Perhaps you ought to respect my intelligence, and my own desires, as well as your own honour. That’s the greatest respect you could give me.”

Max stared at her in wonder. “I’m never going to deny you anything, am I?” he said with a sudden glimpse of their future.

“Doubtful,” she replied gravely, though her eyes twinkled with amusement, and then she pressed her mouth to his.

Oh, the devil take him, he was trying to be good, but he could not resist her, not when they both wanted the same thing, to be close to one another.

She leaned into him, and Max’s arms slid about her slender waist, holding her carefully as she kissed him. He let her lead the way, laying passively beneath her though every fibre of his being demanded he take control of the kiss, that he turn her onto her back and slide his hands under her skirts and… and this was for Kathy, so she would set the pace, she would decide what she wanted, and Max would oblige her, even if it killed him.

“Is this comfortable, Max? I’m not hurting you?” she asked earnestly.

“Fine,” he gritted out. She wasn’t hurting the wound on his back, which he’d frankly forgotten about, but his cock was throbbing uncomfortably, eager for attention. As if she’d read his mind, she hoisted her skirts up and clambered over him, straddling his lap. She sat then, her sex nestled against his hardness, and all the breath left him in a rush.

“Kathy,” he murmured, closing his eyes and savouring the feel of her.

“Am I dreadfully bold, Max? Are you shocked?” she asked, her voice quavering but laced with amusement.

"Dreadfully. Shocked to my bones." The words were strained as he gazed up at her, determined to endure this wonderful torture for as long as she wanted him to.

She laughed and shifted closer, and he bit back a groan.

"Your eyes have gone all dark," she said, watching him with interest. "You look like you want to eat me in one bite."

"Accurate," he said through his teeth.

"Help me, Max." She leaned in and nuzzled at his throat, pressing little kisses along his jawline. "Show me what to do."

Max swallowed. "Well, j-just for a moment. But then we are going to visit your parents and I will try to persuade them to allow us to marry. Because if they say no…." he said, trying to act upon some remaining shred of good sense and proper behaviour.

"They won't say no. Not when they realise you make me happy. Papa and Hart just might make you sweat a bit, that's all."

He was sweating now, but he refrained from mentioning that as she kissed him again. Oh, and she was getting the hang of this now, her tongue sliding against his, sleek and curious. Max's hands went to her waist, holding her there for a moment before dropping to her bottom. There were far too many layers of skirts and petticoats between him and that glorious part of her anatomy, but he pulled her closer and rocked his hips into her. She gasped, breaking the kiss to stare down at him.

"Oh," she said.

"Your eyes are very dark as well," he observed with delight.

"Well, I could eat you in one bite, too. I want to touch you everywhere, and I want you to touch me everywhere too," she said breathlessly and with such disarming candour, he could hardly breathe himself.

She ran her hands down his arms, squeezing his biceps, and oh, lord, she would be marvellous in bed, for she was clearly not the least bit shy, but honest and giving and… and please God, let him be able to talk her father around and stop her brother from cutting him into little pieces.

She put her mouth upon his again, kissing him feverishly as she pressed her hips closer, seeking her pleasure against him.

"Yes, love, like that," he murmured. "Use me however you need."

He tugged her skirts up out of the way to allow her closer and she gasped, her eyes closing when she discovered only the cotton sheet and his small clothes kept them apart. Max could feel the heat of her, the place where he longed to be burning through the fine layers of cotton, and gritted his teeth. He would bloody well endure this, he would give her this, and then he'd go directly to speak to her father.

"Max." She said his name dreamily, her gaze heavy lidded now. "Max, please."

He hesitated, not wanting to misbehave, but wanting to give her pleasure, what she so obviously needed from him.

"*Please*," she said again.

Max slid his hands under her skirts, sliding up her thighs as she shivered under his touch. Gently he cupped her sex, desire lancing through him as he found her soft curls damp, the wet heat of her blazing against his palm.

She dropped her forehead to his, whispering his name.

"More?" he asked, his voice hoarse.

Kathy nodded, and so he slid a finger carefully through the curls, seeking the little nub of flesh that would bring her release.

"You are so lovely, so sweet. I don't deserve this," he said, awed by her trust in him.

"Oh!" Her head fell back as she moved against his hand and Max swallowed, unable to take his eyes off her.

"More?" His voice was cracked and unsteady now, rough with desire, and he did not know how he would stop himself from coming. For a man who had been jaded and dissipated by his twenty-first birthday, it was astonishing to realise, but the sight of her taking her pleasure was the most erotic thing he'd ever seen.

"Yes. Oh, yes," she whimpered and then cried out as he slid a finger into the fierce heat of her.

Oh, God. He wanted to be there, wanted to slide his aching cock inside and lose himself in her. *Married*, he reminded himself. When she was his wife, and not before, then he would have the rest of his life to show her how good this could be between them.

"Max," she said, his name a plea as she writhed against his hand, pressing against the heel of his palm as he slid another finger inside her. Max moaned as he felt her muscles tighten around him, felt her shudder as the climax overtook her and she clutched at his shoulders, holding on as she trembled and cried out. He caressed her, gentling his touch as the final ripples of pleasure subsided, not wanting to stop.

She stared down at him, her eyes hazy and sated. "That… That was lovely," she said with a sigh.

"*You* are lovely," Max replied, smiling up at her, his heart bursting with adoration and gratitude.

She slumped against him, and he sucked in a sharp breath as his neglected cock leapt with anticipation.

"Oh," she said, sitting up again, eyes wide. "Oh, Max. I'm sorry. Should I—"

"*No*!" he exclaimed, panicked.

He gave her a little push, tumbling her off him and onto the mattress. She squealed as he flung the covers aside and got out of bed, the pain lancing from the wound in his back taking the edge off his arousal, which was something.

Kathy giggled, and he glanced back at to see her amused expression. "Poor Max. I am a terrible trial to you."

He grinned at her. "The best kind of trial, and everything I want," he promised, before hurrying into his dressing room, calling over his shoulder as he went. "But we need to get married. At *once.* I must speak to your father."

"Today? Are you well enough, Max?"

He snorted as he tugged the bell for his valet. "Right now. This instant," Max replied, trying to ignore the fact his body was screaming at him for being an idiot. "Once we have your parents' blessing, things will be different, but I cannot carry on so when they don't even know we have feelings for each other. Now you'd best get yourself downstairs before all the staff know what we've been up to. I don't want any gossip about you."

"Yes, Max," she replied sweetly, and he smiled as he heard the teasing note in her voice before she let herself out of his room and did as he asked.

Chapter 20

Darling,

I will be with you again soon. I have missed you so much.

I am happy the children have had such a wonderful time. Morven's sons seem fine young men and I am pleased Evie seems taken with Muir. I pray something comes from it. Do you think her attachment is strong enough to make her forget the comte? I had feared there was no hope, for she has been so listless of late, but your last letter relieves my mind that I did the right thing.

Helena, I know you think me too hard, but I cannot think of my darling girl married to such a man. Perhaps that makes me the worst kind of hypocrite but even my past was nothing compared to what I have discovered. I know not all rumours ought to be believed, but I already knew his past was complicated, to say the least. He has been a thief, a circus performer, and owns the most notorious club in Paris, this alone ought to be enough to colour my opinion of such a match for our innocent girl. To discover just how murky the waters are is of grave concern. He is dangerous, my love, far more so than his brother. I do not believe he would ever hurt Evie, but he will draw her into his world and that I cannot allow. We must keep them apart. I would do anything to save her from hurt, but this friendship ought never to have been allowed. It is inappropriate and if the man himself cannot see it, that alone must prove he is not a suitable companion for her.

—Excerpt of a letter from Mr Gabriel Knight to his wife, Lady Helena Knight.

19th June 1842, Church Street, Isleworth, London.

It was almost dinnertime when they arrived at Kathy's parents' house. Max dithered on the doorstep, glancing at her with such obvious anxiety Kathy took his hand.

"All will be well, Max. We'll make them see."

He turned away from the front door, taking her a few steps from it and shaking his head. "What about Grace and Beatrice? I can't tell them myself, for that would be a betrayal when I have sworn to never tell a soul. But your father and Grace's father are close friends. Few people know the baby isn't Sterling's, but her parents do, and she looks like me. What if they guess? I don't want to cause them any more upset."

Kathy squeezed his hand tighter, unable to pretend that wasn't a possibility. "Then we shall face that when it happens. Max, I love you. Let us take it one day at a time, and this is the first step."

He took a deep breath and nodded, and walked up to the front door, giving a sharp rap.

Kathy's heart sank as the door opened, and instead of the housekeeper or a maid, her brother loomed over them. His expression darkened as he stared at Max.

"What the hell is he doing here?" he demanded of Kathy, and then noted the fact they were holding hands. His furious gaze swerved back to Max. "Vane. If you've laid a finger on her, so help me—"

Impatient now, Kathy marched up to her brother and shoved at his chest. "Do get out of the way, Hart, and stop snarling. I know you're trying to protect me but it's terribly tiresome and we need to speak to Mama and Papa."

Shoving at Hart was akin to shoving a brick wall. He'd not budge if he didn't want to, and he didn't want to.

"Hart!" Kathy said, glaring at him. "We're getting married and Max needs to speak to Papa."

"Like hell you are," Hart growled, moving now but only to step between them as if Kathy needed protection from Max, which might have been touching if her brother wasn't such a great, overbearing lummox.

"Hartley, what is going on here?"

Everyone looked around as their mother descended the stairs. She was still a beautiful woman, slender and elegant, and, Kathy hoped, the voice of reason.

"Oh, Mama, do stop Hart from being a brute. Lord Vane has come to speak to you and Papa, and Hart won't let him in."

"Because he's a damned libertine, and he's no business asking you to marry him," Hart said angrily. "And I don't need to speak to our parents to know that's the truth. Father will only say the same thing, I'm just saving him the trouble."

Mama's eyes flashed with interest as she stared between Kathy and Max, and then at Hart. Much to Kathy's relief, she took Hart's arm, patting it gently. "Hart. I appreciate your protective nature as always, but I think we owe Lord Vane the courtesy of listening to him if he wishes to propose to our daughter."

"Ma, you don't understand. He's—"

"A very bad man," Mama said with a wry smile. "Yes, I'm not a complete nincompoop and I do occasionally read the scandal sheets. Now run along and ask Mrs Jones if she would delay dinner, please."

Kathy smirked at her brother, who only glowered and stalked off, muttering under his breath.

"Well, my lord," Mama said, regarding him with interest. "You have set the cat among the pigeons, and we've not even got to Mr de Beauvoir yet. Come along then and let us see what you're made of."

"Thank you, Mrs de Beauvoir. I appreciate the opportunity to make my case."

"You're not on trial," Kathy said, trying to soothe him as she took his arm and escorted him to Papa's study."

"Oh, I think you'll find I am," Max murmured, giving her a small smile as her mother led the way.

"Inigo, we have visitors," Mama announced, holding the door open for them to enter her father's study.

"Who the devil is calling at this hour?" Papa grumbled, getting up from behind his desk and growing still as he saw Kathy escort Max inside. Papa had not been pleased by her work with Lord Vane and only Mama's insistence that Kathy was intelligent enough to manage such a position without getting into trouble had persuaded him to allow it. His current expression suggested he regretted that decision. They walked in and Mama was just about to close the door when Hart reappeared.

"I want to hear what the arrogant bastard has to say," he growled, barging in.

"Language, Hartley!" Mama scolded him, giving him a look he'd do well not to ignore.

Hartley huffed, glaring at Max. "Sorry, Ma, but he's not good enough for Kathy."

"I know that," Max replied before anyone else could speak. "You'll have no argument from me on that point. And I know everything you think of me is true, or at least it was."

"Good enough?" Papa demanded. "Good enough for what?"

"We want to get married, Papa," Kathy said, the words breathless as her father stared at her. "And he *is* good enough."

"The man himself says otherwise. So why should we waste our time listening to him?" Papa asked, walking around from behind his desk to stand in front of Max. He was a tall man and an imposing one, with fierce features and a penetrating gaze that skewered Max immediately.

"Because I'm in love with your daughter, and though I cannot comprehend why she should any more than you can, she loves me too."

Hart made a sound of disgust and folded his arms, but kept his mouth shut thanks to a warning glance from their mother.

Papa looked at Kathy and she nodded, holding Max's arm tighter. "It's true, Papa, and before Hart makes any vile insinuations, Max has been nothing but a perfect gentleman. If not for my insistence, he would have left town by now to take himself away from temptation."

"If not for the fact someone tried to kill him. *Again*," Hart retorted. "It makes one wonder what kind of fellow he is, doesn't it? When people want to go around killing him."

Well, the gossip mills had run at their usual speed, it seemed. Papa looked from Hart to Max and raised one eyebrow. Max cleared his throat.

"I was visited by a Mr Franklin this morning, that is true. He was the man who stabbed me some years ago. It seems he decided to give it another go."

"Why?" Mama asked, concern mingling with curiosity in her gaze.

Max took a breath. "He believed I'd had an affair with his wife. I didn't, though I doubt that makes much difference to you, for there are stories enough about my past affairs. This one, however, seems to be a case of misunderstanding."

"Franklin," Papa mused, meeting Mama's eyes.

"Oh! Linda Franklin," Mama said at once. "*Oh*."

"You know her?" Kathy asked in surprise.

Papa snorted. "Not exactly, but she…."

"She made overtures to your father," Mama said, eyes flashing with annoyance. "I believe she is rather free with her affections. It seems you were unfortunate to be singled out, my lord. I wonder why he chose to target you?"

"Because I was among the worst of the fast set she ran with," Max said with a shrug. "It was a reasonable conclusion to draw that I had persuaded her to join us. Though it seems someone else gave him the idea."

"Surely, Kilbane would have been the obvious choice?" Hart said grudgingly.

Max nodded. "Yes, that's true, but only a madman would go after Kilbane, though I grant you the man I saw today did not seem entirely in his right mind."

There was a brief silence while everyone considered this.

"In the past few years you have become a model of good behaviour, though, Lord Vane," Mama said, turning the conversation in the direction Kathy preferred it to go, and she sent her mother a grateful smile.

"I am trying my best, Mrs de Beauvoir. It may seem an odd thing to say, but I owe Mr Franklin a great debt. There is little as motivating as staring death in the face to make you take a hard look at yourself and the legacy you will leave behind. I made a promise to God that if he gave me another chance at life, I would do better."

"So you're giving your money to charity," Hart said with a dismissive shrug. "Half of the *ton* does that and then carries on with their depraved lives with no pangs of conscience. Why should you be any different?"

"Hart!" Kathy said, the temptation to hit her brother like she would have done when she was eight years old growing harder to ignore.

"No, love," Max said, earning himself a sharp look from Papa at the endearment. "I mean, Miss de Beauvoir. It's a fair question. I think, or at least I *hope* I am different, because I have learned how to see from another's perspective. I spent some time with the man who saved my life after I was stabbed, living and working as he did in the Seven Dials. In part because my memory was shattered, but even after that, because I was too ashamed to return to my own life. I learned a great deal during those months. Burt Clump taught me it costs nothing to be kind, and that generosity—not just financial generosity, but a generosity of spirit—gives a man peace. I have tried drinking and losing myself in debauchery to quiet my demons, and nothing ever worked. But this does, and I don't mean to go back. I'm happy for the first time in my life, and Miss de Beauvoir has played an enormous part in finding that happiness."

He turned to smile at Kathy and her heart turned over at the adoration she saw in his eyes. She thought Mama had seen it too, for Kathy heard her give a wistful sigh.

"That's all well and good, Vane," Papa said, bringing them back down to earth with a bump. "But you're a nobleman. An earl, no less. Kathy is worth ten times any woman you care to mention among the *ton*, but the rest of your kind won't see it that way, because she was born in the workhouse. People can be cruel, as you know. Would you really submit her to that, all the sly comments and the snubs?"

Max frowned and Kathy felt a tremor of unease as he turned to look at her. "Your father makes a valid point, love. I've no particular desire to socialise on a grand scale, but the position comes with certain responsibilities and some things are inescapable. Would you be happy, do you think? I would protect you as far as I can, that goes without saying, but women can be cruel to each other too, and I won't be able to stop them."

Kathy snorted, rolling her eyes. "Everyone knows my background and I've survived this long. The season is akin to swimming in shark-infested waters. I'm no shrinking violet and, if I can manage a lot of unruly builders, I think a few catty comments will not bring me to my knees. Besides, I'll be the Countess of Vane, and if they're too horrid I shall be a terrible snob myself and remind them of that fact."

She put her nose in the air and adopted a snooty expression with the express intention of making him laugh, for he looked so worried and serious.

It worked, and he grinned at her. "You are a marvel. I do believe you'll have the *ton* eating out of your hand in no time at all."

Papa grunted, exchanging a glance with Mama. "She would, I swear," he agreed, amusement in his voice.

"You're not thinking of agreeing to this nonsense?" Hart demanded, incensed.

Her father regarded her for a long moment and went to sit on the edge of his desk.

"Looking at this logically," he said. "If I do not agree, Kathy will make our lives hell on earth until we give in, or she runs out of patience and forces Vane to elope with her."

Kathy smothered a giggle as her father sent her a wry smile before turning to Mama.

"Minerva, my dear. You're the only one with any sense around here. What do you think?"

Mama looked back at Max. "You love her?"

Max nodded. "With all my heart. I won't let her down, or you, if you give me this chance. I cannot change my past. What is done I cannot undo, and I cannot promise that… that things will not emerge in the future that will make you think ill of me, but I promise you I will devote my future to your daughter's happiness, to being worthy of her. She makes me a better man, Mrs de Beauvoir."

Mama smiled, and Kathy felt the tension in her shoulders ease.

Max looked a little uneasy as her mother stood close to him, forcing him to meet her eyes as she studied him closely. "He reminds me of you, Inigo," she said after a long moment. "He needs looking after."

Her father snorted. "That's it, Lord Vane, you're done for now. Once Minerva has decided you need looking after, there's no escape."

"Oh, Papa! Thank you, thank you!" Kathy cried and flung herself into her father's arms.

"I don't believe I gave my consent just yet, my love," Papa said gently.

"Oh, but—"

Papa silenced her by putting a finger to her lips.

"I think your mother and I would appreciate a few words in private with his lordship."

Kathy turned back to look at Max, who nodded, giving her a small smile. "Very well, then," she said reluctantly, before lowering her voice. "But don't be too hard on him, Papa. I'm not a fool and he isn't the spoilt boy he once was. Please give him a chance."

"And if I get it wrong, and my beloved daughter is married to a man that makes her unhappy?" he asked, his eyes implacable, though his words were kind.

"He won't," Kathy said, putting her heart and soul into the words, hoping he could hear the belief she had in Max.

"We shall see," Papa replied.

Kathy sighed and went to Max, squeezing his fingers in silent encouragement before heading to the door. "Come along, Hart," she said, gesturing for her brother to leave.

Max did not need him here stirring up trouble.

Hart folded his arms. "I'm staying," he said, planting himself in the middle of the room.

"No," Mama replied, taking his arm, and steering him to the door. "You are not."

"But, Ma—"

"No." Mama cut him off, gesturing for him to leave.

Kathy smirked at him as her brother stalked past her and out of the study.

Chapter 21

Bainbridge,

You are an interfering busybody and, if I did not know your intentions were kindly meant, I should call you out.

I would never offer such an insult to Lady Rosamund. My intentions are honourable and only that of a friend. She is the sweetest young woman I have ever met, and I would cut my throat before I did her harm. If I believe the gossip risks doing just that, I shall of course keep my distance, but the lady needs a guiding hand to navigate the cruel world of the ton and I wish to help her. She is too kind-hearted, too open, and I fear for her happiness. She has set her heart on marrying a man I am coming to believe will not suit her and I pray I might save her from making a mistake I understand all too well.

You may put your wife's mind at rest. I am not seeking to ruin the child and make her my mistress. I know you did not ask this in so many words, but cut line, my lord. That is what you meant. I am married, for better or for worse, and I assure you that is something I cannot easily forget.

—Excerpt of a letter from The Right Hon'ble Sebastian Fox, Lord Hargreaves, to The Most Hon'ble Lawrence Grenville, The Marquess of Bainbridge.

19th June 1842, Church Street, Isleworth, London.

An hour later and Max felt like a wet rag. Mr de Beauvoir had undertaken a cross-examination of everything from his financial position to his opinion of Kathy's desire to carry on working and how he would feel if she did not wish to work for her husband. He wanted to know how he would educate their children—especially any daughters — what provision would be made for Kathy's security in the event of Max's death, what his political affiliations were, and a dozen other pertinent questions. Mrs de Beauvoir had politely enquired what his opinion was of Mary Smith's 1832 women's suffrage petition. As it was something Max hadn't thought about at all, he'd had to think on his feet.

"I have not seen the petition, ma'am, but I do know your daughter, and I can tell you that I believe her to be my equal. I confess I have not considered the question in any depth, but I believe a woman like Kathy ought to exist in the eyes of the law, not just as the property of her father or husband." Max hesitated, uncertain of the atmosphere in the room. "Does that answer your question?" he asked, nervous now.

Mrs de Beauvoir turned to her husband and beamed at him. Max let out a breath of relief as Mr de Beauvoir sighed, apparently accepting the inevitable. Or so Max thought, until the next question made his blood run cold.

"You said things might emerge in the future that would make us think ill of you. I suspect you had something specific in mind. Am I correct?"

Max swallowed. Kathy had said her father was perceptive, and she had not exaggerated. He nodded, a hollow sensation opening in his gut.

"Don't you think it would be wiser to make a clean breast of it?" he asked, his intent gaze making Max feel like something loathsome that ought to crawl at his feet.

"I would," he replied, his voice unsteady. "But the information does not affect me alone. If it were only my reputation at stake, I would tell you, I swear, but I cannot. I can only tell you my behaviour, everything that happened because of my selfishness, makes me ashamed. I acted dishonourably, and for that I will spend my life atoning."

"You have a child," Mrs de Beauvoir whispered.

Shame washed over him in a wave of heat, and he struggled to meet their eyes. Humiliation was a sour taste in his mouth, and he could do nothing but give a taut nod.

Mr de Beauvoir's eyes darkened, and Max felt terror roll down his spine. He was about to get thrown out and he'd never see Kathy again.

"They are safe?" her father asked.

Max cleared his throat, forcing himself to answer. "The woman married a good man, a better man than I. He is a wonderful father. They are happy."

"Does Kathy know?" Mrs de Beauvoir asked, her expression unreadable.

Max nodded again. "Everything," he said unsteadily. "She knows everything. I would not have her hurt by discovering something she could not forgive me for when it was too late."

There was a long silence as they considered him.

"I cannot defend my past or make excuses. I was selfish. I understood nothing, valued nothing. I can only tell you I am no longer that man."

"Will you take a mistress?"

Max's eyes widened at the bald question, especially coming from Kathy's lovely mama, but this one he could answer with ease. "No. I could never betray her that way. If I make Kathy vows before God, I'll keep them. And, besides which, I cannot imagine ever wanting anyone else. I love her. I did not know what that meant until now. I did not realise I had never seen what it looked like, how it felt to stand in the light of it, until I met your daughter. I know I am not what you wanted for her and, if you refuse me, I will understand. But know this: I will love her alone until the day I die, and I shall always be grateful for having known her."

"Oh, Inigo," Mrs de Beauvoir said with a sigh. "I believe him."

She turned to her husband, who was still looking deeply unhappy. Mr de Beauvoir got up and moved towards Max, who stood too, uncertain whether the man was going to break his nose or shake his hand.

"Listen to me, Lord Vane," he said, his voice dark and threatening.

"Max," Max croaked. "Call me Max."

"Hmph. Well, *Max,* if you ever give me cause to regret this decision, I will come for you. I'm a scientist, you know, and I can make a body disappear, bones and all. No one would ever know. You have a think about that."

"Oh, Inigo!" Mrs de Beauvoir bustled over and sent her husband a look of fond exasperation before turning to Max. "Welcome to the family, my dear. I only hope you don't live to regret the association."

Max gave a startled laugh, disbelieving. "I never shall, but… but you mean it? I have your blessing?"

"You do. *Doesn't* he, Inigo?" she said, elbowing her husband.

Mr de Beauvoir grunted, a noncommittal sound but one that Max was only too happy to take as acceptance.

"Thank you," he said, his heart thudding erratically in his chest. "I won't let you down."

"See that you don't," Mr de Beauvoir said gruffly, and held out his hand.

26th June 1842, Vane Hall, Chiswick, London.

They were married a week later at Vane Hall. It was to be a quiet affair, which they all agreed was for the best. Max had no close family he wished to invite, but the staff were all welcomed to attend the ceremony in the family chapel, and Max had ensured they would have their own celebration below stairs, too.

Stuck for a choice of best man, Max had taken a chance and gone to see Louis César. He'd only just returned from Scotland but had seemed touched by Max's request and had happily agreed. At this moment, Max was relieved he had. The Frenchman's calm presence was a balm to his jittery nerves as he stood waiting for his bride.

Mr Franklin had evaded capture, a fact which was disturbing, but Max had put security in place now, both for him and Kathy, to ensure the man would not get near them again. Now Franklin's words about another Frenchman being obsessed with Louis came back to him, and Max resolved to mention it to him… but not now. Today was for celebrating, for marking a new beginning in his life, one he did not deserve, but that he intended to do all in his power to come as close to deserving as possible.

"*Et la voici,*" Louis murmured, smiling at Max and gesturing to the aisle.

Max turned, his heart leaping into his throat as he saw the most beautiful sight he'd ever laid eyes on, dressed in ivory silk. His chest felt tight, pride and love and too many emotions fighting for predominance.

"I'm not worthy of this," he whispered, his voice rough. "I don't think I ever will be."

The Frenchman returned an understanding smile and shrugged. "*Mais non.* Of course not. None of us are, *mon ami*. But we must turn our backs on the past and do the best we can. And remember, those of us who have survived the worst of human nature, and the worst of ourselves, know just how fortunate we are. A better man may never appreciate the gift of such a woman as we can."

Max let out a breath, wondering who the woman was that Louis did not deserve.

"Yes. Thank you, Louis. You've eased my mind, and I wish you all the best too, whoever the lady is."

Louis inclined his head, accepting his good wishes. "*Merci,* my friend, and you are welcome."

Max's heart leapt as the little chapel fell silent, and Kathy took her father's arm and walked down the aisle.

Kathy stared at Max as he raised his hand to wave goodbye to her parents as their carriage pulled away from Vane Hall. Hart was with them, his distrust of Max obvious, though he had grudgingly accepted this was Kathy's decision to make and held his tongue. As a peace offering to her, he had provided her bouquet. White roses for purity, peonies for compassion and a happy marriage, and orange blossom for eternal love and faithfulness. Kathy had cried when she'd seen it and her brother had hugged her, enfolding her in his bearlike embrace.

"If he hurts you, I'll kill him," he said simply, before kissing the top of her head and walking away to join her mother in the chapel.

And now she stood beside her husband, on the steps of Vane Hall, as the last of their wedding guests finally left. They were alone. Well, apart from about fifty servants, but she supposed she would get used to that. Besides, they were all celebrating below stairs and the upper house was empty.

"Your father looked like he might burst with pride when he walked you down the aisle," Max said, sliding an arm about her waist as the carriage turned the corner and out of sight.

Kathy nodded. "I know. He's such a darling man. I could not have asked for a more wonderful father. And Mama," she sighed, smiling. "Mama is quite taken with you, I think."

"She's been so generous, welcoming me as she has. Even your father looked less like he wanted to murder me today."

"You've made me a countess. I'm wealthy, my future secure, and he thinks I'm more than capable of handling you," she added dryly.

Max gave a bark of laughter. "He said that?"

"He did." Kathy grinned, smug now.

"Well, he's not wrong," Max whispered, pulling her closer. He reached up to touch her hair, which had been simply arranged in a low chignon. "I've never seen your hair loose, Kathy. Is it very long?"

Kathy blushed, suddenly shy, which was ridiculous, as she had been dying from impatience for this day. "Why don't you come and find out?" she said, her voice unsteady.

Max bent his head and brushed his mouth against hers, a barely there kiss that still sent her blood surging in her veins. "You're not sorry?"

"I'll never be sorry," she replied, sliding her arms about him and holding on tight. His heartbeat thrummed in his chest, strong and even, reassuring. A moment later, she gasped as Max swung her up into his arms.

"Oh, Max, your back! You'll hurt yourself."

He sent her a look of mild reproach. "I'm not in my dotage yet, love." Kathy rolled her eyes. "I meant the knife wound. You'll make it bleed again."

Max shook his head. "That's healing well. Stop fretting. It's traditional to carry you over the threshold and I mean to do everything right in this marriage, beginning now."

"Everything?" she repeated sceptically.

Max nodded, his expression grave. "I shall be the perfect husband."

He carried her over the threshold and up the stairs. "I'm not certain I like the sound of that," Kathy grumbled, looping her arms about his neck.

"Whyever not?"

"Because if you're perfect we can't ever argue, and I enjoy arguing with you, and also we can never make up again, which seems a shame, and—"

"Good heavens, there's more?" he demanded, amusement glinting in his eyes. "And here I was thinking you'd be pleased."

"Oh no, and this is the most important point of all."

"Go on then."

Kathy lowered her head to whisper in his ear. "I am reliably informed that reformed rakes make the best husbands, and I want you to teach me to be wicked with you."

His eyes darkened, and he chuckled as he pushed open his bedroom door. "Well, I promised to never let you down, and if you *want* me to be wicked, I suppose I shall have to indulge you."

"You shall," she said, struggling to keep her expression serious as he lowered her gently to the floor. Kathy smiled, rediscovering the room she had seen once before. It was comfortably, if sparsely furnished.

He caught her curious glance about and shrugged. "When I returned after—well, after everything—I cleared out a lot of furniture and belongings. Reminders of the past. Through that door is your bedroom, and you must decorate it, and anywhere else, just as you please. Though, I confess, I hope you will spend your nights here, with me."

Kathy glanced at the enormous bed, mingled anticipation and nerves swirling in her belly.

"It's new," he said hastily, and rubbed the back of his neck, looking awkward. "The bed, I mean."

"Thank you," she said, realising he had not wanted them to begin their married life in a bed where he'd entertained so many other women.

Kathy moved about the room, inspecting the paintings on the walls, the books he'd left on his bedside table. She opened the book on the top of the pile and smiled as she saw a neatly folded sheaf of papers with her handwriting on. All the lists she'd given him, progress reports and orders to be made, tucked carefully into a book of love poetry.

She turned back to him. "You kept all my notes."

Max cleared his throat and nodded. "Er… yes. I did."

Oh, he was adorable. And nervous, she realised. She considered this, realising her virginal state and his past were conspiring to make him awkward. Somehow, the knowledge made her feel less anxious. Lifting her arms, she took the pins from her hair, allowing it to tumble free, over her shoulders, down past her waist.

"Oh." Max's breath caught, and he moved towards her. Bolder now, she flashed him a grin and then kicked off her shoes, gathering up her skirts and climbing onto the enormous bed.

"My, but it's huge," she said, flopping backwards so that her skirt and petticoats billowed about her. She sat up on her elbows and patted the space beside her.

Max removed his coat and waistcoat before he sat on the edge of the bed and pulled off his boots. Kathy watched as he slowly turned around, as if not to startle her, before lying down at her side. She stretched out beside him, so they lay facing each other.

"Good evening, Lord Vane," she said politely.

His lips quirked and he reached out toying with her hair, curling it about his fingers, his expression intent. "Good evening, Lady Vane," he said, his voice low and husky.

"Oh," she said, her eyebrows going up. "How strange, to be a lady, a countess, no less."

Max sat up, head resting on his elbow. "You've always been a lady, my love."

"Perhaps, but not officially," she replied, touching his mouth, tracing the shape of it until he growled and nipped at her finger.

Kathy laughed, a little breathless. "What now?" she asked.

Max sighed and trailed a finger along the neckline of her gown, raising goosebumps and making her shiver. "What should you like, do you think?"

She sent him an arch look. "For you to take control of this so I don't feel silly."

He smiled. "You could never be silly, my love. Why don't we start by taking off this lovely gown?"

"Yes, and it is lovely, isn't it?" she added, sitting up and then smoothing her hands over the figured silk.

"Not as lovely as you, not as silky as your skin," he murmured, sitting behind her and ducking his head to kiss her shoulder, the curve of her neck.

He made quick work of undoing the bodice, making her laugh as he got her to stand on the bed and disappeared into the mountain of silk as he pulled the gown off her. Layers of petticoats, her stays and chemise were all tossed aside to land in the pile of fabric by the bed until she lay back down in just her stockings. Max reached for the ribbon on a garter and tugged. It came free, and he gathered it in his hand, leaving one silky length of ribbon free. Kathy watched as he trailed it up the inside of her thigh, over the triangle of curls between her legs, and circled her navel with it. Her breath caught, and she laughed at the teasing, tickling sensation. Max watched her, his gaze intent, like a cat watching a mouse as his hand trailed the ribbon higher, tracing a line beneath the underside of her breasts and then circling the plump mound, the ribbon making tantalising ever decreasing circles around her nipple. A quickening sensation began at her core, the place between her thighs alive with anticipation, every fibre of her being straining for his attention.

"Max," she whispered, fidgeting beneath the titillating flutter of the ribbon. "Don't tease."

He lifted one eyebrow, his lips quirking. "But teasing is part of the fun, and you did request wickedness, did you not?"

"Yes, but," she said doubtfully. "But I want—" Colour flooded her cheeks, and she decided she was not quite as bold as she'd believed.

"What do you want?" he asked, his eyes very dark now. She gave a nervous laugh and shook her head. He grinned, lowering his head to hers. "Whisper it to me, if it's so very naughty."

Kathy squirmed, both inside and out, scolding herself for being silly and missish. "Touch me," she said, hoping that was enough of a command to get things moving.

"How?" he asked, all innocence, the rat. "And where?"

"How?"

"Yes, how? With my hands? My mouth? My tongue? Gently, firmly, impatiently? And where? Shall I suckle your breasts, put my mouth upon your quim?"

She gasped at that last and covered her face with her hands to hide the scald of her cheeks.

"Ah," he murmured, moving down the bed. "That shocked you. Intrigued you too, I think."

He leaned over her, nuzzling into the soft curls and pressing a kiss there. Anticipation and scandalised curiosity surged beneath her skin. Her mama had explained he would probably enjoy kissing her in places that she might not expect but somehow she had not considered that. Kathy peered through her hands to see him lift his head.

"Open your legs for me, little love."

She bit her lip, still too mortified to do as he asked.

"Hmmm, stubborn, eh?"

He bent his head again and licked along the crease of her sex, then slid his tongue inside. Kathy gasped and clutched at the bedcovers. She felt rather than saw the smile that curved over his mouth as he did it again, and again, provoking the most delicious sensations and a deliberate throbbing ache that seemed to pulse through her to her bones.

Max sat up, watching her with amusement. "Now will you do as I ask?" he enquired politely. "I promise you'll like it."

Kathy stalled, uncertain. She wanted him to do that again, but surely it was shameless to lie in such a pose. He seemed to read her uncertainty and laid a warm hand on her belly.

"You can't keep your dignity intact if we're to enjoy each other," he warned her, stroking her stomach, her hip and down her thigh with soothing caresses. "But you can trust me, as I trust you. There's nothing awkward or shameful or wrong, so long as we please each other."

She nodded, seeing only the tenderness in his expression, his desire to reassure her.

"But I am trusting you to be honest with me too, love. If you want me to stop, or if you don't like something, you must say so. I would be unhappy if you didn't tell me. Do you understand?"

"Yes," she said.

"Well then," he replied, sitting back and waiting.

Kathy took a deep breath and spread her legs for him. Max grew very still and expelled a long, shuddering breath, his expression one she could only describe as ravenous as he moved into the space she had made for him.

"So beautiful," he murmured, his voice gone deep and husky. "Every part of you is perfection."

He trailed his fingers along the tender skin at apex of her thigh before bending to follow the same line with his tongue.

"Especially here," he added, pushing her thighs wider and parting her with gentle fingers. "You're sweetest of all, here."

She swallowed a cry of pleasure as his mouth settled against her but the next escaped despite her best efforts as his tongue slid over her with a long, decadent lick.

He raised his head for a moment, eyes glinting wickedly. "Don't keep quiet on my account. I want to hear you scream for me."

"Oh, my wo—" she began, only to oblige him at once as he returned his mouth to her aching flesh and the words were lost in a moan.

In a matter of moments, it seemed to Kathy he had stripped away all layers of civilised behaviour and reduced her to some primitive state, where all she cared about was the gratification of her own desires. She writhed beneath him, canting her lips higher, demanding more, clutching at his hair to keep him where she wanted him, and giving him instructions.

"More, yes, yes, harder, don't stop."

Words she had never considered she could ever say in such circumstances poured from her and only seemed to please him more as he obeyed her every command without hesitation.

Sensation built and built until she could no longer fill her lungs but held her breath, suspended on some precipice, waiting, until he closed his mouth over her and suckled.

The cry that tore from her throat would likely shock her when she came back to her senses, but for now she was helpless, her body at the mercy of the waves of pleasure that flooded her, drowning her. Kathy could do nothing but let it happen, swept away on a surge of joy so profound she felt it must change the fabric of her soul.

She lay in a state of utter abandon, all shyness washed away, uncaring how wanton she must appear. Sighing, she tried to open her eyes, but she was boneless, intoxicated with the delicious feelings still rippling through her, the insistent throb of pleasure still pulsing in the place where his mouth had been. Though living in a daze, she became aware of movement and forced herself to focus, finding Max, stripping off his shirt and undoing the fall on his trousers with such urgency he'd likely rip the buttons off.

She grinned at him. “You’re in an awful hurry,” she remarked lazily.

He laughed, tugging his trousers off and kicking them aside with his small clothes. “Says the contented cat. Some of us are feeling a little less relaxed.”

Kathy watched, a strange possessive feeling stealing over her as she took in the sight of her husband. Oh, but he was splendid, his body hard and muscular. Her gaze travelled over him, resting on his arousal with interest.

“Not disappointed, I hope?” he asked with a wry smile as he knelt in front of her.

“Not a bit. So far, at least,” she added, feeling coquettish.

“Ah, I see how it is,” he murmured, prowling over her. “You’ll reserve judgement until the performance is over, is that right?”

He lent down and nipped at her ear, and she giggled. “Perhaps.”

“Well, in that case. I had better be sure I give you my best effort.”

He kissed her then and Kathy lost herself in the caress of his tongue, in the press of his hot flesh against hers. He lowered his weight onto her, carefully, and yet the shock of his arousal pressing against her sex made her gasp.

Max soothed her, stroking her face and kissing her deeper, his hand falling to her breast to squeeze and stroke, gently pinching her nipple. She arched up into his touch, amazed that her previous languor had vanished, and that desperate, demanding sensation was tugging at her again.

“Max,” she said, arching her hips against his, moaning as he slid his aroused flesh back and forth over hers until she thought she run mad. “Max!” she said again, a complaint this time, a demand for more.

"What love? Tell me," he whispered, lowering his head to her breast and suckling.

She made a sound of approval, sinking her hands into his hair as he nuzzled and licked, toying with the delicate flesh until she was dizzy, her blood fizzing in her veins.

"What do you want?" he asked again.

"You," she said urgently. "Please!"

"Where, where do you want me? I'll do anything you ask, my love, only tell me."

She murmured a rude word, and he chuckled. "Kathy, love, stop holding back. It's me, there's nothing you can say to shock me, I swear."

"Inside me! I want you inside me!" She almost shrieked the words at him, clutching at his shoulders.

"Thank God," he murmured, finding his place between her thighs. "Because that's just where I want to be."

Kathy held her breath as he nudged inside her, staring up at him.

"Kathy?" There was a question in his eyes, in his voice as he pushed inside.

"Yes," she managed. "Yes."

With one hard thrust, he filled her. Kathy gasped, holding on tight against the strange sensation. Too full, too much. Max paused, limbs trembling with effort, until she released the breath again, her body relaxing with the exhalation, and she closed her eyes on a sigh.

"More?"

"Mmm," she replied, nodding. Her tension melted away under his clever hands, hands that touched her tenderly, that moulded her anew, turning her into something other than her usually earthbound body. She felt ethereal and wondrous, floating in a daze of pleasure, as he loved her with such reverence. Her hands coasted down over his broad shoulders, following his powerful back to stroke his flanks. He was so warm, his skin soft, the muscles shifting beneath her hands as he moved, thrusting into her. The scent of him filled her, masculine musk, spice and sex, and it was intoxicating. Kathy revelled in it, in her power over him as he groaned and made a primal sound of pleasure that thrilled her. She slid a hand down his front, over the hard ridges of his abdomen, to the place where their bodies joined, feeling the strength of him, the force behind each push of his hips.

"Christ," he groaned. "So good. I love you."

He ducked his head, kissing her before she could reply, but he knew it already.

The world narrowed, shrinking until nothing but the two of them existed. It grew darker and wilder, and Kathy lost herself in it, in him and the pleasure he took in her. Though she'd not thought such another explosion of joy possible, she felt the exquisite tugging at her core again and impatience filled her. His pace grew faster, more erratic, and she sensed the same desperation in him too, a reckless race to the glittering pinnacle combined with a reluctance to ever let this end. His breathing was harsh and uneven, his hot breath coasting over her skin until he shuddered, and his fractured cry delighted her so much that she went too, tumbling into happy oblivion to float in some place only they could go to.

Max eased away from her and rolled to the side before reaching for her, gathering him to her with her back to his front. He held her close, his breathing still too fast after the effort he'd expended on loving her.

Kathy sighed, her arms settling over his and feeling safe and warm, sleepy and dazedly content. "Thank you, Max," she said with a sigh.

He chuckled, nuzzling her neck. “The pleasure was entirely mine, I assure you.”

“Not entirely,” she countered, making him laugh.

“I’m glad. I wanted it to be good for you.”

“Good? Heavens, any better and I might have died from it.”

He laughed again, and the sound rumbled through her, making her smile.

“I’m so happy, Max. Thank you.”

He propped himself on one elbow, leaning over her and Kathy shifted to look back at him, sighing with contentment at the sight of her handsome husband. “Thank you, my love,” he said, his expression grave. “For forgiving me, for daring to give me this extraordinary chance. I won’t ever take it for granted. I won’t let you down.”

“I know,” Kathy said simply, seeing sincerity in his eyes, and the desire to be everything she needed. “You’re mine now. My sweet devil, my Max. Whatever comes, we shall face it together. I will always be by your side.”

“Keeping me on the right path,” he murmured, bending to steal a kiss.

Kathy shook her head. “Not that. You don’t need that. You see the path clearly now. I shall be there because I want to be, because there is nowhere else on earth I would rather be.”

Max smiled at her and kissed her again, and proved to her, as if proof were needed, exactly why that was.

Epilogue

Dear Monsieur,

Thank you so much for the lovely outing yesterday. I had a wonderful time and the picnic by the Serpentine was quite delicious, though I wished Miss Knight had been with us. It's always so lovely when she can come too, for she is such fun and she always makes you laugh so. Please do not scold me for impertinence, though I know it is impertinent of me to say it, but I wish you would marry her. She is the only person who truly makes you happy, and I think you should ask her at once before someone else does. I don't want her to marry this Muir, or some other Scottish fellow who will take her away from us, somewhere we will never see her. She ought to be with you, and you <u>must</u> make that happen.

The good news is that you will have your chance. I received a letter from her this morning. She bids me to tell you she is coming home in time for her birthday on the 15th of July and will be at Lady Grasmere's ball. I wrote this letter at once, for I know how much you have missed her too. How wonderful it will be to see her again after so long.

Please consider what I have said. I know you think me only a child, but I am not so silly that I cannot see what is in front of me.

—Excerpt of a letter from Miss Agatha Smith to her guardian, Louis Cesar de Montluc, Comte de Villen.

10th July 1842, between Bond Street and Church Street, Isleworth, London.

Kathy sighed, closing her eyes as Max nuzzled the tender spot beneath her ear that always made her shiver.

"Max," she murmured, wishing they'd gone home once they'd finished their shopping instead of asking the coachman to take them to her parents' house.

They had been in Warwickshire for the last ten days, and Kathy had fallen hopelessly in love with the house there. This was where they would make their home, once the school project no longer needed their attention. They had not planned to call on her parents today, for Mama had invited them for dinner tomorrow, but Kathy was full of plans for their new home, and wanted to tell her family all about it, so she'd decided on a surprise visit.

"Mmm?" He nipped at her ear, his warm hand gathering her skirts up and slipping beneath.

"Max!" she giggled, scandalised. "We mustn't."

"I want to touch you," he whispered against her mouth, kissing her as his hand skated higher. "I always want to touch you."

"Yes, but not right before I have to face Mama and Papa," she said, gasping as his hand glided up the inside of her thigh to stroke the little nest of curls between her legs.

"Shall I stop, then?" he asked, raising his head to look at her.

Kathy stared at him, seeing the echo of the man he'd been, wickedness glinting in his eyes, but tempered now with love and understanding, and a generous heart.

"No," she sighed, giving herself over to him, even though it seemed dreadfully outrageous to let him touch her so with the coachman and half the world outside the thin curtains.

Kathy held her breath as his clever hand worked between her legs, caressing and toying with her until she was writhing with pleasure, and he slid two long fingers inside her. He nuzzled his face against her hair and moaned.

"God, you feel so good. I shall never have enough of you."

Kathy grasped his arm, holding him still as the climax took her, swift and fierce, rolling through her with pulses of pure joy, leaving her sated, pliant and sleepy. She rested her head on his chest and let out a shuddering sigh.

"Good?" he asked her, a touch of smug satisfaction lingering in the words as he stroked her inner thigh, reluctant as always to stop touching her.

Kathy snorted and glanced up at him. "Marvellous," she said dreamily. "Though I am afraid we are almost there, unless you want to ask the driver to go around the block a few times," she added with a saucy grin.

Max grinned and bent his head to kiss her. "No. I can wait. There's always the drive home, after all."

She buried her face in his coat and smothered a shocked laugh. "I can't wait," she mumbled, blushing as Max lifted her head, his eyes dancing with laughter.

"So wicked you are, Lady Vane. I am the luckiest husband that ever lived."

"Indeed, you are," she said, putting up her chin and attempting to look haughty, an effect he ruined by tickling the curls between her thighs and making her squeal and giggle.

"Stop it," she ordered him, trying to restore some order to them as they turned onto Church Street. "Behave, you dreadful man, or I shall be too flustered to talk to them."

Max did as she asked, making use of his handkerchief and helping her to restore her clothing to its proper place and put her bonnet on. His expression grew serious as the carriage halted.

"You *are* happy, love?"

Kathy stared at him, so astonished by the question, she gave a startled laugh. "You can't doubt it, surely?"

Max shrugged, looking apologetic. "I hadn't, but we're seeing your parents, your brother, for the first time since we married and… I'm nervous," he admitted.

"Foolish man," she chided. "I am so happy I could burst, so there."

She kissed him, waiting until he returned a pleased smile, and then hurried him out of the carriage.

The downstairs maid let them in, bobbing a curtsey.

"They're in the front parlour, my lady," the girl said.

"They have visitors?" Kathy asked, hesitating.

"Yes, but Mr and Mrs Oak are just leaving," the maid replied. "Excuse me while I run and fetch the baby's doll. Miss Beatrice got jam on it, the little dear. I was just sponging it clean."

She hurried off, leaving them alone.

Kathy turned a panicked gaze upon Max, who snatched up his hat and gloves from the sideboard where the maid had put them. As one, they turned towards the door, but voices in the corridor behind them told Kathy it was too late. They were trapped.

Max reached for Kathy's hand, holding on tight, as Grace appeared first with Sterling carrying Beatrice. Everyone froze, except for Kathy's mother, who came out, exclaiming happily as she saw them.

"Well, what a surprise! I didn't think to see you both today. But whatever is the matter? You look like you've seen a ghost."

Her father and brother had appeared after Mama, their attention on Grace and Sterling, and instantly aware of the tension vibrating between in the air.

Kathy gathered herself first, forcing a smile to her lips. "Good afternoon, Mama," she said, kissing her mother's cheek. "I'm sorry to surprise you. We just had such a wonderful time, and I wanted to tell you about my new home."

"Well, that's nothing to worry about. We like surprise visitors. Especially like the ones we've had today, and little Betty here has been…." Mama turned back to the family in the corridor and her words trailed off.

The silence felt like a weight bearing down on them.

"We did not think you would be back until tomorrow," Grace said, looking almost apologetic, though why on earth she should do so, Kathy could not fathom.

"Our fault," Max said, taut as a bowstring beside her, his hand gripping hers as if she were the only thing keeping him tethered to the spot. "We should have waited."

Kathy swallowed, too aware of her brother's sharp gaze moving between everyone, aware of the atmosphere, but not why it existed.

"Bloody hell," her father's quiet curse was barely audible and yet cut the air like gunfire. His sharp gaze moved from Max to Betty, and she knew he'd made the connection. He wasn't the only one, as Hart did the same, and his eyes widened.

"Hart, no," she said firmly, but her words only confirmed what her brother had guessed.

"You son of a bitch," he growled, and moved.

Sterling's arm shot out, holding him back, which was some feat as Hart was a big man, and an angry one now. "Stay where you are," he commanded.

Hart stared at him in fury. "But he—" he began, outraged.

"You think I don't know?" Sterling shot back, his expression furious. "But we have resolved this between us. It's none of your damn business."

"He's my sister's husband!" Hart shot back.

"Yes. *My* husband," Kathy told him, glaring at her brother. "I know, Hart. I know everything. I did before we married. This is nothing to do with you. Stay out of it."

Hart let out a breath of frustration, staring at Max with disgust before turning to his father, who shook his head.

"He told us," Papa said, his expression grim. "He didn't tell us who, but he told us."

"And you still let him marry Kathy?" Hart said, disbelieving.

"Kathy has forgiven him," Mama said, her voice quavering a little. "And if Grace and Sterling can do the same, we can do no less. I think Max is the only person who has not yet forgiven himself, but that is as it should be."

She sent her son a pointed expression, but Hart just folded his arms.

Max's gaze moved to Grace, his expression so wretched Kathy wanted to cry. "I'm so sorry," he told her quietly. Whether he meant for this scene, or for everything he'd done, she did not know, but his sincerity was audible.

Grace put up her chin. "I'm not," she said, holding his gaze. She turned to look at her daughter in her husband's arms and smiled, leaning in to kiss her soft cheek. "I'm very happy. Happier than I could have dreamed possible."

She smoothed a hand over the apparent swell of her stomach and Kathy's breath caught.

"Oh, Grace. Another child? That's wonderful."

Grace beamed, glancing back at her husband, who stared at her with such adoration it was clear he could not believe his luck either. "We are blessed," she said, looking proud and strong, and so fierce Kathy could only admire her. "Now, then. Come along, Sterling, my love. We need to get Betty home for her nap or there will be the devil to pay."

The maid bobbed up from the top of the servants' staircase, bearing the well-worn doll. "Here you are, Mrs Oak. All clean."

"Thank you," Grace said, handing the doll to her daughter, who snatched it with an exclamation of delight and held it against her face, staring at everyone with wide blue eyes. "Good day to you, then."

Sterling followed her out of the house as Betty waved at everyone, oblivious to the stir she'd caused.

The door closed and Kathy faced her parents and her brother.

"I'll let you enjoy your visit," Max said to her, giving her hand a squeeze. "I'll leave you the carriage, I can walk back."

"No," she said, her voice sharp. She shook her head. "No."

Kathy stared at her parents.

Mama, bless her, smiled and walked towards them. "Do come and sit down, then, both of you. I'll order a fresh pot of tea and you can tell me all about your new home, Kathy. You are pleased, I take it?"

"Yes, Mama," Kathy said, her voice quavering. "Very."

"Oh, love." Mama hugged her, stroking her back like she'd done when she was a little girl. "It will be all right. You'll see."

She let Kathy go and looked at Max, who was staring at the floor, unable to meet her gaze.

"Max," she said, and then hugged him.

He stiffened, a flash of bewilderment in his eyes, and Kathy wondered about his parents, about the perfect noble marriage that meant they saw their nicely turned-out son for an hour each day until he was old enough to be sent away, and never hugged him.

"Forgive me," Max said, hugging Mama back awkwardly.

Kathy swallowed hard, her throat tight.

"We did that already, remember?" Mama said briskly. "Now, come along, everyone. I think we all need a cup of tea."

Hart grumbled under his breath but stalked back into the parlour as Mama ushered him ahead of her. Papa hesitated, but reached out a hand and patted Max's shoulder, before he too followed her, leaving Kathy alone with Max.

He looked back at her and swallowed. "Still no regrets, my lady?"

Anxiety flickered in his eyes, and she wanted nothing but to reassure him and chase it away.

She smiled, allowing the tension of the past few moments to leave her, and accepting the happiness that this man had brought into her life. Nothing and no one were perfect, but she knew she could find her future and face it joyfully with her imperfect husband.

"None. You have enough of those for us both. I love you. Nothing has changed, and you make me happy, Maxwell Drake, Lord Vane, my husband."

He reached out and stroked her cheek, his expression one of wonder. "You were my salvation from the start of this journey, my love. From the first moment I heard your voice and decided I wanted to live, to try again, and do it right this time."

Kathy stared at him in shock, turning his words over. "You know," she said on a breath of surprise. "I kept meaning to tell you, but… you know."

"I've known for a long time," he said gently. "You were there, the light in the darkest time of my life, guiding me back."

"I always will be, Max," she said, meaning it.

"Your brother despises me." He gave her a rueful smile, but Kathy only shrugged.

"Hart's stubborn, but he's not stupid. Give him time. He'll see what I see, what even Grace and Sterling saw, and he'll give you a chance too. Don't give up."

"I never shall. Not if you believe in me."

"I do," she said, her heart full of her belief in him, her love for him. "I believe in you."

And to make sure he understood how much, she kissed him, and kissed him some more, until Papa cleared his throat and told them the tea was getting cold.

Next in the Daring Daughter Series…

Sinfully Daring

Daring Daughters Book Twelve

The Perfect Young Lady…

Lady Rosamund Adolphus, daughter of the Duke of Bedwin, will not have the slightest trouble in finding a husband. So says the *ton*. She has beauty, breeding, charm and a dowry weighty enough to sink an East Indiaman. Yet the only man she fancies is the elusive Lord Ashburton, long-time friend of her older brother Jules. Naturally, he is one of the few men who does not see her at all, regarding her only as Jules' little sister.

A Married Man…

Frustrated by her inability to catch Ashburton's attention, Rosamund consoles herself with the company of her new best friend, Viscount Hargreaves. Lord Hargreaves is sophisticated, funny and kind and tries his best to help Rosamund capture Ashburton's eye, to no avail. As their schemes to find her a husband become increasingly silly, Rosamund realises she has forgotten the purpose of this endeavour, for she is enjoying Hargreaves' company far too much to care. Too bad he's already married to a woman who flaunts her affairs and makes the poor man's life a misery.

A Scandal That Rocks the Ton…

When the viscount confesses his feelings for Rosamund have gone far beyond friendship, they both know the only honourable thing he can do is leave. But Lady Hargreaves had already decided her husband is enjoying his new friendship a little too much. Her spiteful retaliation leaves Rosamund's reputation in ruins and Lord Hargreaves issuing a deadly promise of retribution.

A Grave Situation…

When Lady Hargreaves is found dead just hours after a furious altercation with her intoxicated husband, there's only one direction the fingers are pointing.

Pre-order your copy here

Sinfully Daring

The Peculiar Ladies who started it all…

Girls Who Dare – The exciting series from Emma V Leech, the multi-award-winning, Amazon Top 10 romance writer behind the Rogues & Gentlemen series.

Inside every wallflower is the beating heart of a lioness, a passionate individual willing to risk all for their dream, if only they can find the courage to begin. When these overlooked girls make a pact to change their lives, anything can happen.

Eleven girls – Eleven dares in a hat. Twelve stories of passion. Who will dare to risk it all?

To Dare a Duke

Girls Who Dare Book 1

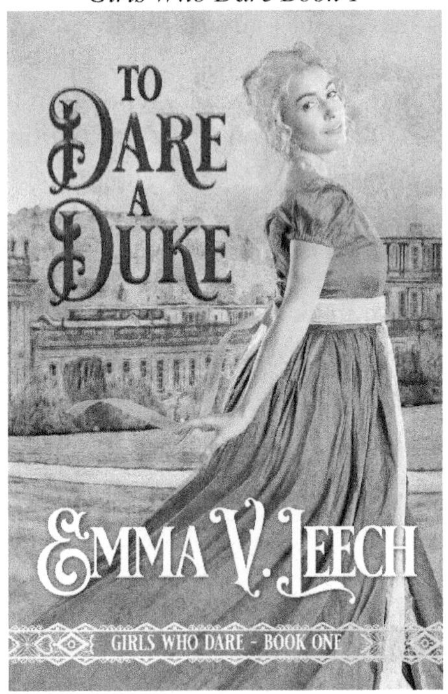

Dreams of true love and happy ever afters

Dreams of love are all well and good, but all Prunella Chuffington-Smythe wants is to publish her novel. Marriage at the price of her independence is something she will not consider. Having tasted success writing under a false name in The Lady's Weekly Review, her alter ego is attaining notoriety and fame and Prue rather likes it.

A Duty that must be endured

Robert Adolphus, The Duke of Bedwin, is in no hurry to marry, he's done it once and repeating that disaster is the last thing he desires. Yet, an heir is a necessary evil for a duke and one he cannot shirk. A dark reputation precedes him though, his first wife may have died young, but the scandals the beautiful, vivacious and spiteful creature supplied the ton have not. A wife must be found. A wife who is neither beautiful or vivacious but sweet and dull, and certain to stay out of trouble.

Dared to do something drastic

The sudden interest of a certain dastardly duke is as bewildering as it is unwelcome. She'll not throw her ambitions aside to marry a scoundrel just as her plans for self-sufficiency and freedom are coming to fruition. Surely showing the man she's not actually the meek little wallflower he is looking for should be enough to put paid to his intentions? When Prue is dared by her friends to do something drastic, it seems the perfect opportunity to kill two birds.

However, Prue cannot help being intrigued by the rogue who has inspired so many of her romances. Ordinarily, he plays the part of handsome rake, set on destroying her plucky heroine. But is he really the villain of the piece this time, or could he be the hero?

Finding out will be dangerous, but it just might inspire her greatest story yet.

To Dare a Duke

Also check out Emma's regency romance series, Rogues & Gentlemen. Available now!

The Rogue

Rogues & Gentlemen Book 1

The notorious Rogue that began it all.

Set in Cornwall, 1815. Wild, untamed and isolated.

Lawlessness is the order of the day and smuggling is rife.

Henrietta always felt most at home in the wilds of the outdoors but even she had no idea how the mysterious and untamed would sweep her away in a moment.

Bewitched by his wicked blue eyes

Henrietta Morton knows to look the other way when the free trading 'gentlemen' are at work.
Yet when a notorious pirate bursts into her local village shop, she

can avert her eyes no more. Bewitched by his wicked blue eyes, a moment of insanity follows as Henrietta hides the handsome fugitive from the Militia.

Her reward is a kiss, lingering and unforgettable.

In his haste to flee, the handsome pirate drops a letter, a letter that lays bare a tale of betrayal. When Henrietta's father gives her hand in marriage to a wealthy and villainous nobleman in return for the payment of his debts, she becomes desperate.

Blackmailing a pirate may be her only hope for freedom.

******Warning**: This book contains the most notorious rogue of all of Cornwall and, on occasion, is highly likely to include some mild sweating or descriptive sex scenes. ****

Free to read on *Kindle Unlimited*: The Rogue

Interested in a Regency Romance with a twist?

A Dog in a Doublet

The Regency Romance Mysteries Book 2

A man with a past

Harry Browning was a motherless guttersnipe, and the morning he came across the elderly Alexander Preston, The Viscount Stamford, clinging to a sheer rock face, he didn't believe in fate. But the fates have plans for Harry whether he believes or not, and he's not entirely sure he likes them.

As a reward for his bravery, and in an unusual moment of charity, miserly Lord Stamford takes him on. He is taught to read, to manage the vast and crumbling estate, and to behave like a gentleman, but Harry knows that is something he will never truly be.

Already running from a dark past, his future is becoming increasingly complex as he finds himself caught in a tangled web of jealousy and revenge.

A feisty young maiden

Temptation, in the form of the lovely Clarinda Bow, is a constant threat to his peace of mind, enticing him to be something he isn't. But when the old man dies, his will makes a surprising demand, and the fates might just give Harry the chance to have everything he ever desired, including Clara, if only he dares.

And as those close to the Preston family begin to die, Harry may not have any choice.

A Dog in a Doublet

Lose yourself in Emma's paranormal world with The French Vampire Legend series.....

The Key to Erebus

The French Vampire Legend Book 1

The truth can kill you.

Taken away as a small child, from a life where vampires, the Fae, and other mythical creatures are real and treacherous, the beautiful young witch, Jéhenne Corbeaux is totally unprepared when she returns to rural France to live with her eccentric Grandmother.

Thrown headlong into a world she knows nothing about she seeks to learn the truth about herself, uncovering secrets more shocking than anything she could ever have imagined and finding that she is by no means powerless to protect the ones she loves.

Despite her Gran's dire warnings, she is inexorably drawn to the dark and terrifying figure of Corvus, an ancient vampire and master of the vast Albinus family.

Jéhenne is about to find her answers and discover that, not only is Corvus far more dangerous than she could ever imagine, but that he holds much more than the key to her heart …

Now available at your favourite retailer.

The Key to Erebus

Check out Emma's exciting fantasy series with hailed by Kirkus Reviews as "An enchanting fantasy with a likable heroine, romantic intrigue, and clever narrative flourishes."

The Dark Prince

The French Fae Legend Book 1

Two Fae Princes
One Human Woman
And a world ready to tear them all apart

Laen Braed is Prince of the Dark fae, with a temper and reputation to match his black eyes, and a heart that despises the human race. When he is sent back through the forbidden gates between realms to retrieve an ancient fae artifact, he returns home with far more than he bargained for.

Corin Albrecht, the most powerful Elven Prince ever born. His golden eyes are rumoured to be a gift from the gods, and destiny is calling him. With a love for the human world that runs deep, his friendship with Laen is being torn apart by his prejudices.

Océane DeBeauvoir is an artist and bookbinder who has always relied on her lively imagination to get her through an unhappy and uneventful life. A jewelled dagger put on display at a nearby museum hits the headlines with speculation of another race, the Fae. But the discovery also inspires Océane to create an extraordinary piece of art that cannot be confined to the pages of a book.

With two powerful men vying for her attention and their friendship stretched to the breaking point, the only question that remains...who is truly The Dark Prince.

The man of your dreams is coming...or is it your nightmares he visits? Find out in Book One of The French Fae Legend.

Available now to read at your favorite retailer

The Dark Prince

Want more Emma?

If you enjoyed this book, please support this indie author and take a moment to leave a few words in a review. *Thank you!*

To be kept informed of special offers and free deals (which I do regularly) follow me on *https://www.bookbub.com/authors/emma-v-leech*

To find out more and to get news and sneak peeks of the first chapter of upcoming works, go to my website and sign up for the newsletter.
http://www.emmavleech.com/

Come and join the fans in my Facebook group for news, info and exciting discussion…

Emma's Book Club

Or Follow me here…

http://viewauthor.at/EmmaVLeechAmazon
Facebook
Instagram
Emma's Twitter page
TikTok

Can't get your fill of Historical Romance? Do you crave stories with passion and red hot chemistry?

If the answer is yes, have I got the group for you!

Come join myself and other awesome authors in our Facebook group

Historical Harlots

Be the first to know about exclusive giveaways, chat with amazing HistRom authors, lots of raunchy shenanigans and more!

Historical Harlots Facebook Group

Printed in Great Britain
by Amazon